Before 1066 the City of Gloucester paid £36 at face value, 12 sesters of honey at that Borough's measure, 36 dickers of iron, 100 drawn iron rods for nails for the King's ships, and certain other petty customary dues in the hall and the King's chamber.

Now the City pays to the King £60 at 20 (pence) to the *ora*. The King has £20 from the mint.

Domesday Book, Gloucestershire, 1086

DOMESDAY
GLOUCESTERSHIRE

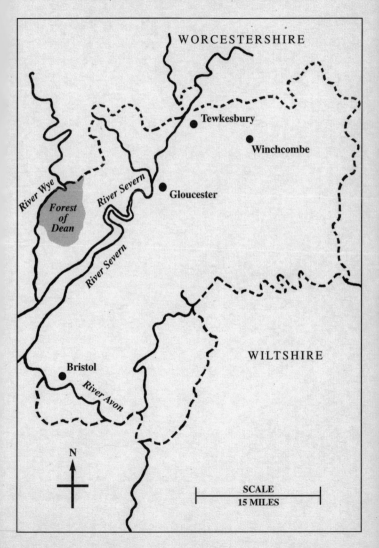

WORCESTERSHIRE

● Tewkesbury

● Winchcombe

River Wye

Forest of Dean

River Severn

● Gloucester

River Severn

WILTSHIRE

● Bristol

River Avon

N

SCALE
15 MILES

Prologue

'Do you want to be beaten again?' asked Brother Frewine quietly.

'No, no!' they cried in unison.

'Well, that is what will happen if I report this to Brother Paul. You know what a dim view the Master of the Novices takes of any laxity or disobedience among his charges.' The monk looked meaningfully at the two boys. 'You also know how strong an arm Brother Paul has. When someone has once been flogged by him, they rarely wish to invite a second punishment. Yet the two of you seem to be almost imploring a further touch of his rod.'

'That is not so, Brother Frewine,' said Kenelm quickly. 'Please do not report us to Brother Paul. Punish us yourself, if you must, but do not hand us over to our master. He is ruthless. My body ached for a fortnight after his last chastisement. It was vicious.'

'Brother Paul was only doing his duty.'

'We will do our duty from now on,' promised Kenelm, turning to his companion. 'Is that not so, Elaf?'

'Yes!' vowed the other boy.

'Spare us, Brother Frewine.'

'We did not mean to offend you,' said Elaf.

'It is God who was offended,' chided the monk, wagging a finger. 'You fell asleep during choir practice. It is an insult to the Almighty to doze off like that when you are singing His praises.'

Kenelm shrugged. 'We were tired.'

'It will not happen again,' added Elaf in an apologetic whisper.

'I will make sure of that,' warned Frewine. 'If I see so much as a flicker of an eyelid from either of you again, I will drag you out of the church by the scruff of your unworthy necks and hand you over to Brother Paul without mercy. Is that understood?'

The boys paled with fear and nodded meekly.

Brother Frewine did not enjoy scolding them. He was the Precentor at the Abbey of St Peter and, like the novices, a Saxon who had been born and brought up in Gloucester. A kindly old man who inclined to leniency, he had neither the voice nor the manner for stern rebuke. The boys liked him enormously, but that did not stop them from mocking him in private. His round face featured two large, dark-rimmed eyes separated by a small, beak-like nose, giving him an unmistakable resemblance to an owl. The Precentor was well aware that his nickname among the novices was Brother Owl. He bore the title without complaint and liked to think that he had acquired some of the bird's fabled wisdom. While the muscular Brother Paul imposed his will by means of a birch rod, the owl could only inflict a sharp peck.

'Are you truly penitent?' he demanded.

'Yes, Brother Frewine,' they chorused.

'This is not the first time you have earned my disfavour but it had better be the last. Remember the words of the great St Benedict himself. "Listen, my son, to the precepts of your master and hear them in your heart; receive with gladness the charge of a loving master and perform it fully so that by the hard road of obedience, you may return to him from whom you strayed along the easy paths of disobedience." Yes, it is a hard road you must follow. I know the temptations which beckon you on every side. But you must ignore them. You must learn obedience.'

Brother Owl delivered a sermon on the virtues of the monastic life and the benefits of true humility. The two boys listened patiently, sensing that this was part of their punishment, and stifling the yawns that would have seen them delivered up to their fearful master. Both were finding life within the enclave too full of constraints. Kenelm was a high-spirited lad with a mischievous nature which had not been entirely curbed by the swing of a birch rod. Elaf, smaller and more tentative, was easily led by his friend, often against his better judgement.

The three of them were standing outside the church in which choir practice had just been supervised by the Precentor. Proud of the high musical standards of the abbey, Brother Frewine worked hard to maintain them. Sleeping novices were not tolerated, especially when, as he suspected, their tiredness was due to the same kind of nocturnal antics which had brought them their earlier beating.

'You are blessed,' he told them softly. 'This abbey is admired and respected throughout the whole realm. It was not always so. When Abbot Wilstan ruled this house, there were only two monks and eight novices here to do God's work. I should know. I was one of those two monks.' He let out a wheeze as ancient memories flooded back. 'Gloucester Abbey was a sorry place in those days. But now, under the inspired leadership of Abbot Serlo, we have a vigorous community with almost fifty monks to follow true Benedictine traditions. You are very fortunate to be part of this community. Show me that you appreciate your good fortune.'

'We will, Brother Frewine,' said Kenelm solemnly.

'We know that we are blessed,' murmured Elaf.

'Remind yourselves of that while you fast for the rest of the day. That is the punishment I order. If your eyes cannot stay open, your bellies will remain unfed.' He saw them wince. 'Now go back into the church and kneel in prayer until you hear the bell for Sext. Give thanks to God that He has chosen you to do His work on this earth. Commit yourselves to Him and beg His forgiveness for your shameful misbehaviour during choir practice.' They were about to move off when he detained them with a raised palm. 'Do not forget Brother Nicholas in your prayers. He has been missing for two days now. Pray earnestly for his safe return.'

The boys nodded and let themselves into the church. Frewine watched them go and smiled. They were twin portraits of obedience. He believed that his sage counsel had brought them both to heel.

As soon as they were alone, however, Kenelm turned apostate. 'I will not pray for his safe return,' he said with vehemence.

'But we must,' said Elaf. 'Even though we don't like him.'

'Not me. I hate him.'

'Kenelm!'

'All the novices do. Pray for him? No, Elaf. I hope that Brother Nicholas *never* comes back to the abbey!'

The monastic day continued at its steady, unhurried, unvarying pace. Vespers was sung in church, followed by a light supper of bread, baked on the premises, and fruit, picked from the abbey garden. The meal was washed down with a glass of ale.

Kenelm and Elaf were absent from the table, however. Hungry by the time of Vespers, they were famished when the bell for Compline summoned the monks to the last service of the day. As they shuffled off to the dormitory with the other novices, they were feeling the pangs with great intensity. Elaf gritted his teeth and accepted the discomfort. It was far preferable to a severe flogging by Brother Paul. He lay in the darkness until fatigue finally got the better of him.

But Elaf was not allowed to sleep for long. His arm was tugged.

'Wake up!' whispered Kenelm.

'Go to sleep,' said the other drowsily.

'Come on, Elaf. Wake up.'

'What do you want?'

'I'm starving!'

'Wait until breakfast.'

'I can't hold out that long.'

'You have to, Kenelm.'

'No I don't. Neither do you. Follow me.'

'Where are you going?'

'To find something to eat.'

'Kenelm!'

'And you're coming with me.'

Elaf's protests were brushed aside and he was more or less dragged from his bed. The other novices were fast asleep, tired out by the rigours of the day and wanting to enjoy as much slumber as they could before they were roused in the early hours of the next morning. Kenelm led his friend along the bare boards of the dormitory, moving furtively in the gloom, one hand on his empty stomach. Elaf followed with the greatest reluctance, wanting food as much as his companion but fearful of the consequences of trying to find it.

They descended the day stairs and slipped out into the cloisters. Moonlight dappled the garth. Keeping to the shadows, they crept along the south walk side by side. Both of them started when an owl hooted. Kenelm was the first to recover. He gave a snigger.

'Brother Frewine!'

'He was good to us, Kenelm.'

'Starving us to death? You call that being good?'

'We could have been reported to Brother Paul.'

'He'd have beaten us *and* starved us.'

'Be thankful for Brother Frewine's kindness.'

'The only thing I'll be thankful for is food and drink.'

Kenelm led the way past the refectory to the kitchen. Its door was unlocked and he opened it as silently as he could. Elaf darted inside after his friend then put his back to the door as it was shut again. Their eyes needed a few moments to adjust to the darkness. Vague shapes began to emerge. Kenelm let out a chuckle but Elaf was having second thoughts about the enterprise.

'What if we are caught?' he said anxiously.

'Nobody will catch us.'

'But they'll see that the food has gone, Kenelm.'

'Not if we choose carefully. Who is going to miss a few apples from the basket? Or some bread from the bakehouse?'

'It is stealing.'

'No, Elaf,' reasoned the other. 'It is taking what we should have enjoyed at supper. There is no theft involved. Come on.'

'I'm not happy about this.'

'Then stay hungry, you little coward!'

Elaf was stung. 'I'm no coward.'

'Prove it!'

'I've done that by taking the risk of coming here.'

'You've been shaking like a leaf all the way,' said Kenelm, growing in confidence. 'But for me, you wouldn't have dreamt of taking what's rightfully yours. Out of my way.'

He pushed Elaf aside and crossed to a basket of apples, picking two at random and sinking his teeth voraciously into each one alternately. His friend could not hold back. Hunger got the better of caution and he dived forward to grab his own share of the bounty. The two of them were soon gobbling food as fast as they could grab it and swilling it down with a generous swig of ale. It was a midnight feast that was all the more satisfying because of the daring circumstances in which it was being consumed. As his stomach filled and the ale made its impact, Kenelm's high spirits increased. He wanted more than a meal. It was time to shake off the strictures of the abbey and play.

The first apple core hit Elaf on the back of the head.

'Aouw!' he cried, turning around. A second missile struck him full in the face. 'Stop it, Kenelm!'

'Make me stop,' taunted the other.

'I will!'

Taking a last bite from the apple in his hand, Elaf hurled the core at his friend and secured a direct hit. Success emboldened him and he searched for more ammunition. Caution was now thrown to the wind. Laughing aloud, the two of them ran around the kitchen, hurling fruit, bread and anything else which came to hand. It was only when Elaf backed into a table that the game was brought to a sudden halt. The table overturned and its rows of wooden bowls scattered noisily over the stone floor. From the empty kitchen, the sound reverberated tenfold. Keen ears picked it up and within minutes a monk came to investigate. A lighted candle in his hand, he flung open the door of the kitchen.

The two novices were hiding behind the fallen table.

'What do we do now?' whispered Elaf, trembling with fear.

'Get out quickly.'

'How?'

'This way.'

Kenelm threw a last apple core to distract the monk then dashed through the door of the bakehouse with Elaf at his heels. They ran into the adjoining brewhouse with its cloying stink and dived behind a barrel to see if they were being followed. Pursuit was vengeful.

'Where are you?' roared a voice.

Elaf quailed. 'It's Brother Paul!'

'Come here, you little devils!'

'No thank you,' said Kenelm under his breath.

Pulling his friend in his wake, he groped his way to the back door and eased it open. The Master of the Novices saw their silhouettes and lumbered after them, tripping over a wooden pail on the way and cursing inwardly. Pain served to add extra speed and urgency to his pursuit. Hauling himself up, he charged after the miscreants and reached the cloister garth in time to see two shadowy figures vanishing swiftly in the direction of the abbey church.

Elaf was now panic-stricken.

'We're trapped!' he said as they entered the church.

'Not if we can find a hiding place.'

'I can't see a thing!'

'Keep quiet!' ordered Kenelm. 'Hold on to me!'

Desperate to elude Brother Paul, he felt his way along the nave and tried to work out where they could best take refuge. Their master was thorough. Aided by his candle, he would search every nook and cranny until he found them. The repercussions were unthinkable. Elaf was now sobbing in despair and Kenelm shook him to instil some courage.

'I know where we can go!' he announced.

'Where?'

'The one place he'll never think of looking.'

Still holding Elaf, he headed towards the bell tower and groped around until his fingers met the steps of the ladder. He made his friend go up first then scrambled after him. The west door clanged open as their pursuer arrived in a tiny pool of light. Elaf hurried through the trap door, Kenelm after him. Clutching each other tightly, they hardly dared to breathe as they crouched on the wooden platform beside the huge iron bell. They ignored the stench of their refuge. Footsteps moved about below them. The candle flickered in all parts of the church as a systematic search was carried out. When the footsteps approached the base of the ladder, Elaf finally lost his nerve and jerked backwards. Something blocked his way and he fell across the obstruction, letting out an involuntary cry of alarm. It turned to a yell of sheer terror when he realised that he was lying across the stiff, stinking body of a man.

Kenelm was as horrified as his friend. As the two of them tried to scramble out of their hiding place, they collided violently with the bell and sent its sonorous voice booming throughout the abbey to tell everyone the grim news.

The missing Brother Nicholas had at last been found.

Chapter One

Ralph Delchard reined in his horse and held up an imperious hand to bring the cavalcade to a halt. Shading his eyes against the afternoon sun, he gazed into the distance. A rueful smile surfaced.

'There it is,' he said, pointing an accusing finger. 'Gloucester. That's where this whole sorry business started. That's where the King, in his wisdom or folly, had his deep speech with his Council and announced the Great Survey which has been the bane of my life for so long. Consider this: if the Conqueror had not spent Christmas at Gloucester, I might not have been forced to wear the skin off my arse riding from one end of the kingdom to the other.'

'Do not take it so personally,' said Gervase Bret, mounted beside him. 'The King did not order the creation of this Domesday Book simply to irritate Ralph Delchard.'

'I am more than irritated, Gervase.'

'You've made that clear.'

'I am appalled. Disgusted. Enraged.'

'Think of our predecessors. They did most of the work. The first commissioners to visit this fair county toiled long and hard without complaint. All that we have to deal with are the irregularities they uncovered. In this case, they are few in number.'

'How many times have I heard you say that?'

'Our task should be completed in less than a week.'

'That, too, has a familiar ring.'

'I have studied the documents, Ralph. Only one major dispute confronts us. It will not tax us overmuch.'

'What about the things that do not appear in the documents?'

'Do *not* appear?'

'Yes,' said Ralph wearily. 'Contingencies. Unforeseen hazards. Like the skulduggery we found in Warwick. The dangers we met in Oxford. The small matter of border warfare in Chester. The foul murder of our dear colleague in Exeter. Our documents failed to warn us about any of those things.'

'Unfortunate mishaps.'

'They were disasters, Gervase. Cunningly devised by Fate itself to torment me. Have you forgotten Wiltshire?' he added, jerking a thumb over his shoulder. 'I shuddered when we rode past the Savernake Forest again. Think of the problems we had there. And in Canterbury. And York. And Maldon. And every other damnable place it has pleased the King to send us.'

'Including Hereford?'

Ralph was checked. 'That was different,' he conceded.

'Very different,' Gervase reminded him with a grin. 'You went to Hereford to expose villainy and found yourself a wife into the bargain.' He glanced behind him. 'And an excellent bargain she was.'

'The best I ever made.'

Golde, the lady in question, was riding at the rear of the column with Canon Hubert, the portly commissioner whose donkey always seemed too small and spindly to bear his excessive weight. While her husband led the way, Golde enjoyed a conversation with Hubert and even managed to prise an occasional word out of Brother Simon, the emaciated monk who acted as scribe to the commission and whose fear of the female sex was so profound that he usually retreated into anguished silence in the presence of a woman. It was a tribute to Golde that she had finally broken through the invisible wall Simon had constructed around himself. He remained wary but no longer felt that the sanctity of his manhood was threatened.

Ten knights from Ralph's own retinue acted as an escort and towed the sumpter horses along with them. Like their lord, they wore helm and hauberk and bore swords and lances. On their latest assignment fine weather had favoured them all the way from Winchester and their hosts along the route had provided good accommodation and a cordial welcome. The pleasant journey had lifted the spirits of all but one of them. Ralph Delchard was the odd man out.

'Hereford was the exception,' he agreed for a second time. 'It gave me the most precious thing I have. My beloved wife. Though there's a strange irony in the fact that I spend most of my life fighting the Saxons then end up marrying one of them.' He gave a wry smile. 'Not that I regret the decision for one moment. It has brought me true happiness. Or it would do, if the Conqueror allowed me the time to enjoy it.' His gaze travelled back to the city on the horizon. 'The one saving grace of Gloucester is that it can be reached easily from Hereford. We have sent word for Golde's sister to meet us there.'

'I look forward to seeing Aelgar once more,' said Gervase.

'As long as she is our only visitor from Hereford!'

'What do you mean?'

'Don't you recall who else we first met there?'

'Archdeacon Idwal?'

'Do not mention that accursed name!' said Ralph with a grimace. 'He was a Welsh demon. Summoned from hell to make my life a misery. He stalked me both in Hereford and in Chester. *Now* can you see why I did not wish to come to Gloucester? Whenever we get near the Welsh border, that fiend of hell pops up in front of me.'

'Idwal is no fiend of hell.'

'His very name unnerves me! Do not mention it!'

'The archdeacon was a devout man.'

'He was living proof that the Devil speaks in Welsh.'

'I liked him,' said Gervase. 'We had some lively discussions. But you're quite safe, Ralph. I doubt very much that we shall encounter him in Gloucester. He is Archdeacon of St David's now.

Far away in west Wales. What possible reason can he have to come to Gloucester?'

'*I* will be there.'

Ralph yelled a command then set the troop in motion once more.

Gervase had more reason than any of them to want a swift end to their latest assignment. Ralph preferred to take Golde with him on the King's business, but Gervase had left his own wife, Alys, alone at home in Winchester, pining for her husband and praying for his quick return. Devoted as he was to her, Gervase never even considered the notion of bringing Alys with him because he knew that he would be so concerned for her safety and comfort that he would be unable to give his work the concentration it needed. Ralph was different, seemingly able to separate his private life from his public responsibilities without any effort.

Marriage was still too fresh an experience for Gervase for him to be able to put its joys aside when his wife was with him, and he knew that Alys, so young and vulnerable, lacked Golde's ability to fade into the background while her husband discharged his duties as a commissioner. And there was another significant factor. Ralph and his wife had both been married before. They were seasoned in the art of togetherness, skilled in the nuances of love, sure enough to give each other space and freedom. Compared to them, Gervase was a raw beginner. He had vowed that Alys would be his one and only wife and he was still learning to understand the limitations of that vow.

Like Golde, and the two Benedictine monks in their black habits, he was an incongruous figure among the armed soldiers. Wearing the sober attire of a Chancery clerk, Gervase Bret was the lawyer in the party, a clever advocate with a subtle mind. He was also the recognised diplomat, able to relate easily to everyone and to reach each of them on their own terms. Ralph Delchard revelled in his mockery of both Canon Hubert and Brother Simon and it was left to Gervase to smooth ruffled monastic feathers on a regular basis. By the same token, he could act on behalf of his fellow commissioner or scribe with the acknowledged leader of the commission, representing their point of view in a way which made Ralph take it seriously. Golde was also very fond of him, not least because he could speak her native language fluently, having been born of a Saxon mother. Ralph Delchard might be nominally in charge but it was Gervase Bret who really bonded the group together.

A steady canter was bringing Gloucester ever nearer. Situated in border country between England and Wales, it occupied a strategic position on the River Severn, a fiercely tidal waterway which swept down to the estuary and made Gloucester a thriving port as well as a crucial Norman garrison.

Ralph came out of his reverie and turned to his young friend.

'We should all stay at the castle,' he said brusquely.

'Hubert and Simon have elected to go to the abbey.'

'Our business can be dispatched more readily if we are all under the same roof. Make that point to them, Gervase.'

'They already appreciate it.'

'Then why must they escape into the abbey?'

'For the same reason that a soldier like you turns instinctively to a fortress. They feel at home there just as you do in a castle. Besides,' said Gervase, 'Hubert is anxious to renew his acquaintance with Abbot Serlo. It is something we should encourage.'

'Why?'

'Because the abbey will be a useful source of intelligence. Nothing eludes the sharp eyes of a monastic community. What we fail to find out at the castle, Hubert and Simon will assuredly learn within the enclave.'

'Two holy spies, eh?'

'No, Ralph. Two Benedictine monks mixing with their brothers.'

'Relishing the latest scandal. Whatever it may be.'

'Picking up useful gossip. Canon Hubert is well known to the abbot. He will be taken into his confidence.'

'You are right, Gervase. Let them go to the abbey.'

'Not that there will be much for them to find out, mark you.'

'How can you be so sure?'

'I sense it,' said Gervase confidently. 'Gloucester will be a benign place for us to visit. No hidden menaces this time – not even a Welsh archdeacon to yap at your heels.'

'God forbid!'

'Take my word for it, Ralph. You may relax.'

'I have lost the art of doing so.'

'Rediscover it again in Gloucester. Trust me. It will turn out to be the least troublesome city we have visited.'

Abbot Serlo stared down at the naked body of Brother Nicholas with a mixture of sadness and anger. In life, the monk had been a plump man of middle height with an abnormally large head. Death seemed to have shrunk him. It was as if the knife that had slit his throat had let out half of his substance. The blood had been washed away and the wound covered but there was still an expression of horror on Nicholas's face. Herbs were scattered on the mortuary floor to sweeten the atmosphere, but the stench of death rose powerfully to the nostrils. Serlo gave a nod and Brother Frewine drew the shroud back over the corpse. The two men left the mortuary and went out into the fresh air.

'This is an outrage,' said Serlo quietly.

'The whole abbey is in a state of shock.'

'One of our holy brothers. Murdered on consecrated ground.'

'It is shameful, Father Abbot.'

'It is abominable, Frewine. A heinous crime. I have schooled myself not to be vengeful, but I do look for justice. Swift and unrelenting justice. I have impressed that upon the sheriff.'

'Who could wish to kill Brother Nicholas?' said the Precentor, shaking his head in bewilderment. 'And for what possible reason?'

'That will emerge in the fullness of time. Meanwhile, we must mourn his death with all due solemnity and assist the sheriff in every way that we can.' He heaved a sigh. 'It will mean that the abbey is invaded by Durand and his men but that cannot be helped. Vital clues may lie here. They must be sought.'

A small, elderly, ascetic man with silver hair encircling his bald pate, Serlo had an extraordinary dignity. He looked around him with proprietary affection. A moribund abbey had been brought back to life by his arrival. It had been testing work and there had been many setbacks along the way, but the abbot had persisted, imposing discipline, raising morale, increasing the number of monks, enlarging the range of their duties and spreading the influence of the abbey throughout the whole county. Within a period of fourteen long years, Serlo had transformed Gloucester Abbey into a highly effective and respected institution, and what pleased him most was the sense of common purpose he had instilled in his monks. But one of them had now been brutally murdered, leaving an ugly stain on the purity of his vision for the abbey. It was a severe personal blow.

Brother Frewine hovered, shoulders hunched, owlish features puckered with concern. He knew better than to interrupt the meditative silences into which the abbot was accustomed to drop, particularly as he knew what thoughts must be racing through the other's mind at this moment. The Precentor had his own grief to nurse, tempered as it was by the very faintest sense of relief that, if any monk had had to be killed, it had been the unpopular Brother Nicholas rather than someone encompassed by the unconditional love he gave to the other monks.

Abbot Serlo understood exactly what he was thinking.

'This loss could not be more grievous,' he said in a chiding tone. 'Thrust aside any bad memories of Brother Nicholas. They have no place here. When one monk dies – whoever he is – a little piece of all of us perishes with him. Nicholas was a conscientious man. Pray earnestly for the salvation of his soul.'

'I will, Father Abbot.'

'Remember what I said during Chapter.'

'The words are engraved on my heart.'

'Consult them often.'

'Yes,' said Frewine, bowing his head in humility. 'There is one matter still to be discussed,' he added, looking up again. 'The two novices, Kenelm and Elaf. Their punishment has not been determined.'

'Punishment?'

'Brother Paul thinks that they should be flogged.'

'And what do you think, Frewine?'

'It is not my decision, Father Abbot. I am not the Master of the Novices. Only you and Brother Paul can pronounce sentence.'

'I would still like to take your counsel.'

'So be it.'

'What punishment should we mete out to these boys?'

Brother Frewine took a deep breath before he plunged in. 'I think that they have had punishment enough already,' he said. 'It was wrong of them to leave the dormitory at night and even more wrong of them to take food from the kitchens. I do not excuse them and feel that they should be given the sternest reprimand. But they are both very young, Father Abbot, still trying to fit their minds to the notion of obedience.'

'Go on.'

'The experience of finding Brother Nicholas has put the fear of God into them. It is something that will live with them for the rest of their days and will, in my view, serve to shape them into true members of the Order. They are in pain, they are in distress. Kenelm and Elaf are covered in contrition.' The black-rimmed eyes widened hopefully. 'I know that Brother Paul feels that the birch rod is called for but they have already been lacerated by the events of last night. Spare them, Father Abbot. Show the mercy for which you are justly admired.'

Serlo ran a contemplative finger across his lower lip.

'Sound advice,' he said at length. 'I will speak with Brother

Paul.' He sensed the Precentor's fear. 'Do not worry, Frewine. I will not tell him that I am acting at your behest. My decision is my own. I had already taken the same path as yourself. I merely needed confirmation that I was going in the right direction. Flogging two novices may give Brother Paul's arm some practice but it will not bring back a murder victim.'

'I could not agree more, Father Abbot.'

'Good. That contents me.' He set off in the direction of his lodgings with Frewine beside him. 'This is a poor advertisement for the abbey.'

'Advertisement?'

'I take such pride in this community. It is a joy to be part of it. But pride and joy have both fled now. I was ready to welcome his visit but now I face it with some trepidation.'

'We have a visitor, Father Abbot?'

'Two, in fact. Members of a royal commission, returning to the city to deal with unfinished business. I am well acquainted with one of them, Canon Hubert of Winchester, a learned man brought to God, like me, in our native Normandy.' He pursed his lips. 'I had thought to show him the beauty of the Benedictine Order here in Gloucester. Instead of that, he will be walking straight into a murder scene.'

'Murder!' exclaimed Canon Hubert, his fat cheeks whitening and his body trembling. 'Murder inside the abbey church?'

'Alas, yes,' said Durand.

'Can this be true, my lord sheriff?'

'Unhappily, it is. The body was discovered last night.'

'How? Where?' gibbered Hubert. 'Has any arrest been made?'

'Not as yet.'

'But we are due to stay at the abbey, Brother Simon and I.'

'That is why I thought it a kindness to warn you.'

'There is no kindness in these tidings, my lord sheriff. They are

17

the unkindest words you could have uttered. I am shaken to the core.'

On their arrival at the castle, Durand the Sheriff had been waiting for them. Ralph Delchard performed the introductions and was pleased with the courteous way in which Golde was immediately conducted to their apartment by a servant. He was also impressed when his men were led off to stable the horses before going to their lodging. They were expected. Preparations had been made. The sheriff himself, a big, brawny, smiling man with a rough handsomeness, was in the bailey to give them a warm greeting after their ride. He was evidently pleased to see them.

Left alone with the commissioners, however, Durand became a different person. The smile was replaced by a scowl, the pleasant manner by a preoccupied air. Instead of actually wanting them there, he was plainly exasperated by their presence. The sheriff's mind was on something else. When he told them what it was, he elicited a variety of reactions. Brother Simon fell to his knees in alarm and began to pray for deliverance. Ralph listened grimly then flung Gervase a look of sharp reproof. After answering it with a shrug of apology, Gervase made a mental note of all the details of the crime. Canon Hubert, quivering all over, needed everything repeated at least three times before he could accept it.

Durand the Sheriff forced himself to sound hospitable.

'It may be better if you and the scribe were to stay here.'

'We will not hear of it,' said Hubert, grabbing Simon by the arm to haul him upright. 'It sounds to me as if the abbey has need of us.'

'It will be a mean lodging at such a time as this.'

'Nevertheless, my lord sheriff, we will seek it out.'

'Will we?' asked Simon, stricken with doubt.

'Most certainly!' asserted Hubert.

The monks took their leave and headed for the abbey. Ralph was pleased to see them go. It enabled him to press the sheriff for more detail about the murder, but Durand had no time for further conversation.

'A crime has been committed, my lord,' he said peremptorily. 'It is my duty to investigate it as quickly and thoroughly as I may.'

'Where will you start?' wondered Ralph.

'In the place where the body was found.'

'The bell tower? How on earth did the victim come to be there?'

'It is too late to ask him.'

'Tell us more, my lord sheriff,' said Gervase. 'We bring fresh minds to this problem. We may be able to help you.'

'I have all the help I need, Master Bret.'

'You have a suspect, then?'

'Dozens of them.'

'How have you identified so many in so short a time?'

'By accepting the obvious solution.'

'What obvious solution?' asked Ralph.

The sheriff spoke with conviction. 'Brother Nicholas was killed by one or more of the other monks,' he declared. 'He was, it transpires, always something of an outsider. Nobody really liked him, not even the sanctimonious Abbot Serlo who purports to like everyone. Brother Nicholas was the rent collector for the abbey, a task which kept him away from it for most of the time. It was no accident. They deliberately wanted him out of the way.'

'Why was he so disliked?'

'That is what I am trying to find out, my lord.'

'I am not convinced by this,' said Gervase. 'I was raised in an abbey myself and almost took the cowl. I know the strong currents of feeling that can run in such places. But I find it very hard to believe that a Benedictine monk could be guilty of murder.'

'Look at the facts,' said Durand coldly. 'The victim's throat was slit within the abbey precincts and his body stowed in the abbey church. Who else would have had access to him there? Who else would know where to hide the corpse? Who else would have had a motive to kill a monk? No,' he decided, mounting his horse, 'there is no shadow of a doubt in my mind. The killer wears the black habit of the Order. Finding him is another matter, however. It is a labour of Hercules. How do you solve a murder when almost any monk in that abbey might have committed it?'

'These are holy men,' argued Gervase. 'They deserve your respect, my lord sheriff, not your derision.'

'I speak as I find. Monks are all alike to me. They look the same, talk the same, think the same, and, when they break wind, smell the same. How am I to pick out the man or men I am after? Monks are trained in deceit. How do I get behind those blank faces and those lying tongues? How do I catch the one who cut the throat of Brother Nicholas?'

He rode off quickly before they could even speak.

Chapter Two

From its vantage point in the south-west of the city, the castle controlled not only Gloucester itself, but the river crossing and the whole of the surrounding countryside. This geographical fact served to increase the power of Durand of Pitres, constable of the castle, sheriff of the county and collector of the King's revenues, offices which his late brother held before him and which made Durand, in effect, the gatekeeper to Wales and the west. The stronghold followed the established Norman pattern of motte and bailey, making use, in this case, of remaining Roman fortifications. Surmounting the high mound of tightly compacted soil was a wooden tower which commanded a superb view in all directions and would be the final point of defence in the event of an attack. The bailey looped out on the eastern side of the motte and was enclosed by a ditch and a timber palisade which boasted a fortified gate and a heavy drawbridge.

Clearly visible from any part of the city, the fortress was a vivid symbol of foreign domination and a reminder that sixteen Saxon dwellings had been demolished to make way for it. A small forest had also been cut down to provide the timber needed for its construction. The Normans were not temporary visitors; they were there to stay.

It was a thought which had often troubled Golde in younger days, and even now, though married to a member of the Norman nobility, she felt the dull resentment of a conquered nation. As she looked out across the city, she remembered the visit she had once made there as a young girl when her father was a thegn in the neighbouring county of Herefordshire and her family had real standing in the Saxon community. Domestic buildings had changed little since then. There were no stone houses in Gloucester; they were either built in the time-honoured fashion with posts hammered into the ground then linked by interwoven wattle, or they were timber-framed. The same sunken floors and thatched roofs predominated.

What differed from her first trip was the fact that the citizens now lived in the shadow of Norman rule as epitomised by its castle. Not for the first time a twinge of guilt unsettled Golde. Marriage to Ralph Delchard brought many benefits and untold pleasures, but it did not leave her conscience unmolested. Gloucester was bigger than Hereford but there were many similarities between the two. But for a happy accident, she would still be working in the family brewhouse or haggling in the market like the crowds she could see in the streets below. Golde turned away from the window. She was in an upper room in the square tower. It was small and cluttered but extremely clean and would be a far more comfortable place to pass the day than on the back of her palfrey. Having shivered in so many draughty Norman castles in wintertime, she was grateful that they were staying at Gloucester during warm weather. It was a great solace.

Footsteps pounded up the steps outside the room, then the door opened and Ralph came bursting in. Golde saw the vexation on his face.

'What is the matter, Ralph?'

'Everything.'

'I thought you would be glad to reach Gloucester.'

'I was, Golde. The sooner we reach the place, the sooner we can leave. At least, that is what I thought. But it seems as if our stay may be longer than I hoped. Gervase has let me down.'

'Surely not.'

'He has, my love. He promised me that we would encounter no problems here. It was a confident prophecy. So much for Gervase Bret's reputation as a fortune teller! I'll never trust him again.'

'Why not?'

'Two unheralded blows have already struck us.'

'Blows?'

'Yes, Golde,' said Ralph, pacing up and down the little chamber. 'While you were being conducted up here, the sheriff confided that we have arrived in the middle of a murder investigation.'

'Heavens! Who was the victim?'

'One of the monks at the abbey.'

'Never!'

'That is what Durand told us – in fairly blunt terms at that. His tone was less than friendly to us and I mean to point that out to him when he returns.'

'What exactly happened, Ralph?'

'Don't worry yourself about it.'

'But I want to know.'

'The details are quite distressing.'

'So?'

'Better that you don't hear them.'

'I'm not a child.'

He gave a tired smile. 'I can vouch for that.'

'Then you know that I don't need to be protected from unpleasant facts. And I'd much rather hear them from you. Since we're staying in the castle, I'm bound to pick them up elsewhere sooner or later.'

'True, my love.'

'Tell me all.'

He nodded. 'Thus it stands.'

Ralph gave her a shortened version of what the sheriff had told him and produced a long sigh of regret. Golde was shocked that murder had occurred within a monastic community. Her questions came thick and fast and Ralph took her by the shoulders to stem the flow.

'Don't interrogate me. I've told you all I know.'

'What of Canon Hubert and Brother Simon?'

'Forget them.'

'Are they aware of this?'

'Durand warned them about it in my hearing.'

'It will make the abbey a frightening place to be.'

'Simon was shaking at the prospect.'

'I don't blame him, Ralph. It's the one place where you would expect to be completely safe. Are there any clues? Any suspects? Does the sheriff think the murderer is still in Gloucester?'

He put a finger to her lips. 'No more questions.'

'What else did he say?'

'Enough!'

He silenced her with a kiss and she responded warmly, sinking into his embrace and enjoying their first moment alone since dawn. Ralph stood back and beamed at her.

'That's the nicest thing that's happened to me all day.'

'There is ample time for improvement on a solitary kiss.'

'I will remind you of that later on, my love.'

'Do you think that I will need reminding?' They exchanged a knowing smile. 'But you said that there were two of them.'

'Two what?'

'Unheralded blows.'

'Yes!' he groaned. 'And the second may be worse than the first.'

'What could be worse than murder?'

'Being haunted by a ghost.'

'A ghost?'

'The most terrifying kind, Golde. A *Welsh* ghost.'

'Stop talking in riddles.'

'He has come back from the dead to harry me.'

'Who has?'

'A certain archdeacon.'

'Idwal?'

Ralph recoiled as if struck by an arrow and clutched at his chest.

'I've asked you not to speak his foul name.'

'But I grew quite fond of Archdeacon Id—' She checked herself just in time. 'Of that prelate from the other side of the border.'

'If only he would stay there!' said Ralph bitterly. 'Gervase assured me that he would. He insisted that I would be completely safe from that garrulous little goat. Yet what happens? No sooner do we reach the castle to be told of the murder at the abbey than a second avalanche falls on me. A letter is handed to us regarding the major dispute we have come here to resolve. We thought we would be sitting in judgement on only three people, but a fourth has now declared himself.'

'A fourth?'

'The Archdeacon of Gwent.'

'But that is not Idwal,' she said, inflicting another wound with the unguarded mention of his name. 'When we met him in Chester, he was Archdeacon of St David's. Before that, during your stay in Hereford, he spoke as Archdeacon of Llandaff.'

'Exactly!' said Ralph, on the move again. 'He changes his title at will in order to pursue me. He is Archdeacon of Gwent now.'

'Are you certain of that?'

'I feel it in my bones.'

'The aches and pains of travel.'

'He is haunting me, Golde. Wherever I go that ugly face of his is leering at me. We all have our cross to bear and mine is hewn from the heaviest Welsh timber. When I first read that letter, I wanted to turn tail and ride back home, but he would follow me even there.'

'What do you mean?'

'I'd probably arrive back to find him Archdeacon of Winchester.'

Golde laughed. 'That's ridiculous!' she said. 'And you know it. I'm surprised at you, Ralph. You're the most fearless man I've ever met. You fought bravely in many battles and would take on a giant in single combat. Yet a harmless Welsh churchman can make you tremble.'

'There is nothing harmless about him.'

'You alarm yourself without necessity. Id—' She bit back the name once again. 'The person we're talking about is not the Archdeacon of Gwent.'

'He could be, Golde.'

'Impossible. Gwent is too small a county for a man of his high ambition. It would be a much lowlier office than the one he already occupies. On that account alone, he would spurn it.'

'I had not thought of that.'

'Rest easy.'

'We are too close to Wales for me to do that.'

'Forget this new archdeacon until you have to confront him at the shire hall. You've been so busy unburdening your bad news that I've been unable to tell you my good tidings.'

'Good tidings?'

'You and Gervase are not the only ones to receive a letter. Mine was waiting for me here,' she said, crossing to the little table to pick up the missive and hand it to him. 'It's from my sister. Aelgar expects to be here within a day or two.'

'These are indeed good tidings.'

'There's more yet, Ralph. She is betrothed.'

'It was only a matter of time.'

'Her future husband will be travelling with her.'

'Then we must give them both a worthy welcome. Gloucester may yet have some joy to offer us.' He enfolded her in his arms. 'I'm sorry to get into such a state, my love. It was the sheriff's manner which put me out of sorts. That and the threat of the mad archdeacon.' A sudden fear made him tighten his grasp. 'Your sister is betrothed, you say?'

'Yes.'

'To whom?'

'A young man from Archenfield.'

'Saints preserve us!' he gasped. 'Is he *Welsh*?'

Golde shook with mirth until he kissed her into submission.

* * *

The abbey was smothered under a blanket of sadness. When the guests arrived, they were given only a token welcome by the Hospitaller, who conducted them in silence to their lodgings. Hardly a monk looked up as they passed, hardly a spark of curiosity was ignited; a melancholy air pervaded the whole community. Those who padded across the cloister garth, shoulders hunched, chins on their chest, were deep in mourning. Even the novices, taking instruction from their master as the visitors went past, were figures of dejection. The atmosphere was in marked contrast to that of the abbey that Canon Hubert and Brother Simon had recently quit on the King's business. Winchester throbbed with a subdued vitality; Gloucester was a charnel house.

'I have never felt so uneasy inside the walls of a religious house,' admitted Simon. 'It is eerie.'

'Sacrilege has taken place here,' boomed Hubert as they followed their mute guide. 'A spiritual refuge has been despoiled.'

'I wish that we had not come, Canon Hubert.'

'Nonsense! We are needed here.'

'By whom?'

'By the abbot, by the brothers, by God. A terrible crime has been committed. Our footsteps have been guided here so that we may help to track down the villain responsible.'

Simon blanched. 'What can we do against a violent killer?'

'Expose him.'

'But we are strangers here, Canon Hubert.'

'That may be an advantage,' said the other blandly. 'An abbey rightly looks inward. Coming from the outside, we may perceive things that elude those who know nothing but life within the enclave. We may be of real help in this investigation.'

'I am unequal to it.'

'Fear not, Brother Simon. I will act for both of us.'

'You are ever my salvation.'

'Let us pray together before I begin.'

When they reached their lodgings, they deposited their satchels of documents before adjourning to the church to kneel in prayer. Tainted with blood, the place sent shivers through the cadaverous scribe and he implored God to cleanse the abbey forthwith and safeguard all within its holy bounds. Hubert soon left him to continue his supplication alone and made his way to the abbot's lodging to present himself to his old friend.

'I am delighted to see you, Hubert!' welcomed Serlo.

'And I, you, Father Abbot.'

'It has been too long a time since we last met.'

'You have ever been in my thoughts.'

'I only wish this blessed reunion could have taken place in happier circumstances. You have heard of our predicament, I daresay?'

'Alas, yes,' said Hubert. 'Durand the Sheriff told us.'

'He is no doubt searching the abbey even as we speak.'

'Looking for evidence?'

'More than that, Hubert,' said the other, his face clouding. 'Durand has seized on the disturbing notion that the killer himself may lurk within these walls.'

'That is a monstrous suggestion!'

'So I told him. I can vouch for every monk and novice at the abbey but the sheriff will not trust my word. He is questioning everyone.'

Hubert was glad to find the abbot alone, but concerned to see the distant anxiety in his eyes. It was the quiet desperation of a father who has been told that one of his sons is a callous murderer.

The room was large, low and musty. A crucifix stood on the bare table, a bible open beside it. When Hubert was waved to a seat, he lowered himself on to the wooden bench. Serlo himself sat beside the table.

'A royal commissioner!' he said with a congratulatory smile. 'You have done well, Hubert. Your talents have received due recognition.'

'Thank you, Father Abbot. I will not pretend that it is work which is close to my heart, but it is a necessary task and the King's bidding must be done. It has also given me the opportunity to expose much fraud and corruption so, in a sense, I am doing God's work as well.'

'Indeed, you are. Loud protests have been raised against this Great Survey but they have not come from me. Though it may lead to more taxes in some cases, this Domesday Book, as they call it, has the virtue of establishing rightful claims to property. I do not mind telling you, Hubert,' he said, lowering his voice to a confidential whisper, 'that this abbey was grossly exploited before I came here. All but ruined, in point of fact. Land was wilfully taken, income diverted from our coffers. I fought hard to regain much of what was lost.'

'You did, Father Abbot,' said Hubert knowledgeably. 'I have seen the returns for this county. You have already recovered the manors of Frocester and Coln St Aldwyn.'

'There are others which were illegally taken during the time of Abbot Wilstan, my predecessor. Nympsfield, for one. Does that come within the scope of your inquiry?' he asked, fishing gently. 'I would be indebted to you if it did.'

'Then I have to disappoint you, I fear. We have not been sent here to adjudicate on abbey property. The first commissioners only identified the worst irregularities and it is those we have come to address.'

'Could you not find time to hear our case?'

Hubert was firm. 'It is outside our jurisdiction, Father Abbot. We are tied by specific instruction. Privately, of course,' he said with a flabby smile, 'I will give you the most sympathetic hearing and advise you how best to represent the abbey's claims. Having acted in a judicial capacity so many times now, I like to think I am well versed in the intricacies of property disputes.'

'Are you the leader of this second commission?'

'Technically, no, but my word carries great weight. The lord

Ralph, our appointed head, is a veteran soldier who lacks an appreciation of legal subtleties. He is forced to turn to me very often,' said Hubert with smooth pomposity. 'But no more of my work. It is an irrelevance at this moment in time. Tell me more about this catastrophe which has struck the abbey. Who was this unfortunate Brother Nicholas of whom the sheriff spoke?'

'Our rent collector.'

'How long had he been dead before he was found?'

'We can only hazard a guess at that, Hubert.'

Serlo ran a palm across his wrinkled brow and gave a detailed account of how the murder victim had been found. Hubert was dismayed at what he heard. After condemning the anonymous killer in the strongest language he felt able to use, he turned his ire on the novices.

'I hope that they have been soundly swinged, Father Abbot,' he said, puffing with indignation. 'Their behaviour was disgraceful. To leave the dormitory like that, plunder the kitchen and flee into the church from the Master of the Novices! Their backs should be raw for a month.'

'Far too Draconian a remedy.'

'Disobedience must be punished. Not,' he added hastily, 'that I would presume to teach you how to rule here when you patently do so in the true spirit of the Benedictine Order. Yet, with respect, I do feel that these miscreants should be shown no mercy.'

'Then you and I must agree to differ, Hubert.'

'I hope not, Father Abbot.'

'Kenelm and Elaf are relative newcomers to the abbey. They have yet to understand the sacrifices which they must make. What they did was deplorable and they realise that now. However,' he continued, rising to his feet, 'I do not feel that a flogging is appropriate here. You may wish their backs to be raw for a month but their young minds will be raw for the rest of their lives. Think of what they endured, Hubert. Finding one of the reverent brothers dead. Lunging against his corpse in the dark. A hideous experience. It cured their misbehaviour in an instant.'

'That is one way of looking at it,' conceded Hubert.

'It is my way. Another consideration also guided me.'

'What was that, Father Abbot?'

'Kenelm and Elaf are key witnesses here. They were the first to be questioned by the sheriff and will certainly be called before him again. What sort of evidence can they give if they are writhing in pain after a beating with a birch rod?'

'I begin to see your reasoning.'

'I am glad you recognise it as reason rather than as weakness.'

'Nobody could ever accuse you of that.'

'The Master of the Novices might. He wanted to flay them.'

'They have vital evidence.'

'Yes,' said Serlo, raising a silver eyebrow, 'and they have yet to release all of it to us.'

'They are holding something back?'

'Not deliberately, Hubert. They are still stunned by their discovery. Still in a daze. They are eager to help yet one senses they have more to tell than has so far emerged. We must wait until the shock wears off. Facts which have so far been locked away inside their heads may then be drawn out of them.'

'Let me speak to them,' volunteered Hubert.

'You?'

'I am a skilled interrogator, Father Abbot, that is why the King has seen fit to employ me in this capacity. I am also used to the wiles and evasions of novices. When they are questioned by the sheriff, or by you and your obedientiaries, they are dealing with people they know, faces from their immediate world. I am a total stranger,' he argued. 'It will put them on their guard against me but it will disarm them at the same time because they will not know what to expect. With skill and patience, I might be able to dig out some of those buried facts.'

'You might be able to, Hubert.'

'Then I have your permission to speak with them?'

'Gladly – if it were not a waste of your time.'

'How a waste?'

'They are Saxon boys, still struggling to learn our tongue and still unequal to the harsher demands of Latin. Kenelm and Elaf would not really know what you were talking about.'

'But the sheriff has examined them.'

'Only through an interpreter, Brother Frewine, our Precentor.'

Hubert felt a thrill of pleasure as he remembered Gervase Bret.

'Then I will use an interpreter as well.'

When Gervase dined with his host that evening, he realised that the county was served by two sheriffs, both sharing the same name and body but quite distinct in personality. The man who had informed them of the murder was a brusque, arrogant man with no time for civilities and no tolerance of interference. In the presence of women, however, he became a considerate and almost playful character, laughing freely and trading on a rather heavy-handed charm. Seated directly opposite him in the hall, Gervase was grateful that Durand was flanked by his wife, Maud, a tall, slim creature with a pale beauty, and by Golde, looking every inch a Norman lady in a chemise and gown of light green hue with a white linen wimple. The interrelationships fascinated Gervase. Durand the Sheriff was humanised by his female companions and he, in turn, helped to take some of the haughtiness out of his wife's manner by gently mocking her when she tried to patronise Golde.

Ralph Delchard was less interested in their host's display of hospitality than in the quality of the food, which was excellent, the taste of the wine, which was above reproach, and the identity of a mystery man. The five of them were alone at table. When his cup was filled once more by a servant, Ralph sipped it with unfeigned satisfaction.

'A splendid vintage, my lord!' he said.

'Thank you,' replied Durand.

'There is nothing to match the taste of Norman wine.'

'I could not agree more.'

'It is unmistakable.'

'Not in this case,' said the other with a grin. 'What you are drinking has not come from Normandy at all but from somewhere much closer.'

'I refuse to believe it.'

'Go to the kitchens and ask them. They will tell you that this wine hails from the vineyard at Stonehouse in the Blacklow Hundred. Ride over there if you do not believe me.'

'Our duties leave no time for excursions,' said Ralph, peeved that he had been deceived. 'Golde has been trying to lure me into drinking ale, as she does, but I have set my face against it. Wine delights my palate.' He looked warily into his cup. 'Though it would delight me more if it had come from Normandy grapes.'

'You must learn to enjoy the pleasures of England.'

'I have, my lord. That is why I married one of them.'

Durand chuckled, Maud gave an ambiguous smile and Golde acknowledged the compliment with a grateful nod.

Ralph took another sip of the wine before trying to rid himself of his abiding fear.

'Who is the Archdeacon of Gwent?' he asked suddenly.

'What a strange question!' observed Maud with a shrill laugh.

'Do you know, my lady?'

'No, my lord. Nor do I care to know. Why do you ask?'

'My husband believes that the archdeacon may be an acquaintance of his,' explained Golde, 'though I have assured him that it is unlikely.'

'Give me certain proof,' said Ralph. 'What is his name?'

'Abraham,' replied the sheriff.

'Thank God!'

'You have met the fellow?'

'Happily, I have not.'

'Abraham the Priest is the Archdeacon of Gwent.'

'You have done wonders for my digestion, my lord,' said Ralph.

'What manner of man is the archdeacon?' wondered Gervase, looking across at Durand. 'It seems that he is to appear before us. What should we expect, my lord?'

'What you expect from every Welshman. Guile and deceit.'

'I have a higher opinion of the nation.'

'I don't!' said Ralph.

'The Welsh have always dealt honourably with me.'

'They deal honourably with me,' asserted the sheriff, lapsing back into his surlier self, 'when I have a sword in my hand and armed men at my back. It is the only way to extract honesty from them. By force.'

'Away with such talk!' complained Maud.

'Of course, of course,' said her husband in retreat.

'It has no place at the table.'

'I am sorry,' said Durand, soothing her with a penitent smile. 'We are here to enjoy our meal and not to raise the disagreeable subject of our neighbours.' He turned to Golde. 'My wife and I have a rule that I never bother her with affairs of state, still less with the trivialities which sometimes clutter up my day.'

'I would hardly call a murder a triviality,' observed Gervase.

'It belongs outside this hall, Master Bret,' chided his host with a glare. 'That is why we treat of more homely subjects such as the quality of the vineyard at Stonehouse.'

'Or the beer in Hereford,' murmured his wife, who did not know whether to be amused or dismissive about the revelation of Golde's earlier career as a brewer. 'I want a husband who can separate his private life from his more worldly concerns. Is it not so with every wife?'

'No,' said Golde loyally. 'I would love my husband whatever he talked about. I set no conditions whatsoever on his conversation.'

'That's just as well!' commented Ralph.

'What of your wife, Master Bret?' asked Maud.

'Alys seems content with me the way that I am, my lady.'

'Newly wed, then, I see.'

'Do not be so cynical, Maud,' teased Durand. 'Our guests will think that you are being serious.' More food was brought in on large platters. 'Ah! Here is the venison! Indulge yourselves, my friends. Eat your fill.'

The rest of the meal passed in pleasant banter. Whenever the talk seemed to be in the slightest danger of edging towards tedium, Durand would leap in with a gallant remark to the ladies or a provocative comment to the men. Time rolled easily by. It was Maud who brought an end to the festivities, stifling a yawn and excusing herself from the table, insisting that Golde went with her so that they could speak alone. Durand escorted them both to the door, bestowing a kiss on his wife's cheek and another on Golde's hand before he bowed them out. Then the smile froze on his lips. It was the other sheriff who came back to the table.

'I bid you good night,' he said off-handedly.

'One moment, my lord,' said Ralph, anxious to hear about the progress of the murder inquiry. 'You have not told us what transpired at the abbey this afternoon.'

'The abbey?'

'You rode off there shortly after we arrived.'

'So?'

'Have you narrowed down the number of suspects?'

'What is that to you?'

'A polite question deserves at least a polite answer,' said Ralph, straightening his shoulders. 'And while we are on the topic of civility, I am bound to say that we found your manner offensive when you rode out of the castle earlier. It is equally unappealing now.'

'It is not my wish to appeal.'

'I can see that.'

'We are curious about the murder, my lord,' said Gervase, eager to prevent a row developing between the two men. 'That is all.'

'Master your curiosity. It is not welcome here.'

'But the crime may have a bearing on our work.'

'How could it?' snorted the sheriff.

Ralph stood up. 'Surely you can tell us *something*,' he urged.

'Indeed I can,' retorted Durand. 'I can tell you in no uncertain terms to curb your interest in matters that do not concern you. I am sheriff here and I brook no intervention, however well intentioned. Your work is confined to the shire hall. Keep that in mind,' he said, heading for the door again, 'or it will go hard with both of you. Good night!'

He left the door wide open but they both felt that it had just been slammed in their faces. Ralph Delchard scratched his head in disbelief.

'Was that really the same man who entertained us so well in here tonight? I begin to think that power sits far too heavily upon him.'

'Yes, Ralph,' said Gervase. 'But not as heavily as his wife.'

Chapter Three

Gloucester was a clamorous city. Shortly after dawn was announced by a veritable choir of roosters, the first carts for market rumbled in through the gates, and their owners joined stallholders who lived within the precincts in setting out their wares and produce. Prompt housewives came in search of early bargains, playful children emerged from their homes, dogs and cats began a new day of foraging or fighting, and birds swooped down on discarded morsels. The quayside, too, was bustling with activity as boats set off with their cargoes, fishermen departed with their nets and the first craft came up the river to unload. Almost 3,000 people lived in Gloucester and it sounded as if they were all helping to swell the tumult.

The mounting cacophony wafted across to the castle on a light wind and brought even the deafest of its inhabitants awake. Ralph Delchard did not complain. He and Gervase Bret were already up at dawn, sharing breakfast alone in the hall so that they could make full use of the day. A combination of soft beds and Stonehouse wine made them sleep soundly, and they awoke refreshed, ready to shake off the memory of their friction with the sheriff so that they could give all their attention to the work which had brought them there. Accompanied by half-a-dozen of Ralph's men, they were soon leaving the castle to ride to the shire hall in Westgate Street. The commotion was now greater than ever and they inhaled the distinctive smell of the city, compounded of fish, flowers, ripe fruit, stagnant water, animal dung, human excrement, filthy clothing and the accumulated refuse over which flies were already buzzing crazily.

'What a stink!' said Ralph, wrinkling his nose.

'We'll get used to it,' said Gervase.

'We'll have to now that our stay is likely to be much longer than we imagined. What fool told me that we would be gone in a week?'

'That may still be the case, Ralph.'

'I doubt it. We could be here for *months*!'

Gervase smiled. 'It will give you time to get to know Durand better.'

'I know his kind only too well already. The sheriff will do little to make our visit more pleasant and much to impede us. Left to him, we would be on the road home this very morning.'

Arriving at the shire hall, they tethered their horses and went inside, taking two men with them while leaving the other four on guard at the door. Canon Hubert and Brother Simon were already there, having walked from the abbey, and they greeted the newcomers with polite nods. Ralph and Gervase took their bearings. The shire hall was a substantial building of timber and interwoven wattle. Open shutters allowed light to flood into the room, but fresh air did not completely dispel the reek of damp. An oak table and bench had been set out facing a series of much longer benches to accommodate any witnesses they had to examine. The place had been recently swept and a jug of wine with four cups provided for them. Apart from its greater size, there was nothing to set it apart from the many other shire halls which they made use of in their travels. It was an adequate but nondescript courtroom.

Ralph was just about to ask where the reeve was when the man himself swept in through the door with a flourish. It was a dramatic entrance by someone who had deliberately waited until they were all present before he saw fit to make his own appearance.

'Good morrow, sirs!' he declared. 'Welcome to our fair city.'

'Thank you,' said Ralph.

'I am Nigel the Reeve. Tell me your requirements and they will be satisfied to the letter. The first commissioners, who included Remigius, Bishop of Lincoln, did not find me wanting. Indeed, one of their number, the lord Adam Fitzherbert, went out of his way to compliment me. I trust I will earn similar approval from you.'

While introducing himself and his companions, Ralph took a moment to weigh the man up. Short, compact, well dressed and clean-shaven, Nigel the Reeve had an air of unassailable self-importance. It was not just the lordly pose he adopted nor the condescending tone in which he spoke. He exuded pomposity. Now in his forties, he had the solid look of a soldier overlaid with the trappings of office. Nigel was a royal reeve who administered Gloucester on behalf of the crown yet who acted as if he were wearing that symbol of majesty. Taking an immediate dislike to the fellow, Ralph sought to put him in his place from the start.

'We sent full instructions from Winchester,' he said, meeting the reeve's supercilious gaze. 'I trust that they have been obeyed.'

'Yes, my lord.'

'Good.'

'The first disputants will arrive when the abbey bell rings for Sext. That will give you and your fellow commissioners plenty of time to settle in here and prepare yourselves. When the Bishop of Lincoln was here—'

'I want no anecdotes about our predecessors,' interrupted Ralph sharply. 'If they had done their job thoroughly – and, by implication, you had been as efficient as you obviously think you are – the problems which we have come to solve would not have existed.'

'I do not think you can fault me, my lord.'

'We shall see.'

'My reputation goes before me.'

'It will be put to the test.'

'Respect my position,' warned the other, drawing himself up to his full height. 'I am not at your beck and call. Many other duties fall to me as well. Important commitments which must be honoured. I have shown you the courtesy of a personal welcome but will have to assign most of your requests to one of my underlings.'

'You will still be responsible for their actions.'

'Naturally.'

'Make sure that they are diligent.'

'Do not try to teach me my occupation, my lord.'

'I merely advise you to answer our demands with celerity.'

Nigel replied with a look of disdain. Gervase stepped in to see what information he could glean from the reeve with a more friendly approach.

'It was kind of you to have the shire hall prepared for us,' he said.

'I did no less for the first commissioners,' said the other, sniffing meaningfully. 'Though they seemed to carry more authority than those that follow them. The bishop had a clerk and two monks in attendance, supported by three lords of high standing. You travel much lighter.'

'Our pronouncements have equal weight,' said Ralph.

'Tell us something about Gloucester,' invited Gervase, riding over his friend's comment. 'As reeve here, you must know it as well as anyone and we are anxious to hear your insights. The sheriff, alas, did not feel able to furnish us with much intelligence.'

'That is not surprising,' muttered Nigel.

'You and he must see a great deal of each other.'

'Yes, Master Bret.'

There was a wealth of regret in his voice but he was too diplomatic to put his hostility into words. Gervase understood the situation at once. Though the reeve held a crucial administrative position, his powers were severely limited by a domineering sheriff. Evidently, there was no love lost between the two men. Gervase introduced some gentle flattery.

'I suspect that you are a surer guide than our host,' he said.

'Durand sees little that happens outside the castle.'

'Whereas you do.'

'Inevitably.'

'What kind of place is Gloucester?'

'It is mine,' said Nigel with a gesture of pride, 'and I have made it indisputably one of the finest cities in the realm.'

'How did you do that?'

The reeve needed no prompting. He described the city, its history and its relationship to the surrounding county. Though his lecture was couched in unashamed self-admiration, it was both lucid and concise. Hubert threw in a few questions of his own and they were answered frankly. By the time the reeve had finished, the visitors had a much clearer idea of the place they had come to and the personalities they would encounter.

Gervase was sincerely grateful. Feeling that he had established his primacy once more, Nigel the Reeve gave a token bow and withdrew with dignity.

'I'll teach the rogue to mend his manners before I'm done,' said Ralph, glowering at the door. 'Those airs and graces will get short shrift from me. Who does he think he is?'

'I found his comments enlightening,' observed Hubert.

'So did I,' Brother Simon piped up.

'He needs to be handled in the right way,' said Gervase.

Ralph gave a grim chuckle. 'Around the throat.'

He called the others to order and they took their seats behind the table, spreading out the documents that related to the first case they were due to investigate and discussing the questions they would need to put to the disputants. Only a minor case was coming before them on their first day and they saw no reason why it could not be dispatched quickly. When they had reviewed some of the other disputes on which they would adjudicate, there was a little time left before their official duties began. Ralph turned to the subject which he had put aside until now.

'How did you find the abbey, Canon Hubert?'

'Sorely troubled, my lord,' said the other. 'It is a sad place.'

'I did not sleep a wink there,' confided Simon.

'The fear is tangible. Abbot Serlo does not believe it will leave the abbey until the murderer has been caught and executed. We talked at length about the crime,' said Hubert solemnly. 'About its nature, its impact and its consequences in the longer term.'

'What are the details?' asked Ralph.

'The story is more complicated than the sheriff made it sound when he first broached the topic to us. Brother Nicholas, it turns out, occupied a somewhat strange position at the abbey.'

Ralph and Gervase listened intently while Hubert explained what he meant. Beside the overwhelming vanity of the reeve, Hubert's flights of pomposity seemed negligible, and his constant reference to his friendship with Abbot Serlo was forgiven because it had yielded so much of interest to his listeners. His account of the murder was indeed far more detailed than the one given by Durand and he was happy to amplify it.

'Let us go back to the spot where the body was found,' decided Ralph. 'On a wooden platform in the bell tower, you say?'

'That is correct, my lord.'

'What reason would Brother Nicholas have to go there?'

'None whatsoever.'

'Did he have duties regarding the bell?'

'No, my lord. They fall to the Sub-Sacristan.'

'Is it not likely, then, that the victim was killed elsewhere and carried into the church so that his corpse could be hidden there?'

'That occurred to me,' said Hubert, 'but the abbot discounted that proposition, arguing that it would be very difficult to carry a dead body up the ladder to the loft.'

'Perhaps he was not carried,' suggested Gervase. 'The killer might have hauled him up with a rope.'

'That, too, occurred to me but the abbot was sceptical. Where was the blood that must surely have dripped from his wound? His throat was slit from ear to ear, his cowl was sodden. Had he been hauled aloft, his blood would have been all over the floor yet there was no sign of it. Nor,' said Hubert, anticipating Gervase's next guess, 'was there any indication of the floor being recently washed to remove stains. The whole abbey has been searched and the only place bloodstains were found was on the timber where he lay.'

'So that is where he was killed,' concluded Ralph.

'Apparently, my lord.'

'What on earth was he doing up there?'

'Abbot Serlo is at a loss to understand that.'

'How long had he been missing?'

'A couple of days.'

'Who saw him last?'

'One of the tenants from whom he collected rent.'

'Close by the abbey?'

'Some miles away, my lord,' said Hubert, with an expansive gesture of his hands. 'The abbey's land is scattered far and wide.'

'I know.'

'It owns seventeen manors in the county,' noted Gervase.

'Far too many,' decided Ralph, fingering his chin as he pondered. 'Could that provide the motive?' he said at length. 'The fact that Brother Nicholas collected rents? Did he upset one of the tenants? Or was his scrip so full of money that it incited someone to theft and murder? No,' he added, thinking it through, 'why would any monk be foolhardy enough to climb up a ladder with a vengeful tenant? What would such a person be doing in the abbey church with Nicholas in the first place? I begin to wonder if Durand's accusation may be just. Perhaps the victim *was* slain by one of his fellow monks.'

'No!' protested Simon.

'It is unthinkable!' wailed Hubert.

'Not to the sheriff,' said Ralph.

'He does not know the monks, my lord. Abbot Serlo does. And there is not one among them on whom the slightest suspicion can fall. Take the abbot's word for it. Brother Nicholas was killed by an outsider.'

'Or by a guest at the abbey,' said Gervase.

'Or by an act of God,' said Ralph with mild sarcasm. 'On the face of it it's a baffling crime, but that only makes me want to get to grips with it. If time serves, I would value a talk with Abbot Serlo myself. Would that be at all possible, Hubert?'

'If the approach were first made through me, my lord.'

'Of course.'

'There's a couple of individuals we're forgetting,' remarked Gervase. 'The novices who stumbled on the body that night. What about them?'

Hubert gave his first smile of the day. 'I'm glad that you mention them. They are young boys, Kenelm and Elaf by name. The abbot has given me permission to question them myself but I need an interpreter to reach them in their own tongue. Brother Frewine, the Precentor, could serve in that office but he is a stranger to me and, from what I can gather, too well disposed towards the boys to be entirely independent in his judgements. I prefer someone of proven skill in translation, someone I know well, someone I can trust.'

'Gervase is the obvious person,' said Ralph.

'That is what I felt, my lord.' Hubert looked at Gervase. 'Will you please help me in the interrogation?'

'Do I have any choice in the matter?' asked Gervase.

'No!' said Ralph cheerfully.

'Then it is settled. I am at your command, Canon Hubert, and glad to be of assistance. Their names are Kenelm and Elaf, you say. What sort of boys are they?'

'Frightened ones.'

It was ironic. Kenelm was the older, bigger and more boisterous of the two novices, and yet he was the one who suffered most. Elaf, who had unwittingly fallen against the dead body of Brother

Nicholas, was still haunted by the memory but he was learning to master his emotions in a way that eluded his friend, making it necessary for Elaf to provide the reassurance which had hitherto come from Kenelm. As they sat with the other novices and took instruction from Brother Paul, it was Kenelm who kept nervously glancing across to Elaf for moral support.

'*Cantate Domino canticum novum: quia mirabilia fecit.*'

Afraid to be caught at fault, they joined the others in their recitation of the psalm, knowing that Brother Paul was keeping a close eye on both of them. The Master of the Novices was a brawny man of medium height, with muscular forearms covered with thick black hair and bushy eyebrows which all but hid his dark, gleaming eyes. Brother Paul believed in summary justice. A sound beating soon after an offence had been committed was, in his opinion, the best way to enforce discipline. Kenelm and Elaf had committed a whole series of offences, ranging from youthful mischief to outright theft, and it pained Brother Paul that he was not allowed to inflict the savage punishment he felt was their due. Instead of howling in agony, they were praising the Lord.

> '*Salvabit sibi dextera eus; et brachium sanctum eius.*
> *Notum fecit Dominus sautare suum; in conspectu,*
> *Gentium revelavit iustitiam suam.*'

The Master listened carefully, hoping for a stumble or stutter from Kenelm or Elaf so that he would have legitimate cause to upbraid them on a minor charge. Paul had not forgotten the wild chase on which they had led him through the darkness and he longed for retribution. But they gave him no opportunity to claim it now. Though their minds were in turmoil, Kenelm and Elaf chanted the Latin with clarity and precision.

'*Iudicabit orbem terrarum in iustitia; et populos in aequitate.*'

It was a long while before the novices were released from their lesson. Elaf used their brief freedom to visit the abbey garden.

Kenelm trotted after him, desperate for a moment alone with his friend. Together they reached the cover of some shrubs.

'How can you keep so calm, Elaf?' asked Kenelm.

'I am not calm underneath.'

'My mind gives me no rest. I cannot stop thinking of what we found in the bell tower. Nor can I get rid of that awful smell of death.'

'I still catch a whiff of that,' confessed Elaf. 'And at night, lying in the dark, I still remember that I *touched* poor Brother Nicholas.'

'That is something else which plagues me.'

'What is?'

'He is poor Brother Nicholas now but he was loathsome Brother Nicholas while he was alive. I despised him as much as anyone. I writhe with guilt about it. He was not the hateful man I took him for, Elaf. His murder has made me see him afresh.'

'It is so with me, Kenelm. I feel nothing but sympathy.'

'Sympathy and fear.'

'Yes, terrible fear. It makes my stomach turn.'

'I have not been able to eat a morsel since that night.'

'Find solace in prayer.'

'I have tried,' said Kenelm. 'I have even sought Brother Owl's advice but he has not been able to help me shake these terrible thoughts from my head. How have you done so, Elaf?'

'By prayer and meditation.'

'All that I can meditate on is that dead body.'

'Our pain will ease in time.'

'Not while we stay here.'

'What do you mean?'

'There are too many reminders,' said Kenelm morosely. 'Every time I see the church, I think of what we found there. Every time one of the brothers walks across the cloister garth, I think it is Brother Nicholas. We will never escape those memories as long as we stay here.'

'We have to stay, Kenelm.'

'Do we?'

A dangerous notion began to form but Kenelm had no chance to discuss it with Elaf. A sudden rustling sound alerted them to the presence of an eavesdropper. Frightened that it was Brother Paul, they were rooted to the spot, but it was not the Master of the Novices who stepped from behind a bush. It was the diminutive figure of Owen, the youngest of the novices, teased by the others for his innocence and persecuted for his rosy-cheeked prettiness. Owen seemed to be on the point of speaking to them but he lost his nerve and turned tail, scurrying off as fast as his little legs would take him.

'Was he listening?' said Elaf in alarm.

'I hope not.'

'Do you think Owen will tell on us?'

'Not if he has any sense,' warned Kenelm, bunching a fist and recovering some of his former bravado. 'Or he'll answer to me.'

The first case which animated the shire hall concerned misappropriation of land in the Bisley Hundred. A Saxon thegn, formerly the owner of the property, alleged that it had been steadily encroached upon by his Norman neighbour until it was all but swallowed up in the latter's estate. The dispute soon moved from reasoned argument to bellowed assertion and Ralph Delchard had to step in to subdue the two men and caution them against any further descent into a verbal brawl. What made the issue slightly more complicated was the fact that a third person, Alfwold, presented himself to the commissioners and claimed that he had the right to the land in question on account of a bequest made over fifty years earlier when a Danish king ruled the country.

It was left to Gervase Bret to study the last will and testament of a certain Leofhelm the Anchorite before translating the Anglo-Saxon aloud.

'Leofhelm the Anchorite, God's exile, greets King Cnut and

Queen Emma very joyfully with God's joy. And I make it known to you that I have entrusted our charitable gift to Christ and all his saints where it shall remain for the comfort and happiness of our soul. First, the estate near Frampton Mansell to the Abbey of St Peter in Gloucester, where our bones shall lie; the remainder of our property, the manors of Sapperton and Westwood, to our heirs in perpetuity . . .'

Cries of outrage from the other two disputants greeted this new claim and Ralph had to impose himself even more strongly. He had grave doubts about the validity of the document and was supported by Canon Hubert, who, knowing that Sapperton was firmly in the possession of the powerful Robert de Tosny, did not wish to draw in a fourth person to further enliven the debate. It was Gervase who eventually ruled out the will of Leofhelm, finding inaccuracies in the wording and the calligraphy which confirmed his suspicion that the document was a blatant forgery. The bold Alfwold tried first to bluster then to bluff his way out of the situation but Ralph was merciless. Summoning his men, he had the supposed descendant of Leofhelm the Anchorite placed under arrest and hauled off to cool his heels in a dungeon at the castle.

With one claimant out of the way, the commissioners swiftly disposed of another, restoring it to the thegn from whom it had been illegally taken and chastising his rapacious neighbour in round terms. When the shire hall was cleared of witnesses, the four men were able to relax in the knowledge that it was only mid-afternoon yet their work was done for the day. Ralph wanted to make good use of their leisure time.

'We must go to the abbey, Gervase,' he announced, gathering up his documents, 'and inspect the scene of the crime in the hope of picking up clues which others may have missed.'

'I was about to urge that idea on you,' said Gervase.

'It may not be altogether welcome,' warned Hubert.

'Why not?' said Ralph.

'Because the abbot is already unhappy about the way that the sheriff and his men are trampling all over the abbey. It is very unsettling. The last thing he wants is more lay people intruding.'

'Intruding? Did I hear you aright, Hubert? You call us intruders? Doesn't the abbot *want* this dreadful crime to be solved?'

'It is his dearest wish, my lord.'

'Then he must endure the curiosity of those who wish to help.'

'You would need to secure his permission first.'

'Perhaps you could be our ambassador there, Canon Hubert,' said Gervase politely. 'Since you have privileged access to Abbot Serlo, you would be the ideal person to put our request before him. And while we are in the abbey, of course, I could find a moment to question the two novices with you. Could that be arranged as well?'

Hubert was persuaded. 'It will be, Gervase.'

'Then what are we waiting for?' said Ralph impatiently. 'Lead the way, Hubert. I long to see this bell tower and, if possible, to view the body of the deceased.'

'That is something I am not able to guarantee, my lord.'

'At least, get us inside the church.'

Canon Hubert nodded confidently and left the hall, picking his way through the crowd with surprising nimbleness and towing Brother Simon behind him. Ralph went out to the sentries and sent them back to the castle with the satchels which he and Gervase had brought. The two of them then mounted their horses and ambled off in pursuit of their colleagues, noting that the streets were busier than ever and that the city smells had taken on a greater pungency. When they reached the abbey, they did not have long to wait. Hubert appeared to confirm that the abbot's permission had been granted, and he conducted them to the church as if he were a long-standing member of the community and not merely a recent visitor. Ralph and Gervase easily tolerated his customary self-importance. Compared to Nigel the Reeve, the canon was modest and unassuming.

Shafts of sunlight shone through the windows to pierce the gloomy interior of the church and illumine the way to the bell tower. Hubert was hovering at Ralph's elbow. Gervase could see that his friend was becoming increasingly annoyed by their colleague's presence and he moved in tactfully before Ralph resorted to language unfit to be heard on consecrated ground.

'Since you know the abbey so well,' said Gervase, taking Hubert gently by the arm, 'perhaps you could track down those two novices, Kenelm and Elaf. We will talk with them anon.'

'Am I not needed here?' said Hubert.

'No!' Ralph was blunt.

'But I could be of assistance.'

'Do as Gervase bids and you will be.'

Hubert's pride was hurt. Gathering his paunch in both hands, he plodded off on his errand without a backward glance.

Ralph looked around the church to see what other exits it possessed, then he turned his attention to the ladder which led up to the loft, testing it for strength and reliability. Satisfied that it was robust enough, he turned to Gervase and took a firm grip on him.

'What are you doing, Ralph?' protested the other.

'Proving something to myself.'

'Does it involve assaulting me?'

'Relax and have faith in your friend.'

Having secured a hold, Ralph suddenly hoisted Gervase over his shoulder and held him there with one hand as he began to climb the ladder. It was a slow and perilous ascent, leaving Gervase to stare down at a slowly receding stone floor while having no control over his limbs. The rungs of the ladder creaked ominously under the combined weight and it bent and swayed from time to time, but Ralph went purposefully on, making light of the problems. When he reached the top, he eased Gervase carefully on to his back on the wooden platform then clambered up to join him.

'There!' he said triumphantly. 'I knew it. It *was* possible for the killer to carry his victim up here.'

'Only if he was as strong and wilful as you, Ralph,' said Gervase, head still pounding from the ordeal. 'I'll tell you this. You are certainly not going to carry me down again.'

'It will not be necessary. I've proved my point.'

'What about the dripping blood?'

'Easily stemmed by wrapping a cloth around the victim's neck.'

'I remain to be convinced.'

'Then let's look around.'

There was not much room for two adults in the confined area. The huge iron bell took up most of the available space, hanging silent and lifeless now but capable of rousing the whole city when rung in earnest. Light was poor but they could see far more than the two novices who had used the place as a nighttime refuge. Several bloodstains were visible on the timber and they examined them with care, noting their position and texture. For the rest, there was nothing else in the loft apart from a coil of rope, which would, in time, replace the existing bell rope, and a new stay, hewn out of ash and, judging by the one already in position to prevent the bell from turning full circle when it was rung, soon to be brought into use instead of its battered predecessor.

'It's far too dark up here,' said Ralph. 'We should have thought to bring a candle with us.'

'We have at least established one thing,' observed Gervase.

'Yes, you don't like to be carried up ladders.'

'That, too, I grant you. No, sit down and you will see what I mean.' Ralph lowered himself into a seated position beside Gervase. 'It is a perfect hiding place. Even during the day it is impossible to see anyone up here if they are crouched down.'

'Or lying full-length in their own blood.'

'Quite.'

'The killer knew exactly where to stow the body. Had it not

51

been for those two boys, it might have lain undetected for much longer.'

'Until the stink became too unbearable!'

Ralph got up and kept a steadying hand on the bell as he manoeuvred his way around to the other side of it. Even more shadow obscured his view there so he relied on touch rather than sight, feeling his way gently along each timber. The oaken beams were thick and well-seasoned and he admired the skill with which they had been chiselled into shape and shorn of their roughness. When he came to the largest beam of all, he used both hands to explore it, finding nothing untoward until he slipped them under the timber to feel the other side. His fingers met something which caused him to stop in surprise.

'Now that's interesting,' he said, identifying his find.

'What is it, Ralph?'

'Something I didn't expect on the back of this beam.'

'A bird's nest or a couple of bats?'

'No, Gervase, these were put here by the hand of man, but for what possible purpose I can't rightly say. Nobody would fix them on the wrong side of the beam like this.'

'Why? What is it that you've found?'

'Hooks,' said Ralph, still fingering his discovery. 'Two large hooks.'

Chapter Four

Travelling with Ralph Delchard on royal business brought setbacks as well as benefits for Golde. Although she could enjoy the pleasure of her husband's company, she also endured the discomfort of watching him plunge regularly into situations that were fraught with danger. Nor had her journeys been entirely free from personal slights and humiliations. On her first outing with Ralph, to York, she had lacked the wedding ring that made her his legitimate bride and she was, accordingly, treated as his mistress by the disapproving wife of their host. It had caused Golde intense embarrassment and there were other places where her presence had not been wholly welcome. After her initial meeting with the critical lady Maud, her hostess, she feared that Gloucester might be another venue where her Saxon origins aroused muted hostility or covert derision.

Golde was pleased, therefore, when Maud approached her with the offer of a guided tour of the city that afternoon. Maud was polite rather than friendly, and there was the faint sense of an effort being made, but that did not detract from the nature of the invitation. Golde willingly accepted. It would give her an opportunity both to re-acquaint herself with a city she had once visited with her father and to win over her hostess. When the two met in the bailey, horses had already been saddled for them, ostlers waited to help them mount and four soldiers were in attendance to escort them.

'You have been here before, you say?' recalled Maud.

'Yes, my lady. Many years ago.'

'You may notice some changes since then.'

'This castle is one of them,' said Golde without rancour. 'When King Edward sat on the throne, he held his Witenagemot – his Great Council – at the Palace of Kingsholm.'

'Those days are over.'

'So it seems.'

'This castle is now the most important building in the county.' She gave a smile. 'The abbot would dispute that, of course, and rightly so, but this is where affairs of state are decided. A castle can never be an ideal home for a woman but one has to make the best of it. I suspect that the lord Ralph's manor house is a far more comfortable place to live.'

'It is, my lady.'

'Where are his estates?'

'In Hampshire. A beautiful county.'

'Gloucestershire, too, has its charms.'

Maud's manner was pleasant and Golde detected none of the resentment she had felt during the meal on the previous evening. What impressed her hostess was Golde's easy mastery of Norman French, a language which she had learned from her husband while simultaneously instructing him in her own. Neither Durand the Sheriff nor his wife made the slightest effort to understand the native tongue of their citizens, still less their culture and customs.

Assisted into the saddle, the two ladies were about to ride off when the sheriff came striding across to bid them farewell. Durand's grin was restored along with the flirtatious glint in his eye.

'Are you deserting me?' he asked with mock distress.

'We are going to see the sights,' said his wife.

'Am I myself not one of them?'

'Do not fish for compliments, Durand.'

'How else will I get them?'

'They are yours by right, my lord,' said Golde.

'That is what I tell Maud but my virtues stale with time.'

His wife gave a shrug. 'That is the way of the world.'

'Then why do I see your beauty afresh every morning?'

She accepted the compliment with a smile, extended a hand for him to kiss then said something under her breath to Durand. His quiet laugh made Golde feel that she was intruding on a private moment between man and wife. Approaching hoofbeats were heard and all three of them turned towards the gate. The drumming on the drawbridge timbers suggested a rider who was in a hurry. Entering the bailey at a steady canter, he reined in his horse when he recognised the sheriff. Judging by the sweat on his brow and the lather on his mount, the messenger had ridden far and fast. He pulled a letter from his belt and handed it to Durand. The seal indicated the urgency of the missive.

Opening the letter, Durand read it quickly then registered great surprise. The messenger dismounted to await his response. The sheriff signalled for him to follow then strode off swiftly towards the keep.

'What is it, Durand?' asked his wife.

But her beauty was no longer enough to detain him. Spurred on by some unexpected news, he was blind to anything but his duty. Golde could see how peeved her companion was at being so rudely ignored and she wisely restrained herself from attempting conversation with Maud when they set off. As they rode along, Golde wondered about the contents of a letter which could turn an amorous husband into an indifferent one.

Ralph Delchard stepped inside the abbot's lodging and took a quick inventory of its contents while exchanging niceties. Serlo kept him standing while he appraised him, knowing that a man chosen to lead the second team of commissioners must rank high in the King's estimation. Ralph withstood his scrutiny without flinching under the searching gaze.

'Canon Hubert tells me that you wish to speak to me,' said Serlo.

'That is true.'

'Everything about you indicates a soldier so I can hardly suppose you wish to join the Benedictine Order. That leaves two possibilities. Either you have come here to endow the abbey, or, as I suspect, you are curious to learn more about this fearful crime which afflicts us.'

'Your suspicion is well-founded, my lord abbot.'

'Has the sheriff requested your assistance?'

'Not in so many words.'

'I thought not.'

'But I am sure he would give this visit tacit approval.'

'And I am equally certain that he would not,' said the abbot levelly. 'Durand has many good qualities but tolerance is not among them. He is, by nature, unduly possessive. My guess is that he would make no bones about the fact that he does not want your interference.'

'Help is not interference.'

'Our sheriff would identify them as one and the same thing.'

'And you, my lord abbot?'

'What about me?'

'You want this killer caught as soon as possible?'

'Of course.'

'Then you need additional assistance.'

'Why should it come from you, my lord?'

Ralph spread his arms. 'Why not?'

'I can think of a number of reasons,' said Serlo, lowering himself into his seat. 'First, you have important business here in the city which should preclude anything else. Second, you are a complete stranger and cannot possibly expect me to place the confidence in you that I place in the sheriff. Third, you are profoundly ignorant of the way that this abbey is run and fourth, if I am to believe Canon Hubert, your general attitude towards religious houses falls far short of respect.'

'I plead guilty to that last charge,' said Ralph with a grin, 'but, then, I am not alone in wanting to mount an investigation. My dear friend and colleague, Gervase Bret, is at my side and, as Hubert can tell you, Gervase has enough respect for both of us. He cannot pass an abbey without genuflecting. Until wiser counsels prevailed, he all but took the cowl himself. In short, my lord abbot, his instincts are sufficiently sacred to offset my leanings towards profanity.'

'You are an honest sinner, I'll say that for you.'

'Honest and cheerful.'

'And altogether too glib, my lord.'

'I stand rebuked. Talking of which, may I sit down?'

'When I decide if you are staying,' said the abbot, raising a hand to check his movement. 'State your business, please.'

'I want to solve a murder.'

'Why?'

'All just men abhor violent crime.'

'They do not all seek to catch an offender.'

'I cannot rest while a killer is on the loose.'

'Durand the Sheriff has sworn to track him down.'

'We may move at a swifter pace.'

'Your host would not thank you for saying that.'

'No,' said Ralph happily. 'Nor will he raise a cheer when we do his job for him more successfully than he himself but that thought will not hinder us. Bringing a murderer to justice takes priority over anxieties about ruffling the feathers of a sheriff.'

'From the way you say that, I deduce that he would not be the first sheriff on whose toes you have unwittingly trodden?' Ralph beamed at him. 'Your position differs from ours, my lord. Durand's word is law in these parts. When you have thoroughly upset him, you can ride away and forget all about him. It is those of us who stay here who will suffer the consequences of his wrath.'

'You will easily cope with Durand,' said Ralph. 'Hubert has been talking about you all the way from Winchester. He reveres you. No aspect of your good work here has been obscured from us. To do so much in such a short time indicates a man of true

Christian purpose and with enough guile to lead a sheriff by the nose.'

'I doubt if Canon Hubert used the word guile.'

'He called you a supreme diplomat.'

'It is not a phrase I can apply to you, my lord.'

'I'm delighted to hear it. Politicians have their place but so do men of action. I am one of them. That is why I cannot resist getting involved in a murder inquiry. It is not mere curiosity, believe me.'

'Then what is it?'

'Disgust at the nature of this particular crime.'

'We all share that disgust.'

'Let me help you, my lord abbot,' said Ralph, taking a step towards him. 'What can you lose? If I fail, the worst that I will have been is a nuisance. If I succeed – and I usually do in such cases – the whole abbey will sleep more soundly in its bed.'

'That is certainly a desired end,' admitted the other. 'It has been a shattering experience. We feel invaded. The sanctity of our church has been vitiated. One of my greatest ambitions is to build a fine new abbey church and this outrage has reinforced the strength of that ambition. I want the murderer to be caught swiftly so that we can begin to put this whole hideous business behind us.'

'That is why you need me and Gervase Bret.'

'I remain unconvinced.'

'We have sharper eyes than the doughty sheriff.'

'Prove it.'

'Easily,' said Ralph. 'Durand still believes that Brother Nicholas was killed by one of the other monks. We do not. No member of the Order would defile consecrated ground in this way.'

'I am glad that you agree with me on that point.'

'Brother Nicholas was the one member of the community who went outside the enclave on a regular basis. That is where we must look for his killer. Among the tenants whose rents he collected and among the other people he would normally meet in the course of his travels. Does that not set us apart from Durand?' he said, showing his palms again. 'While the sheriff's officers are causing havoc within the abbey, we will be out hunting the murderer where he is likely to be.'

Abbot Serlo pursed his lips as he studied Ralph afresh. After a full two minutes, he eventually reached a decision and indicated the bench.

'Perhaps you had better sit down, after all,' he said.

The meeting took place in the Precentor's lodging, a room too small to accommodate all five of them with any comfort and obliging the novices to stand with their backs pressed up against the wall. Ranged against them were Canon Hubert, Gervase Bret and Brother Frewine, who looked less like an owl on this occasion, and more like a mother hen worried about the safety of her chicks. The boys were deeply grateful that the Precentor was there to support them. Gervase's manner was friendly but Canon Hubert's bulk and stern judicial gaze made him an intimidating figure in such a cramped area. Hubert conducted the interrogation with Gervase acting as his interpreter and turning to Frewine each time he translated a question to collect his approval of the wording. While he could have wished for a less menacing inquisitor, Brother Owl had no reservations about the skill of the interpreter.

Kenelm and Elaf were tired and scared. They had already been subjected to close questioning by the abbot, the Master of the Novices, the Precentor and the sheriff. Hoping for some relief from the endless enquiries, they were disheartened to be hauled in front of Canon Hubert. Gervase did his best to gain their confidence by talking about his own time as a novice but the boys remained on guard and Kenelm, in particular, was difficult to draw out.

'Ask them when they last saw Brother Nicholas,' said Hubert.

Gervase translated and the boys looked blankly at each other.

'Three days ago,' prompted Frewine.

'Let them answer for themselves,' said Hubert.

'Well?' encouraged Gervase.

'Three days ago,' agreed Elaf.

'Where?'

'Here in the abbey.'

'Where exactly?'

'Crossing the cloister garth.'

'Was he alone?' asked Gervase.

'Oh, yes, Master Bret.'

'You sound as if Brother Nicholas was usually alone.'

'He was.'

'Why was that?'

Elaf looked guiltily across at Frewine. Hubert grew impatient.

'What is he saying, Gervase?'

After translating for him, Gervase suggested that he be allowed to put a series of contiguous questions himself to speed up the examination and extract more out of the boys. Reluctant to yield up control, Hubert nevertheless saw the virtue in the proposal and accepted it. Gervase turned back to Elaf, still having a silent conversation with Frewine.

'Tell me the truth,' said Gervase softly.

'Brother Nicholas . . .' The boy faltered. 'He preferred to be alone.'

'You mean that the other monks did not like him?'

'Well, yes, I suppose so.'

'That is not the case at all,' said Frewine loyally.

'The sheriff thinks otherwise,' countered Gervase. 'And with great respect, Brother Frewine, I would like to hear Elaf and Kenelm answer. They may perceive Brother Nicholas in ways that are different from you.'

'Understandably.'

'Is that not so, Kenelm?' continued Gervase. 'You have said little enough so far. Whom do you agree with here? Elaf or Brother

Frewine? Do you think that Brother Nicholas was unpopular?'

'Yes,' murmured Kenelm.

'Why was that?'

'I don't know.'

'Elaf?'

'Nor me.'

'But you must have some idea.'

'We didn't know Brother Nicholas very well.'

'You knew him well enough to identify him in the cloister garth. And you must have picked up the gossip. I know that I did during my novitiate. We were always searching hungrily for scraps of information about our holy brothers. Which ones were kind, which ones were critical, which ones sounded like wild animals caught in a snare whenever they tried to sing.' Kenelm smiled and Elaf gave an involuntary giggle. 'I see that you have some toneless monks here as well. We certainly did at Eltham. What sort of a voice did Brother Nicholas have?'

'A funny one,' volunteered Elaf.

'Funny?'

'He was not in the choir,' explained Frewine quickly. 'Brother Nicholas's voice was not suited to choral singing, I fear. He had other virtues by way of compensation but his voice was a little odd.'

'Odd?'

'High and quavering.'

'Could you not train it, Brother Frewine?'

'I lacked both the time and the skill. My hands were already full getting the best out of the other choristers and making sure that two of them did not fall asleep during rehearsals.' He threw a meaningful glance at the novices. 'At least that will not happen again.'

'No, Brother Frewine,' promised Elaf.

'Describe him to me,' said Gervase to him. 'In your own words. How tall was Brother Nicholas?'

'Not very tall.'

'Short, then?'

'No, not short. In the middle.'

'Was he fat or thin?'

'He was quite—' His hands mimed a paunch but words failed him as he saw the generous expanse of Hubert's midriff. 'Wasn't he, Brother Frewine?'

'A little plump,' conceded the Precentor.

'Heavier than me, then?' said Gervase.

'Yes. Much heavier.'

Gervase nodded and ruled out the possibility of Brother Nicholas's dead body having been carried up the ladder. Even someone as strong as Ralph Delchard would have difficulty coping with a substantially heavier load than Gervase represented. After breaking off to translate for the benefit of Canon Hubert, he resumed his questioning.

'Let me turn to you, Kenelm.' The boy gave a little shudder. 'This is a fine abbey. Do you like it here?' Kenelm nodded without conviction. 'In other words, you like some things and don't like others?'

'Yes.'

'That's only to be expected. It was so with me. I used to chafe at the loss of freedom. The sense of being trapped. Does that worry you?'

'Sometimes.'

'What about you, Elaf?'

'Sometimes,' echoed the other.

'Did you not draw inspiration from the monks around you?'

'Yes,' said Kenelm.

'Which ones?'

'Brother Frewine.'

'He is our best friend,' said Elaf proudly.

'Who else?' Between them, the boys listed ten other names. 'You see?' said Gervase. 'You know the holy brothers far better than you imagined. There was no mention of Brother Nicholas, of course. I take it that neither of you drew inspiration from him?' They shook their heads. 'You were too busy laughing at his funny voice.'

Elaf licked his lips. 'We never dared to laugh at him.'

'Why not?'

'No reason, Master Bret.'

'I'm sure you can recall one, if you try.'

'We hardly ever saw him.'

'But when you did, you were afraid to mock him.'

'Yes.'

'Why? Did he threaten you?'

'Not really.'

'So what was the reason?'

There was a long pause. Hubert grew frustrated at being unable to understand what was going on. He leaned forward to speak but Gervase waved him back into silence, certain that he was on the verge of learning a significant piece of information. The two boys were trading glances.

'Brother Nicholas was cruelly murdered,' Gervase reminded them. 'You had the misfortune to find him and I know how gruesome a discovery that must have been. But you're also in a position to help us catch his killer. Any fact about Brother Nicholas is vital, including his relationship with the novices. So tell me, please, because it may be of crucial importance, why you never laughed at Brother Nicholas.'

'Go on,' said Frewine gently. 'Speak honestly.'

Kenelm tried to speak then bit his lip in embarrassment.

'Elaf?' invited Gervase.

'We didn't like him,' confessed the other. 'None of us did.'

'Why not?'

Elaf licked his lips again and took a deep breath before speaking.

'It was the way that Brother Nicholas looked at us.'

* * *

The bulbous eyes of Brother Nicholas were no longer able to cause any disquiet. They were covered forever by lids which had been drawn down by a compassionate finger and thumb when his corpse was brought to the mortuary. Nicholas lay beneath a shroud on the cold stone slab, his wound bandaged and his body washed. Herbs sweetened his noisome stink. Candles burned at his head and feet, throwing a flickering light over the last remains of the abbey's ill-fated rent collector.

When the door opened, Abbot Serlo led his visitor in, pausing to offer up a silent prayer before he reached down to pull back the shroud. Ralph Delchard looked down at the naked body with mingled sadness and interest. Brother Nicholas was a plump man in his forties with a pasty complexion which owed nothing to the pallor of death and a body of unusual whiteness, allowing blue veins to show through on his chest. The body was almost entirely devoid of hair. What Ralph noticed was the absence of any real muscle in the arms and legs. Here was one monk who had not toiled in the fields or taken on one of the more physically demanding tasks at the abbey. Soft white hands confirmed that Brother Nicholas was a stranger to strenuous exercise.

The thickness of the bandaging showed how comprehensively the throat had been cut but there were no other marks of violence upon him. Ralph studied the face: big, round, podgy but surprisingly untouched by the march of time. Even in repose, there was a religiosity about the man. It was a quality which Ralph had never been able to understand or to appreciate but Brother Nicholas seemed to possess it. He reached out to feel the spindly legs and the weak forearms then he pulled the shroud back over the body and turned to his companion.

'Not a strong man,' he commented. 'Brother Nicholas would not have been able to put up much resistance.'

'We are monks, my lord, not soldiers.'

'Even a monk should fight to save his life.'

'He entrusts its safety to God.'

'Then the Almighty was lax in his vigilance here.'

'Do not presume to question divine dispensation.'

'I dare not. Canon Hubert is an example of it.'

'Let us step outside again.'

Abbot Serlo guided him out of the mortuary and back into the fresh air. Both inhaled deeply. Their long conversation had persuaded the abbot that Ralph's help in solving the crime might be extremely useful but he wished that his visitor could take a more reverential approach. He was not quite as brusque and headstrong as the sheriff but his attitude towards the Benedictine Order had worrying similarities.

'I must leave you, my lord,' said the abbot. 'Other duties await me.'

'It was kind of you to spare me so much time.'

'Repay me by finding the murderer.'

'I will, my lord abbot. The more information I have, the easier the task will be. Do not forget your promise to give me a list of all of the tenants from whom Brother Nicholas collected rents.'

'Canon Hubert will bring it to you in due course.'

'Thank you.'

'What will you do now?'

'Go back to the church.'

'Why?'

'To pray for the salvation of Brother Nicholas's soul,' said Ralph.

'A worthy motive.'

'It was something I omitted to do on my first visit there. Having seen the body, I am anxious to repair that omission.'

'Then I will not detain you, my lord.'

Ralph waved a farewell and headed back to the abbey church, untroubled by guilt at having to conceal the real purpose of his return visit. Pleased to find the church empty, he approached the altar rail and knelt before it, offering up the prayer for the murdered man and feeling a genuine surge of grief on his behalf. It soon passed. Ralph made sure that nobody was watching him before moving up to the altar to borrow one of the large candles which burned there. He bore it off to the bell tower and carried it carefully up the ladder.

Having viewed the body, he, too, was having second thoughts about his earlier theory. It was not that Brother Nicholas was too heavy for him to bear. He simply doubted that the rungs of the ladder would cope with the additional weight. Ralph got up to the wooden platform and used the flame to illumine every section of it. The blood was more vivid by candlelight and its extent far greater. It was when he went to the other side of the bell that he made an interesting new discovery. Holding the candle beneath the beam, he ducked his head so that he could actually see the two hooks which he had earlier felt with his fingers. Something else caught his eye. Lying directly below the beam was a small, thin strip of leather. Ralph picked it up and laid it on his palm to inspect it.

After a thorough search, he slowly descended the ladder, glad that he had taken the trouble to pay a second visit to the murder scene. He pondered on the significance of the strip of leather and was far too preoccupied to realise that he was being watched from the shadows. Wide-eyed and tremulous, Owen, the novice, stayed hidden until Ralph had walked back to the altar. The boy took a last fearful look up at the bell tower then slipped quietly out. Tears coursed freely down his hot rosy cheeks.

'When do you expect your sister to arrive?' asked the lady Maud.

'Almost any day now,' said Golde.

'Is that why you were so keen to accompany your husband?'

'It was one of the reasons, though I would willingly go wherever Ralph asked me to go. I love to be near him.'

'I enjoy Durand's company but I have to put up with less of it. When he goes away from Gloucester, I am never invited to go with him.' Maud shook her head sadly. 'I have endured some lonely weeks at the castle. The worst of it is that my husband is so secretive about his work. Most of the time, he will not even tell me where he is going, simply that he has to leave on urgent business.'

'Being a sheriff carries huge responsibilities.'

'We have learned that,' said the other with a rueful smile. 'The honour was thrust unexpectedly on Durand when his brother, Roger, died before his time. My husband feels that he has a sacred duty to carry on where his brother left off.'

'That is to his credit.'

Golde found the visit to Gloucester interesting and enlightening. When her companion had shaken off her irritation, she was friendly and talkative and had clearly taken the trouble to learn something of the city's history. Some of the glances which they collected along the way were tinged either with bitterness or envy but they ignored them for the most part. It was only when Golde heard some harsh words muttered in her own language that she flushed with discomfort. On the leisurely ride back to the castle, they were conversing more easily with each other.

'What did you say your sister's name was?'

'Aelgar, my lady.'

'And this young man?'

'Forne.'

'When are they to be married?'

'I do not know,' said Golde. 'I am hoping that my sister will tell me. All she has said in her letters is that she loves him dearly and wishes to spend the rest of her life with him. And since Forne, apparently, feels the same way about her, it sounds like a promising start for any marriage.'

'Promising starts sometimes end in disappointment.'

'Not in their case, I hope.'

'So do I,' said Maud, her cynicism tempered with goodwill.

'But where will they stay? Room could be found for them at the castle.'

'That is very kind of you, my lady, but they have already reserved accommodation. Forne, it seems, has a kinsman in Gloucester and they will stay under his roof. The truth is,' she said quietly, 'that Aelgar would feel out of place in a Norman castle. Even though she has been supplying the one in Hereford with its beer.'

Maud gave a sudden laugh. 'Is your sister really a brewer?'

'It runs in the family, my lady,' explained Golde. 'I took over the business after the death of my first husband then handed it on to Aelgar when I left. Not that she has to work in the way that I did. Thanks to the judgement of the commissioners, Aelgar inherited property on her own account. She can afford to employ others to brew the beer for her now.'

'What of her betrothed?'

'His interest is only in drinking it.'

Maud laughed again as they clattered across the drawbridge and went in through the gate. She gave their escort a wave of gratitude, allowing the four men to trot off in the direction of the stables. Maud looked up at the keep with a determination tinged with anger.

'Please excuse me, Golde.'

'Of course, my lady. Thank you again.'

'It was a pleasure to get out of the castle for once.'

'I did appreciate it.'

'So did I. But we are back where we started now.'

With the help of an ostler, she dismounted and went off in the direction of the keep to confront her husband. Golde wondered why Durand kept his domestic and official duties so rigidly separate. It led to obvious friction with his wife. Not for the first time, she was grateful to be married to a man who took her into his confidence instead of using his work as a means of shutting her out. Hers was one story, Maud's quite another. As she was helped down from the saddle, she found herself wondering what kind of story Aelgar and Forne were about to write.

Ralph Delchard waited until they left the abbey before he started to hurl a stream of questions at Gervase Bret.

'What did you learn?' he said.

'A great deal.'

'Did they tell you anything new? What sort of boys were they? How freely were you able to talk to them? Why did they climb up that ladder in the first place? Had they ever been up in the bell tower before? Well, Gervase? Aren't you going to tell me?'

'I will, when I'm allowed to speak.'

'Who is preventing you from speaking?'

'You, Ralph.'

'Me?' Righteous indignation showed. '*Me?*'

'Who else?'

Ralph unleashed another flurry of questions at him and only stopped when Gervase burst into laughter. Seeing himself through his friend's eyes at last, Ralph joined in the mirth. They mounted their horses and let them walk slowly off along the street.

'Let us start again,' suggested Gervase. 'What did you find out?'

'That I could never be a monk.'

'Was that ever in doubt?'

'It's this rule of complete obedience. Abbot Serlo seems like an intelligent and caring man, but I could never treat him as my father and bow to his every wish. He was not easy to woo but I managed it in the end. He told me all I wished to know and even allowed me to view the body in the mortuary.'

'Did that reveal anything?'

'I think so.'

Ralph described his assessment of Brother Nicholas then explained how much the abbot had helped him. He considered the promise to provide a list of abbey tenants to be the greatest concession he had wrung out of Serlo. Gervase talked of his own findings.

'It was a valuable meeting.'

'Good.'

'Give or take a few problems.'

'What sort of problems?'

'Canon Hubert was the main one,' said Gervase. 'It was he who asked me to act as his interpreter so he controlled the interview at the start. I had to wait some time before I could work in questions of my own, questions which Hubert would not have asked on his own.'

'At least he got you close to those novices.'

'I could not get too close, Ralph. There was another problem.'

'What?'

'The Precentor. Brother Frewine.'

'What was he doing there?'

'Protecting the novices. They obviously trusted him and looked for his support whenever the questions had them in retreat. Brother Frewine is a good man, honest and fair-minded, but he did defend them well.'

'Would you have got more out of them had he not been there?'

'I don't know. Kenelm and Elaf may have shut up completely. They were both very shocked by what happened. I don't think there will be any more midnight antics from them.'

'So what did you glean from the wretches?'

Gervase told him in as much detail as he could remember. Ralph was a restive listener, constantly throwing in additional questions or asking for fuller explanations. When his friend came to the end of his litany, Ralph thought about the pale, hairless body stretched out on the mortuary slab. Brother Nicholas was an enigma.

'They didn't like the way he *looked* at them?'

'That's what they said, Ralph.'

'Why not?'

'They were too embarrassed to explain.'

'Could the Precentor throw no light on the subject?'

'No,' said Gervase. 'He spoke fondly of the deceased.'

'So did Abbot Serlo, yet we know for a fact that everyone else seems to have disliked Brother Nicholas. Why? Did he look at *them* in a strange way as well? What was so unsettling about him?'

'I don't know.'

'It seems he was an excellent rent collector,' said Ralph. 'It was not just a case of someone not wishing to speak ill of the dead. Abbot Serlo could not praise him enough for his efficiency in bringing money into the abbey coffers. A fair amount of money at that,' he recalled, 'when you think how many sub-tenants inhabit abbey land.'

'Brother Nicholas must have been trusted. His satchel would have been bulging with money when he returned to the abbey. A robber would have made off with an appreciable haul.'

'Yet nothing was stolen from him, apparently.'

'Was the abbot certain of that?'

'Yes, Gervase. As soon as he got back to the abbey, Brother Nicholas would hand the day's takings over so that they could be entered into the account book then locked away.'

'So he could not have been killed for gain?'

'Unlikely.'

'What, then, was the motive? Anger? Enmity?'

'I will know more when I speak to the people he visited on his rounds. That is where the real clues lie, Gervase, outside the abbey.'

'There is still much more within those walls to be dug out,' said Gervase. 'I would like to speak to Kenelm and Elaf alone at some stage and I would value another talk with Brother Frewine. He is a sage old man who has been here longer than anyone else. Nobody is so aware of the undercurrents of monastic life as the Precentor.'

'Will you take Hubert with you next time?'

Gervase smiled. 'I will omit to remember to do so.'

Their conversation had taken them as far as the castle but Ralph called a halt before they entered it. He had been keeping his most telling find until the last moment.

'When I climbed up that ladder, I chanced on something else.'

'Another dead monk?'

'Nothing quite as dramatic as that, Gervase. No,' he said, opening a palm and stretching it out to his friend, 'I found this.'

'Where?'

'Directly below those two hooks I mentioned.'

'May I see it?' Gervase picked up the strip of leather and turned it over. 'Where could this have come from?'

'You tell me.'

'Look at that frayed edge. It was torn off something.'

'Yes, but what?'

Gervase handed it back. 'This could be a vital clue.'

'That's why I'll treasure it.'

'What about the sheriff?'

'Durand? There's no way I'll treasure that rogue. Oh,' he added with a grin, realising what Gervase had meant. 'Will I tell our host about this little strip of leather?'

'Will you?'

'No, Gervase.'

'Why not?'

'Because it was up to him to find it for himself.'

'What about those hooks?'

'Those, too. They are *our* clues. He has enough of his own.'

'But we're withholding evidence, Ralph.'

'So we are.'

'Durand will be livid if he finds out.'

'He'll turn purple with rage if he discovers that we've been snooping around at the abbey and he's bound to do that if we tell him about the hooks and the strip of leather. Serlo won't betray

s, neither will Canon Hubert. There's no need for the sheriff to
arn about this.'

'It's inevitable at some stage.'

'By that time, we'll have handed the killer over to him.'

'Can we keep him in the dark that long?'

'We'll have to, Gervase.'

'Our time is limited, remember. We sit in judgement on the
major dispute tomorrow. Once that starts to unfurl, we'll not be
ble to pay any more visits to the abbey or to its holdings outside
the city.'

'We'll find the time somehow.'

'I foresee difficulties.'

Ralph gave him a hearty slap on the back. 'Be more positive,
Gervase,' he said, nudging his horse forward again. 'If we wish
something to happen, it will. I have picked up the trail. I'll not
lose the scent now.'

'Nor will I,' vowed Gervase.

As soon as they entered the bailey, they were spotted by one of
Ralph's men awaiting their return. He ran across to them.

'The lord sheriff is anxious to see you, my lord,' he said.

'Did he tell you why?'

'No, but he impressed the urgency of the summons upon me.'

Ralph was worried. 'Did you tell him where we were?'

'No, my lord.'

'Are you sure?'

'I led him to believe that you were still at the shire hall.'

'Good man!'

He and Gervase dismounted, left their horses with an ostler
and set off towards the keep. Ralph had no qualms but Gervase
did not share his confidence.

'What if he *knows*, Ralph?' he asked.

'How can he?'

'He may have sent someone to follow us.'

'Then he would have known we were at the abbey and jumped

to the obvious conclusion. Some of his men would have hauled us out of there before we could ask our first questions.'

'I hope that you are right.'

'Trust me, Gervase.'

'It's the urgency of the summons that alarms me.'

'Sheriffs like people to dance to their command.'

'There's more to it than that.'

Durand the Sheriff was in the hall, issuing instructions to his steward who was nodding seriously. When the newcomers entered, the steward was sent on his way. Ralph and Gervase stood before their host, not knowing whether they would be given glad tidings or berated for their audacity for interfering in a murder investigation. The grim expression on Durand's face seemed to exclude the first possibility. Ralph continued to smile blandly but Gervase braced himself for a searing attack. The sheriff walked right up to them.

'What I tell you is in strictest confidence,' he affirmed.

'Of course, my lord sheriff,' said Ralph.

'Nothing will go outside this room,' added Gervase.

'It will have to, I fear,' confided Durand, 'but we must do our best to keep it within the castle. A letter was delivered to me earlier. From Winchester. Nothing is certain but I have been ordered to make the necessary preparations.'

'For what?' said Ralph.

'A royal visit.'

Gervase was astonished. '*Here?*'

'Yes,' said the sheriff uneasily. 'I may soon have another guest under my roof. The King himself.'

Chapter Five

On the following morning, work began in earnest at the shire hall. As the commissioners assembled to sit in judgement on the most complex case which confronted them, they put aside all thought of a murder at the abbey and gave their full attention to the matter in hand. Ralph Delchard was relieved to be able to do so because it rescued him, temporarily, from the moral dilemma of whether or not to tell Golde about the possible visit of King William. Ordinarily, he concealed very little from his wife and she, in turn, was refreshingly open with him. He decided that the latest tidings should be kept from her, because he had given his word to that effect. Besides, there was some doubt about the King's arrival in Gloucester and thus no point in alerting Golde to an event which might not even take place.

Gervase Bret was untroubled by any qualms on the subject. In his opinion, a vow was a solemn undertaking. Having been sworn to secrecy, he did not consider for a moment the notion of divulging the news to anyone else, not even to Canon Hubert and Brother Simon, both as trustworthy as himself. Like Ralph, he did speculate in private on the motives for the King's rumoured visit but he put none of his conclusions into words. Once inside the shire hall, he forgot all about the warning imparted to them by Durand as he tried to assess the irascible man who first came before them.

Strang the Dane had a loud voice and forthright manner.

'The land has been mine since I received it from King Edward's own hand,' he asserted. 'I have the charter which proves my incontestable right to it. For some reason, your predecessors chose to question that right and I am now put in the invidious position of having to defend my claim once again. I hope that you have sufficient intelligence to see what is before your noses.'

'Do you dare to malign our intelligence?' snarled Ralph.

'The first commissioners were found lacking in that respect.'

'On the contrary, they were remarkably astute men which is why they identified so clearly the many irregularities and corrupt practices which have been going on in this county. Your name is linked to them.'

'Wrongfully.'

'That remains to be seen.'

'I demand justice.'

'We will give you no less.'

'Your predecessors did. They were purblind.'

Ralph was trenchant. 'By insulting them, you insult us and – by extension – the King who initiated this Great Survey. We speak for him. Do you wish to rid yourself of any more jibes before we begin?'

'All I wish for is what is legally mine.'

'That is what we are here to determine.'

Ralph's glare silenced him at last. Strang the Dane was a hefty man in his fifties with long grey hair and a full grey beard. His attire suggested a degree of wealth and his bearing was that of a soldier. Gervase wondered why someone who was bristling with defiance before his Norman conquerors had taken the trouble to learn their language so well, unless to be able to abuse them roundly in their own tongue. He glanced down at the document in front of him and saw that Strang had scattered holdings throughout Gloucestershire as well as in one of the Welsh commotes attached to it. The invaders had deprived him of far less land than most other thegns. Strang was determined not to yield up another acre. He was accompanied by his reeve, Balki, a slightly younger and much quieter individual with a long, thin face to which a ragged red beard clung like so much ivy.

After a muttered conversation with his master, Balki took over. His smile was ingratiating as he approached the table where Ralph sat with the other commissioners and their watchful scribe. The red-haired Balki, too, spoke Norman French almost fluently.

'We appreciate the difficulties involved here,' he began.

'Do you?' said Ralph gruffly.

'Yes, my lord. We have lived in the county for many years and know how complicated the pattern of land-holding is. We would be the first to admit that there have been many irregularities – downright acts of theft in some cases – because we have been the victims of them. The property under discussion is a perfect instance. It was granted to my master, Strang the Dane,' he said, producing a charter from his satchel, 'in recognition of services rendered. Here is proof.' Handing the document to Ralph, he smirked helpfully. 'Would you like me to translate it for you, my lord?'

'That will not be necessary,' said Ralph, passing the charter to Gervase. 'We have our own interpreter.'

'Then I hope his translation is sound.'

'It had better be,' rumbled Strang, stroking his beard.

After a glance through it, Gervase rendered the wording carefully into language that his colleagues could understand.

' "I, King Edward, greet Bishop Aldred and all my thegns in Worcestershire and Gloucestershire. And I give you to know that Strang my housecarl has been granted a certain piece of land, namely eight hides in the manor called Westbury to be held and enjoyed for three lives, and after that time the estate is to return to the disposal of whoever is in control of the bishopric of Worcester . . ." '

Hunched in concentration, Balki nodded in approval at the accuracy of the translation. Strang stood proudly with hands on his hips as if the mere recitation of the charter's contents would be enough to secure the property under discussion. When he realised that the Dane had been one of the royal housecarls, Ralph viewed him with slightly more respect. Housecarls were elite soldiers, members of a standing bodyguard who had been selected for their courage, loyalty and military skills. Strang must have given good service to be repaid so handsomely with various grants of land. Qualities which aroused Ralph's admiration only served to increase Canon Hubert's antipathy towards the first claimant. He resented his insolent manner and his total lack of deference before them. Nor did Hubert warm to the oleaginous reeve whom he suspected of being far too devious to be trusted. He decided to wipe the irritating grin off Balki's face.

'How do we know that the charter is genuine?' he asked.

'Because you have my word that it is,' roared Strang.

'Why else should it be presented to you?' said Balki, hurt by the very suggestion. 'That property was acquired by fair means and lost by foul ones. I swear that the document is authentic.'

'It has every appearance of being so,' admitted Gervase, subjecting it to close scrutiny, 'but I would value more time to examine it.'

'You shall have it,' announced Ralph. 'And if it is found to be a clever forgery, those who perpetrated it will be duly arraigned. We have already uncovered one grotesque attempt at deception.'

'There is no deception here,' said Strang, simmering with anger.

'We speak before you under oath, my lord,' added Balki.

'Find in my favour and let us away.'

'Before we have even questioned the others?' asked Ralph. 'What kind of justice is that? All four of you will be given a fair hearing.'

'Four?' repeated Strang. 'Four? We know of only two rivals. The first is Hamelin of Lisieux who unjustly seized the land from me and the second is Querengar the Breton.'

'They still contest your claim.'

'Then where does this fourth person come from?'

'Wales.'

Strang was derisive. 'Do you jest with me, my lord?'

'Not on the subject of a Welshman, I do assure you.'

'What is the man's name?'

'Abraham the Priest.'

Strang let out a long hiss of disgust and Balki turned an anxious eye towards his master. Ralph found their different reactions interesting. Evidently, they knew and disliked the Archdeacon of Gwent. While Strang dismissed him with contempt, however, Balki was quietly alarmed by the mention of his name. His master rebuked him with a long stare then turned his ire upon the commissioners again.

'Are you not capable of making a decision?' he demanded.

'Of course,' said Ralph sternly, 'and we have already decided that your manner is too bold and your words too ill-chosen. Whatever the merits of your claim, you will not advance your cause by unseemly behaviour.'

'No offence was intended,' said Balki with an apologetic smirk.

'I'll speak for myself,' contradicted Strang. 'And I do so honestly and fearlessly. If some are offended by what I say, it is of no account to me. I'll not be muzzled.'

'Remember who we are,' warned Hubert.

'I can see all too well!' sneered the other.

'We'll brook no disrespect.'

'Nor will you have to,' said Balki, trying to calm his master. 'Simply ask the questions you have no doubt prepared and we will answer each and every one of them to your satisfaction.'

'I doubt that,' said Ralph.

'Those hides in Westbury belong to me!' insisted Strang.

'Then how do they happen to be in the possession of Hamelin of Lisieux?' asked Gervase quietly, introducing a more moderate note. 'You have one charter, he, it seems, another. Which should we accept?'

'Mine!'

'Why?'

'Read it, man.'

'I have already done so.'

'It bears the King's seal.'

'That of King Edward,' agreed Gervase, glancing at the charter, 'but Hamelin of Lisieux has a document which bears the seal of King William. I do not need to remind you which of the two now occupies the throne.'

'Hamelin took my land by force.'

'Do you have any proof of that?' said Ralph.

'Yes, my lord,' replied Strang, rolling up his sleeve to display a long, livid scar on his forearm. 'Here is one piece of evidence. I have others on my body. I fought to protect what is rightly mine but I was outnumbered. Hamelin of Lisieux is a barefaced robber.'

'That is slander!' said Hubert.

'It is the truth.'

'I can vouch for that,' said Balki. 'You have two witnesses here.'

Strang glowered. 'I have not been the only person in this county to suffer. Consult the returns from the first commissioners. The name of Hamelin appeared many times regarding land which he did not acquire by legal means. He is a master of unjust seizure. Because he is rich and powerful, most people are too frightened to resist him, let alone challenge him openly. I am not.'

'Nor,' observed Ralph, 'is Abraham the Priest.'

'Not to mention Querengar the Breton,' Gervase reminded them. 'Both of them are prepared to stand up against Hamelin of Lisieux and, of course, against you.'

Strang was about to issue a tart rejoinder but Balki put a hand on his arm to restrain him. He contrived his most obsequious smile yet.

'My master is sorry if his passion spills over but he has been most grievously treated. He looks to you for retribution. Now,' he said, gazing at each of them in turn, 'you have the charter before you. We have a dozen witnesses who will vouch for the fact that the land in question was once – and still should be – the property of Strang the Dane. How else can we convince you of the strength of our claim?'

Though he took his duties very seriously, Brother Frewine carried them lightly. Since he was in charge of the church services, the Precentor was the most important of the obedientiaries. It fell to him to arrange the daily services, to take charge of the abbey's music, to teach the monks how to sing, to decide the readings in church and to provide materials for the repair of books from the choir and the cloister. Responsibilities which would have weighed heavily on a lesser man were discharged with ease by a man whose philosophical calm was the envy of his holy brothers.

'Are the funeral arrangements complete, Brother Frewine?'

'Yes, Father Abbot.'

'I will not pretend that I am looking forward to the service.'

'No more am I. The nature of Brother Nicholas's death makes it a peculiarly sad occasion. But I am sure,' he said with gentle sincerity, 'that you will find exactly the right words of consolation.'

'I hope so, Brother Frewine.'

'You have a gift, Father Abbot.'

'I pray to God that it will not desert me now.'

They were in the abbot's lodging and, in the course of a busy morning, the Precentor somehow found the time to visit Serlo with a request. When they had discussed the details of the funeral service, he raised the subject which had brought him there.

'I came in search of your permission, Father Abbot.'

'To what end?'

'It concern's Brother Nicholas's cell,' explained Frewine. 'I know that it was searched by the sheriff's officers and that you gave orders for it to be swept clean. But the officers did not really know where to look and those who went in with brooms were too scared to stay there long enough to be thorough.'

'Too scared?'

'To linger in the cell of a murder victim.'

'Why?'

'They are superstitious.'

'Superstition has no place in a religious house,' said Serlo with uncharacteristic acerbity. 'God has cleared our minds of such nonsense. I am glad you brought this to my attention, Brother Frewine. Who were the weak vessels? Name them to me and I will make sure they go back to sweep and scrub the cell properly.'

'That is not my request, Father Abbot,' said the other with an appeasing smile. 'Give me a broom and I will gladly do their office for them. No, what I seek is permission to search the cell. Not that I expect to find anything,' he added quickly, 'but at least I would know where to look. The sheriff's officers would have been repelled by the very bareness of Brother Nicholas's abode. I doubt if they gave it more than a cursory glance. I have lived in this abbey many years, remember.'

'More than any of us. What has it taught you?'

'That secretive people can often find the most ingenious hiding places and Brother Nicholas was unduly secretive.'

'Granted. But what would he have to hide?'

'Who knows until we find it?'

'Do you really expect that there is anything to find?'

'I am not sure, Father Abbot,' admitted Frewine, 'but it worries me that we are leaving this investigation to the sheriff and, it now seems, to the royal commissioners. Forgive me for saying so, but we should not be absolved from the duty of searching for evidence ourselves. After all, we *knew* Brother Nicholas and that surely gives us an advantage over anyone else.'

Abbot Serlo watched him shrewdly for a few moments, hands clasped and forefingers meeting at the tiny cleft of his chin. Frewine waited patiently like an owl perched on the branch of a tree.

'There is something behind this,' said the abbot at length.

'A desire to solve a dreadful crime.'

'Something else. Something you are not telling me.'

'I am not dissembling, Father Abbot.'

'Of course not, I accept that.' His forefingers tapped his chin. 'Let me approach it another way. What first put this idea into your head?'

'The need for a motive.'

'Motive?'

'Why was Brother Nicholas murdered?'

'You obviously have your own theory on the matter.'

'I believe the killer wanted something from him.'

'What was it?'

'I wish I knew, Father Abbot.'

'Brother Nicholas had nothing of his own. Like the rest of us, he took a vow of poverty. No earthly possessions. The only thing a killer could take from him was his own life.'

'You are probably right,' sighed the Precentor.

'But you would still like to search his cell.'

'With your permission, Father Abbot,' he said respectfully. 'And I promise to sweep it clean before I leave.'

'It will be a wasted visit. You realise that?'

'I do.'

'You will search in vain.'

'I know.'

'So why do you bother?'

'To put my mind at rest.'

'Instinct tells me that you will not find a thing.'

'I, too, am impelled by instinct.'

Serlo was cautious. 'But if, by chance, you do,' he said, locking eyes with his Precentor, 'send for me at once.'

Hamelin of Lisieux took them all by surprise. Having seen his name recurring time and again in the returns for the county sent to the Exchequer in Wiltshire, they knew him as a leading landholder and one of the few who actually lived in

Gloucestershire itself. Hamelin was no absentee landlord. His manor was at the heart of the county. Strang the Dane painted his portrait in such dark colours that they half-expected Hamelin to prance into the shire hall on cloven feet, swishing his forked tail behind him. No such malignant creature appeared. The man who sailed in to greet them was a tall, well-favoured, elegant Norman lord in his forties, immaculately dressed and accompanied by his wife, Emma, a woman of such startling loveliness that she caused Ralph Delchard's jaw to drop in wonderment and Canon Hubert's eyebrows to shoot up in disbelief. Even Gervase was momentarily taken aback, but it was Brother Simon who suffered the greatest impact, recoiling from her beauty as if from a physical assault and screwing his whole body into a tight ball so that more of it could be comprehensively covered by his cowl.

With a grace singularly lacking in his Danish predecessor, Hamelin introduced himself and his wife then left Emma to distribute a generous smile between the four men behind the table. Ralph responded with a broad grin but his scribe yelped like a branded animal. The newcomers were waved to seats on the front bench then Ralph went through the preliminaries, introducing his companions and explaining the methods they would adopt during their inquiry. He also found himself apologising profusely for the dinginess of the hall and the inadequacy of the seating arrangements. Both man and wife were clearly accustomed to far more comfortable surroundings than those they now shared with the four commissioners.

It was Canon Hubert who initiated the questioning.

'Now that the formalities are finally out of the way,' he said with almost imperceptible sarcasm, 'perhaps we can address the problem which brought us here? I take it that you are familiar with Strang the Dane, my lord?'

'All too familiar!' said Hamelin, suppressing a sigh.

'He was here before you.'

'I hope that does not betoken an order of merit, Canon Hubert.'

'Far from it. Every claimant has equal status.'

'How can that be when our claims do not have equal validity?'

'Relative validity has yet to be decided, my lord.'

'Not by me,' said Hamelin politely. 'I willingly concede that Strang the Dane did, at one time, have a legitimate right to that land in the Westbury. It is unfortunate for him that his right melted in the heat of conquest. As for Querengar the Breton,' he continued, with a fond glance at his wife, 'you must not ask me to take his claim at all seriously. And I can muster even less respect for Abraham the Priest.'

'You know that he is also represented here?' asked Ralph.

'Naturally.'

'How?'

'I am well informed, my lord.'

'More so than we ourselves. We did not learn of the Welshman's intervention until we arrived and Strang the Dane was astonished to hear of it. Why did you catch what eluded his ears?'

'I have many friends in Gwent.'

'Enemies, too, if Strang is to be believed.'

Hamelin laughed. 'Several enemies. He is one of them.'

'You do not seem perturbed by that thought.'

'Why should I be, my lord? You and I are two of a kind, Norman lords in a land we first had to subdue. Our very presence here makes us despised intruders. Where would we be if we could not cope with a little enmity?' he asked, bestowing another fond look on his wife. 'Especially when we can offset all that hatred with so much love.'

'Have you and Strang ever come to blows, my lord?' said Gervase.

'Unfortunately, we have not.'

'He says otherwise.'

'Then he is lying, Master Bret.'

'Strang the Dane is an appalling man,' said Emma demurely. 'I know that it is not my place to speak here but I feel it my duty to tell you that his word is not to be trusted.'

'He spoke under oath, my lady,' said Hubert.

'So does my husband.'

'And I say, under oath,' continued Hamelin pointedly, 'that I have never crossed swords with Strang. More's the pity! Had I done so, that verminous Dane would not now be alive to poison your ears with his wicked lies.'

'He showed us a wound, my lord,' said Gervase.

'It was not inflicted by me.'

'By one of your men, perhaps?'

'That is not impossible. Strang has trespassed on my estates.'

'Did he have to be expelled by force of arms?'

'How else, Master Bret?'

'Recourse to law.'

'That is why I am here,' said Hamelin blandly. 'To attest the legal basis of every hide in my possession. Most of the country is howling in protest at this Great Survey, fearful that it will cost more in taxes and knight-service. My voice is not raised in complaint, as my wife will tell you. I appreciate the true value of this Domesday Book.'

'It is good to meet someone who does!' said Ralph.

'You draw clear lines, my lord. You clarify who holds what where. Once you have pronounced, nobody can lay false claims to my land any more. That is why I welcome this inquiry.'

'Even if we find against you?' probed Hubert.

'That is out of the question.'

'Why?'

'I will show you, Canon Hubert.'

'Why did you not show the first commissioners?'

'Unhappily, I was not in a position to do so when they first visited the shire,' said Hamelin easily. 'I was visiting Normandy to deal with a problem concerning my estates there. My reeve spoke on my behalf before your predecessors but he lacked conviction, I am told. That is why I replaced him on my return and why I come before you in person this time. To eliminate even the slightest possibility of error.'

'Do you fear we will make an error?' probed Ralph.

'The first commissioners did.'

'How?'

'By having insufficient evidence set before them.'

'What new evidence do you have to add?'

'First, peruse this,' advised Hamelin, rising to give Ralph the charter which he held in his hand. 'You will recognise the hand and seal of King William and note that I am granted fifteen hides in the Westbury Hundred. Much of the land which abuts mine is held directly by the King himself so I have one neighbour with whom I am on very friendly terms.'

Ralph skimmed through the charter then handed it to Gervase, who, having read it more carefully, passed it on to Canon Hubert. When Gervase looked back at them, Hamelin, seated once more, was smiling complacently and Emma was looking earnestly at the commissioners.

'Is any more proof than that required?' she asked softly.

'I fear that it is, my lady,' said Gervase.

'Why, Master Bret?'

'Because the document is not as specific as it might be. Fifteen hides are indeed granted to your husband but it is not clear that they include the eight hides formerly given to Strang the Dane.'

'It is clear to us.'

'But not to Strang himself.'

'What irks him most,' said Ralph, taking over, 'is that some of this land lies close to the Severn, down which his boats sail with cargoes of iron ore. Among other things, Strang has the right to mine ore in the Forest of Dean.' His eyes flicked to Hamelin. 'The loss of those hides in Westbury have caused him great inconvenience. He has to transport the ore a longer distance over land, adding to his costs.'

'That is not my concern, my lord,' said Hamelin.

'But it is the consequence of your annexation of the land.'

'It was not annexation. I merely took what is mine.'

'Which, according to Strang, amounted to rather more than the twenty hides to which this document refers.'

'That is palpably untrue,' said Emma with feeling. 'Go to Westbury yourselves and you will surely find as much.'

'We would rather determine this matter here, my lady,' said Hubert as he finished studying the charter. 'We do not have unlimited time at our disposal and cannot ride around the county to measure hides and count the heads of those who work on them.'

'Then tell us this,' requested Hamelin. 'Apart from Strang, has anyone else in Westbury raised objections against me?'

'Querengar and Abraham the Priest.'

'I discount them. Neither actually holds property in the hundred. Both merely claim to do so. Of those that do – the King excepted, of course – which have spoken against me? Go further afield, Canon Hubert. Name me anyone in the Berkeley or Bledisloe Hundreds who accuses me of seizing their land.'

Hubert gave a shrug. 'I cannot, my lord.'

'Does that not say something in my favour?'

'It might indicate that people are too afraid to challenge you.'

'Why should they be afraid of my husband?' asked Emma with apparent surprise. 'He is the most amenable of men. Talk to any of his sub-tenants and they will tell you the same.'

'I'm sure that they will,' commented Gervase quietly.

'Let us go back to the charter,' decreed Ralph, reclaiming it from Hubert. 'Perhaps you can tell us the circumstances in which the King saw fit to grant you such valuable holdings, my lord.'

'Certainly,' said Hamelin of Lisieux.

And he delivered his speech with ringing confidence.

It took Elaf a little while to find his friend. When he finally did so, he was alarmed to see the expression of utter dejection on

Kenelm's face. The mettlesome boy who had led him on so many exploits was now hiding in the abbey garden, wrestling with his guilt and contemplating a bleak future in the Benedictine Order. When Elaf touched him on the shoulder, Kenelm let out a gasp and jerked involuntarily away.

'It's only me,' Elaf reassured him. 'What are you doing here?'

'I wanted to be alone.'

'Why?'

'To do some thinking.'

'About what happened to Brother Nicholas?'

'What else, Elaf?'

'It preys on my mind as well.'

'It is gnawing its way through my brain,' confessed Kenelm, turning to face him with hollow eyes. 'There is no respite. Whatever I am doing, it is there, nibbling away like a rat inside my skull.'

'Brother Owl says that we must seek help through prayer.'

'How can I pray when my mind torments me?'

'I have managed to do so,' argued Elaf, 'and I was the one who actually touched Brother Nicholas that night. The very thought makes me shiver afresh but I am learning to banish the thought.'

'That is because you have less to banish than me.'

'Less?'

'Yes,' said Kenelm, his face ashen with dismay. 'The shock of finding the dead body is all that you have to chill your heart. I have a deeper source of guilt, Elaf, one that will not be so easily forgotten.'

'What do you mean?'

'I did something unpardonable.'

'When?'

'When we were sent into church by Brother Owl to pray for the safe return of Brother Nicholas. I didn't only wish that he would never come back. I prayed,' he admitted, chewing his lip, 'I actually beseeched God to kill Brother Nicholas.'

Elaf was shaken. 'Is this true?'

'To my eternal shame, it is.'

'Kenelm!'

'Now do you see why I am in such despair? I prayed for his death, Elaf. I willed his murder.'

'But you didn't.'

'I did. I'm responsible for it.'

'How can that be? You had nothing to do with it.'

'I feel that I did.'

'No, Kenelm.'

'And I can see no way to atone.'

'There's no need for atonement.'

'Isn't there?' said the other vehemently. 'When I'm an accomplice in his murder? I wished him dead and God answered my prayer. I feel as if I slit his throat with my own hands.'

'That's ridiculous!'

'Not to me.'

'Then you have learned nothing since you became a novice here,' chided Elaf. 'God is bountiful. He responds to pleas for help, guidance and forgiveness. God is the supreme giver of life. He would never take it away in an act of foul murder simply because someone prayed for that to happen. God is not so cruel, Kenelm.'

'But I am.'

'You do yourself a wrong here.'

'That is my punishment.'

'An undeserved punishment.'

'I see it differently.' He looked furtively around him. 'This place oppresses me more and more each day. I will never be content within its walls while the ghost of Brother Nicholas stalks the abbey.'

'What else can you do?'

'Leave.'

'That's impossible.'

'Is it? Don't you remember what he told us, the man who came to question us with Canon Hubert?'

'Gervase Bret?'

'Yes,' said Kenelm. 'He was once a novice at Eltham Abbey but he left at the end of his novitiate. He decide that the Order was too strict a place in which to spend the rest of his life. He was very honest about it and I must be equally honest.'

'But his case is different from yours. Worldly concerns stopped him from taking the cowl. You were placed here by your parents because it was their dearest hope that you became a monk and you have many times confided to me that it is what you really want. It is so with me,' said Elaf wistfully. 'It was my father's dying wish that I be made an oblate here and I would never betray that wish.'

'Even if it meant a life of purgatory?'

'There is no purgatory here, Kenelm.'

'There is for me. I must get away somehow.'

'That is futile talk.'

'Is it?'

'Your parents would never allow you to leave.'

'I will not seek their permission.'

'How else can you go?'

'The way that others have done so before me.'

'No!' exclaimed his friend.

'Siward was one,' recalled Kenelm. 'Before him, it was Dena. Both of them simply took to their heels and fled from the abbey.'

'Where to, though?'

'Does it matter? Escape is escape.'

'Yet nothing was ever heard of Siward and Dena again. Doesn't that worry you? Some terrible harm may have befallen them. And what of their grieving families? Think of the pain they inflicted on their loved ones by running away like that. Do you *want* to hurt your parents in that way? Do you intend to desert all the friends you have made here?'

'Only because I am forced to, Elaf.'

'By whom? By what?'

'My conscience.'

'Salve it with a penance.'

'It is too late for that.'

'But you mustn't go,' said Elaf fervently. 'We need you, we love you.' He saw the tears in his friend's eyes and reached out to embrace him. 'Stay with us, Kenelm. Stay with me, please. I, too, have my doubts but I can fend them off if you are beside me. Let us help each other. We can do anything together. I'd never forgive myself if you ran away. Promise me that you'll stay here. Will you, Kenelm? Will you?'

Kenelm nodded gently but his mind was still in turmoil. Touched by his friend's display of affection, he was willing to soothe Elaf with a token agreement but he was not sure that he could keep his promise.

'Hamelin of Lisieux presented his case very effectively,' said Ralph.

'Almost too effectively,' said Gervase. 'I had the feeling that every word had been rehearsed beforehand with the assistance of his wife.'

'The lady Emma had no place here,' complained Canon Hubert.

Ralph chuckled. 'I disagree. She lit up this cheerless place like a roaring fire. The lady Emma is welcome to decorate the shire hall whenever she wishes. She was a joy to look upon.'

'That was the intention, my lord. She was there to divert you.'

'What an absurd suggestion, Hubert!'

'It is not absurd at all,' said Gervase. 'Hamelin brought his wife here with a purpose, though it was not merely to distract us. The lady Emma was there to lend her husband a softness and appeal which he lacked in Strang's report of him. That's what worries me about Hamelin's claim. If it really is as incontrovertible as he believes, why did he need the support of his wife? The lady Emma was clearly schooled by him.'

'Then she is an apt pupil,' said Ralph with admiration.

'She is an irrelevance,' argued Hubert.

'A terrifying one,' said Brother Simon under his breath.

The four commissioners were taking a short break at the shire hall and enjoying some light refreshment. As they supped their wine and nibbled the pastries which had been provided, they reflected on the long and searching examination of Hamelin of Lisieux. Even when pressed, the man had remained courteous and obliging, deflecting some of the more testing questions with a combination of charm and skill. Emma, too, had shown herself a clever advocate. Individually, each could have mounted a more persuasive argument than Strang the Dane. Together, they were formidable. Gervase was troubled.

'They were too plausible,' he ventured. 'Too good to be true.'

'The lady Emma was true enough,' said Ralph through a mouthful of pastry. 'As large as life and twice as beautiful.'

'I think they were hiding something.'

'What could it be?'

'Only time will tell.'

'Hamelin was more affable than the Dane,' noted Hubert, 'but the affability was worn for our benefit. Another face greets those who dare to trespass on what he believes is his land.'

'Who do you believe, Hubert? Strang or Hamelin?'

'Neither.'

'You think they are both lying?'

'No, my lord. I think it would be foolish to make a judgement before we have examined all four claimants. Querengar would seem to have a more slender case, and we do not even know what the Archdeacon of Gwent is going to argue, but both deserve to be given the same opportunities as their rivals.'

'That is ever our policy. Let all speak before a verdict is reached.' He drained his cup. 'Besides,' he added, 'perhaps this

Querengar will also produce a wondrous wife to brighten up our day.'

Simon gulped. 'She would only darken mine.'

'One thing is certain. Abraham the Priest will come alone.'

'Do not be so sure, Ralph,' teased Gervase. 'Some of the older Welsh clergy are married. Idwal is.'

Ralph choked on his last pastry. 'That name again!'

'He spoke very fondly of his wife.'

'What kind of woman would marry someone like that?' asked Ralph incredulously. 'It defies logic. She must have one eye, no teeth and swing from the trees by her tail!'

'That is ungentlemanly,' reproved Gervase.

'Priests should be celibate,' said Hubert seriously. 'It is quite disgusting for them to have carnal relations with a woman.'

Ralph was jocular. 'It all depends on the woman, Hubert. When you saw someone as gorgeous as the lady Emma sitting before you, I suspect that even you began to regret your vow of chastity.'

'I did no such thing!'

'Nor did I!' murmured Simon.

'No urgent little twitch beneath your cowls?' asked Ralph.

'Fleshly desire is beyond my ken,' insisted Hubert.

'The lady Emma will be disappointed,' mocked Ralph. He looked up as one of his men came into the hall. 'Ah, it seems that Querengar has arrived. Let us start anew, my friends. Take your places.' The other three returned to their seats and Ralph waved to his knight. 'Is the Breton alone?'

'Yes, my lord.'

'No wife, no concubine?'

'None.'

'Send him in while we master our regret.'

Hubert reprimanded him for his levity but Ralph took no notice. Resuming his own seat, he consulted the papers before him and waited for the arrival of the third claimant. It was a lengthy wait and Ralph became restive. He was about to go in search of Querengar when the man finally entered. The delay was explained at once. While Strang had marched and Hamelin had glided, Querengar had to drag himself into the shire hall on his crutches. One leg heavily bandaged and dangling uselessly, he made his way with painful slowness to the bench in front of them. They could see the effort that it cost him.

Gervase leaped up and went forward to help him but Querengar brushed him away with a shake of the head. He was too proud to accept any assistance. A short, compact man, he was shrunk by his injury into an almost dwarfish shape. Each of the commissioners felt a sharp tug at their sympathy. Lowering himself gingerly on to the bench, the newcomer set his crutches aside and turned a wizened face up to the table.

'I am Querengar the Breton,' he said firmly. 'I expect justice.'

It was not until dinner was over that Brother Frewine was able to slip away on his errand. Having eaten a frugal meal of fish, vegetables, cheese and milk, the Precentor left the refectory and made his way to the cell vacated by the untimely death of Brother Nicholas. When he reached the door, he paused out of respect rather than fear, halted by the grim thought that he would never again see alive the monk whose corpse lay in the morgue awaiting burial. Death had robbed him of any personal reservations he had about Nicholas. Frewine mourned him like a brother.

Letting himself into the little room, he gazed sadly around it. Built of stone, it was cool in summer but icy in winter; there was no source of heat. The ceiling was low, the floor sunken. All that the cell contained by way of furniture was a small table, a stool and a rough mattress. A crucifix stood on the table, its shadow magnified on the wall behind it by the shaft of light which came in through the little window. It was a bleak room but contained all that a monk would need. Frewine wondered if it might also contain something unsanctioned by the Benedictine Rule. Brother

Nicholas would not be the first monk to harbour forbidden items in his private abode.

His search began on the ceiling then moved to the walls. Frewine's old fingers probed for loose masonry or chance crevices. None could be found. Lowering himself to his knees, he began to grope around the floor of the cell, wishing that there was more light to assist him. What he could see was that the place had been only superficially swept. A thick layer of dust was largely untouched in some areas of the room. It was especially noticeable at the foot of the bed and he brushed it away with his hand to reveal something which had been invisible before. The floor was scored with parallel lines as if the mattress had been dragged out from the wall and replaced again many times.

Frewine's curiosity was set alight. Grabbing the edge of the mattress, the Precentor eased it into the centre of the room then walked to the end which had been pressed against the wall. Nothing unusual presented itself. The section of wall now uncovered was as bare and uneven as the rest. A spider was scurrying across it on long legs. It was only when Frewine began to explore with his fingers that he noticed something suspicious. One of the stones in the wall was protruding slightly, allowing him to get a purchase on it. When he jiggled it to and fro, he got more and more movement until it suddenly popped away from the wall altogether. He was right. Brother Nicholas did have a hiding place after all.

Frewine set the stone down and reached inside the cavity until his hand closed on something soft and pliable. When he extracted it, the object was much heavier than it had felt at first. Holding it on one palm, he shook it slightly and heard the telltale chink. He did not know whether to be pleased that his instinct had been sound or shocked by the nature of his discovery. It gave him something to think about as he hurried off to report to Abbot Serlo.

Chapter Six

'Did you explain this to the first commissioners who visited the county?'

'No, my lord.'

'Why not?'

'I was unfit to travel,' said Querengar, indicating his wounded leg. 'The accident happened only days before your predecessors arrived. I sent my reeve to the shire hall to represent me.'

'Unsuccessfully.'

'Alas, yes.'

'Did you berate him?' asked Ralph, remembering that Hamelin of Lisieux had seen fit to dismiss his own reeve for his inability to win ratification from the earlier commissioners. 'Is he still in your employ?'

'Of course.'

'You bear him no ill will?'

'Why should I? He did his best.'

'Yet he failed.'

'Not entirely,' said the Breton. 'My reeve must have made some impression or I would not be given this second chance to attest my claim. The fate of those hides in the Westbury Hundred remains in the balance.'

'True.'

'Until I persuade you who has the moral right to them.'

'The *moral* right?' echoed Canon Hubert.

'Moral and legal,' said Querengar, 'though I'm sure that you will agree with me, Canon Hubert, that all law should have a moral basis.'

'Quite so.'

'I knew that you would appreciate that.'

He gave a little nod of gratitude. Querengar the Breton was an enigma. Unlike the two claimants already questioned, he said nothing to the detriment of his rivals. Where the testy Strang had fulminated and the urbane Hamelin had airily dismissed, Querengar made no mention of the others, preferring simply to state his own case to the commissioners and to rely on their estimation of its worth. He was a curiously modest man, one of the many Breton mercenaries who had fought at Hastings and been repaid with grants of land in England and, in his instance, in Wales. Yet there was nothing boastful or belligerent about him. He spoke with quiet authority.

Ralph Delchard looked down at the bandaged leg.

'How serious was your wound?' he asked.

'Very serious, my lord. I all but lost my leg.'

'Where did you come by it?'

'A hunting accident.'

'Were you hunting your lost hides, by any chance?'

'No,' said Querengar. 'Wild boar. I have limited hunting privileges in the forest and try to make the most of them. My horse was startled by something and threw me. I fell awkwardly.'

'You are not the only person to appear before us with a wound. Strang the Dane stripped his sleeve to show us a battle scar from a visit to the Westbury Hundred. According to him, it was inflicted by men in the service of Hamelin of Lisieux.'

'They were not involved in my accident, my lord.'

'Are you sure?'

'Unless they lay in the bushes to frighten my horse.'

'Strang thought your claim worthless,' said Gervase, trying to gauge his opinion of the Dane. 'He shrugged it off completely.'

'He is entitled to do so.'

'It does not annoy you?'

'No, Master Bret. Nor does it goad me into angry words about him. I am conscious that Strang did have a legitimate right to those hides at one time. What he forgot to tell you was that they were subsequently taken from him and granted to me.'

'Hamelin of Lisieux makes an identical claim.'

'Have you no abuse to unload on him?' said Ralph.

Querengar smiled wryly. 'None that could compare with what Strang will already have offered. He has a sharper tongue and a hotter temper than me. Let them rail at each other. I refuse to engage in a war of words with either of them.'

'What about Abraham the Priest?' asked Gervase.

A long pause. 'Is he involved here?'

'Did you not realise that?'

'No, Master Bret.'

'Hamelin of Lisieux did.'

'He has friends in high places. Nigel the Reeve is one of them.'

'You seem surprised to hear the archdeacon's name.'

'I am.'

'Could he have a genuine claim to the land?'

'Only he can tell you that.'

'But you are sceptical?'

'The only claim which concerns me is my own, Master Bret. As for the Archdeacon of Gwent,' he said thoughtfully, 'he will certainly fight tooth and nail for what he believes may be his.'

'Not another bellicose Welshman!' groaned Ralph.

'A civilised fellow. You will like him, my lord.'

'I doubt that.'

'What of you?' said Gervase. 'Do you like Abraham the Priest?'

The wry smile. 'It is difficult not to, Master Bret. Even when you lose an argument with him, and I have lost a few in my time. He is a gentle soul with a gift for persuasion. It is impossible to take offence against the man.'

'Wait until I meet him!' warned Ralph.

'We are straying from the point,' said Hubert, examining the charter which the Breton had brought for their perusal. 'This document is similar to the one offered by Hamelin of Lisieux yet they cannot both be authentic. Which takes priority? Before we can decide that, we will need to study both charters in detail. Each bears the royal signature.' He sighed. 'It is a pity that the King is not here himself to tell us why he gave away the same land twice.'

Ralph shot Gervase a covert look, unnoticed by the others.

'If that is what he did, Canon Hubert,' said Querengar.

'Can you offer another explanation?'

'No, but having met you and seen what upright men you clearly are, I am sure that you will find that explanation.' There was no hint of flattery in his comment. 'What else do you wish to ask me?'

'Nothing at this point,' said Ralph, 'but we will need to call you before us again. I take it that you are remaining in the city?'

'Yes, my lord. Nigel the Reeve knows where I stay.'

'Then we can thank you for your testimony and bid you good day.'

During a flurry of farewells, Querengar the Breton struggled to his feet and used the crutches to propel himself towards the door. Gervase had to control the urge to offer his help. He admired the man, not least because of his own Breton ancestry, but he felt there was something missing from Querengar's deposition. Strang the Dane and Hamelin of Lisieux had said far too much. Their rival was more economical with his words and less grandiose in his claims. It remained to be seen how the Archdeacon of Gwent measured against the others, but that treat, it soon transpired, would have to be postponed.

Nigel the Reeve made one of his ostentatious entrances.

'I fear that I bring bad news,' he announced, striding towards them. 'Abraham the Priest has been unaccountably delayed and will not be here before nightfall.'

'We are ready to examine him now,' said Ralph.

'That will not be feasible, my lord.'

'Did you not summon him in time?'

'Of course. He had ample warning.'

'Yet he fails to present himself on the appointed day. What are we to make of this?' he asked, turning to his colleagues. 'Is this a deliberate attempt to flout our authority or is the Archdeacon of Gwent so absent-minded that he forgot that he was due in Gloucester today?'

'You will have to ask him,' suggested Nigel.

'Not if it means sitting on our arses in here until it grows dark,' said Ralph sourly, rising to his feet. 'We will have to delay the ambiguous pleasure of making his acquaintance until tomorrow.' He glared at Nigel. 'See that he presents himself here when the abbey bell rings for Prime.'

'Yes, my lord.'

'If he does not, he will not be heard at all.'

'I will emphasise that to him,' said Nigel, turning to leave.

'One moment,' called Ralph, checking his departure. 'Hamelin of Lisieux was here earlier and seemed to know that Abraham the Priest was now included in this dispute, a fact of which the other two claimants were noticeably ignorant.'

'What point are you trying to make, my lord?'

'That you disclosed privileged information to Hamelin.'

A curled lip. 'Did I?'

'He probably knew about the archdeacon before we did.'

Nigel was unruffled. 'Does that matter?'

'Yes,' said Ralph angrily. 'You are there to serve us, not to show favour towards someone who is due to appear before the commission. Impartiality is our touchstone and it should be yours as well.'

'It always is, my lord.'

'Not in this case. What else did you tell Hamelin of Lisieux? What other unfair advantage did you give him over his rivals? Are all your dealings based on whispered warnings to your friends?'

'I deny that I have done anything wrong,' said Nigel haughtily. 'Please excuse me while I attend to more pressing matters.'

'I'll give him pressing matters!' growled Ralph as the reeve went out of the door. 'I'll press that stupid head between my hands until his eyes pop out! I'll wager he told Hamelin who sat on the commission and how best he could win us over.'

'By dangling his pretty wife in front of you,' said Hubert sharply. 'Come, Brother Simon,' he added before Ralph could reply, 'we must take advantage of this early end to our deliberations. If we hurry back to the abbey, we may be in time to attend the funeral of Brother Nicholas.'

Gathering up their belongings, they exchanged farewells with their two colleagues and bustled out of the hall. Ralph was still fuming in silence. Gervase searched in his satchel.

'Canon Hubert is right,' he said, taking out a small parchment. 'We must put aside our own concerns and think of Brother Nicholas instead. Here is the list of tenants you requested from Abbot Serlo,' he continued, holding it up. 'Why do we not make best use of this unexpected freedom and ride out to the holding last visited by Brother Nicholas?'

'I am not in the mood for social visits.'

'Then I will go alone, Ralph.'

'Do so.'

'I feel that it's important.'

'Wait,' said his friend as Gervase was about to move off. 'Forgive my choler. Our royal reeve made my blood boil with his impudence. You are right, Gervase. This matter must be pursued. Besides, a ride will help to clear my pounding head. Instead of contemplating murder, as I am doing now, I will be more usefully employed trying to solve one.'

'Try to forget Nigel the Reeve.'

'I will, Gervase, and I'm sorry to be so churlish.'

'Turn your thoughts elsewhere.'

Ralph grinned. 'I will. To the lady Emma. She was an angel. I could have sat there and looked at her all day.'

'That was her husband's intention. Let us go.'

* * *

Abbot Serlo opened the neck of the pouch and tipped its contents on to the table in his lodging. Even though he knew what to expect, Brother Frewine was duly surprised. The hoard was far bigger than he had imagined. The abbot reached down to pick up a handful of coins.

'New-minted here in Gloucester.'

'How much is there, Father Abbot?'

'The amount is immaterial,' said the other, dropping the coins back on to the pile. 'The fact of its existence is shocking enough. Is this what you hoped to find when you searched Brother Nicholas's cell?'

'I hoped to find nothing at all.'

'But you sensed that you might. I am grateful to you, Brother Frewine. Your instinct was more reliable than my own. I was foolish enough to think that I had established complete discipline in the abbey and that all the monks were wholly committed to our common purpose. Obviously,' he said, his voice heavy with sadness, 'I was mistaken. Brother Nicholas rebelled against my leadership.'

'It may look that way, Father Abbot.'

'No other conclusion can be drawn. A hoard of coins was found hidden in his cell. Private possessions are strictly forbidden by the rules of the Order.' He pointed at the table in disgust. 'What use is money to a Benedictine monk? How could it be spent?'

'On the abbey, perhaps,' said the Precentor tentatively. 'Who knows? Could not Brother Nicholas have been saving it up in order to present it to us?' He saw the disbelief on the other's face. 'No, probably not. I just hate to assume the worst about our dear departed brother, especially when his funeral is shortly to take place.'

'You are a kind man, Brother Frewine,' said the abbot, 'and always search for the goodness in human beings. But the evidence is too overwhelming. Brother Nicholas betrayed his vows. Though we will mourn his death, we must also ask one of the questions it leaves behind him.'

'What is that, Father Abbot?'

'Where on earth did this money come from?'

'I think that we can both hazard a guess at the answer.'

'The rents?'

'How else? Brother Nicholas must have been overcharging our tenants, entering the correct payments in the accounts and keeping the difference for himself.'

Serlo shook his head. 'Look at the coins.'

'What do you mean?'

'They are fresh from the mint. Which of our tenants has shiny new coins in his pocket? They usually pay us in old and battered coinage with hands made filthy by work on the land. And there is another thing,' he said wearily. 'Tenants are quick to complain. If they felt that Brother Nicholas was putting up their rent unfairly, they would be banging on our gates in protest.'

'All this is true.'

'Put the money back in the pouch. It offends my sight.'

'Yes, Father Abbot,' said Frewine, gathering it up. 'You will have to report this to the sheriff.'

'Not until after the funeral. That takes precedence.'

'What of the royal commissioners?'

'Who?'

'Those colleagues of Canon Hubert. They have shown a keen interest in the murder and are making enquiries on their own. Should they not be told about this distressing evidence?'

Abbot Serlo frowned. 'I will need to think about that.'

'Did you know that Brother Nicholas was murdered?' asked Gervase.

'Yes.'

'How?'

'The sheriff's officers told me when they came to question me.'

'What did you tell them?'

'The same as I will tell you. I had nothing to do with his death.'

'You were the last person to see him alive.'

'So I am told.'

'It is natural that enquiries should start here.'

'Why?' said the man resentfully. 'There is no proof that I was the last person he met that day. Others must have seen him after me. The killer certainly did. Why bother me?'

'Because we need your help, Osgot.'

'I have work to do.'

'So do we,' snapped Ralph.

Osgot was taken aback to hear himself addressed in his own language by a Norman lord. Ralph Delchard had been silent until now, letting Gervase put all the questions to the truculent Saxon. His answers had been reluctant. Osgot was a tall, stringy man in his thirties, worn out by toil but sustained by an innate pride. Needing to repair some fencing on the land he rented from the abbey, he was peeved at the interruption. Arms folded, he eyed both of them sullenly.

'When did Brother Nicholas leave you that day?' said Gervase.

'Ask the sheriff.'

'We are asking *you*,' declared Ralph. 'When was it?'

A silent battle of wills was resolved when Ralph took a menacing step towards him. Osgot's reply was grudging.

'Towards evening, my lord.'

'Did he head back to the abbey?'

'Probably.'

'Did he?'

'I expect so.'

'Let me ask you for the last time,' cautioned Ralph. 'Did he?'

'No,' said Osgot. 'He rode south.'

'You remember that now, do you?'

'I watched him go,' said Osgot, pointing to the road. 'That way.'

Gervase was puzzled. 'Away from the abbey? Where could he have been going? This was the last holding he was due to visit that day. Why ride off in the wrong direction?'

Osgot gave a shrug, his face still a mask of indifference.

'You didn't like him, did you?' said Gervase.

'None of us did.'

'Why not?'

'He collected rents.'

'Any other reason?'

'Does it matter?'

'Very much, Osgot.'

'He's gone. I'm glad. That's all I have to say.'

'Glad that a monk was cruelly murdered?' pressed Ralph.

'Glad that he won't come here again.'

'Someone else will.'

'I don't care. I pay my rent.'

'But you'd rather not pay it to Brother Nicholas, is that it?'

'You say that none of you liked him,' resumed Gervase. 'What was the cause of his unpopularity? Was he harsh? Bullying? Sly?'

'Not really.'

'Did he ever try to charge you too much rent?'

'No, never.'

'So why this general dislike?'

There was a long pause, ended by Ralph's snort of impatience. 'Well?' he demanded.

'Something about him,' admitted Osgot. 'I can't say what it was. But it made us all feel uneasy. Brother Nicholas was strange.'

'In what way?'

But the man had elaborated all he could. Though they searched for more detail, Osgot had none to give. It was clear that he spent as little time as possible with the rent collector and was glad to see him ride away each time. Ralph and Gervase thanked him for his help and mounted their horses again. They were about to leave when a young boy came bounding into the field, flaxen hair shining in the sun and trailing in the breeze. Osgot's son had the vitality and innocence which he himself must have possessed at one time. As the boy called out to him, Osgot threw a worried look up at his visitors. In that moment, they learned exactly why he despised Brother Nicholas so much. Osgot had seen the monk as a threat to his son's innocence.

Now that the novelty had worn off, Golde was finding her stay at the castle slightly tedious. Maud was doing her best to entertain her guest but the latter soon tired of watching her hostess work at her embroidery and answering questions about her first marriage. There were moments when Golde felt as if the needle was threading its way through her heart. Willing to discuss her life with Ralph, she was very reticent on the subject of the husband who preceded him, a man whom she had not chosen and could never love and whose early demise she was unable to mourn with the full commitment of a grieving widow. Her discomfort was intensified by anxiety about her sister, due to arrive in Gloucester at any moment but so far unseen and unreported. Fears for Aelgar's safety lapped at Golde's mind. Even with an escort, travellers were never entirely safe on the open road.

'Were you sorry to quit Hereford?' asked Maud, sewing away.

'In some ways, my lady.'

'It must have caused you much regret.'

'Occasionally.'

'Have you been back to the town since?'

'Only once,' said Golde. 'When the commissioners visited Chester. Ralph provided me with an escort and I stopped off in Hereford on the way before riding on to rejoin them.'

'Marriage has given you many opportunities for travel.'

'And much more besides.'

'I wish that I could say the same of my husband. The journey from Normandy was the only one of significance that I have made. For the rest, my wanderings are largely circumscribed by the city boundaries.' She looked up as if the thought had struck her for the first time. 'To all intents and purposes, I am a species of prisoner.'

'Surely not, my lady!'

'How else would you describe me?'

Golde was spared the problem of manufacturing a tactful reply. After knocking at the door, a servant entered the chamber with the news that two visitors were at the castle gate, asking to see Golde. Delighted that her sister had at last arrived, Golde excused herself and followed the man along the passageway and out into the fresh air. As she skipped down the steps which led from the keep, she caught a distant glimpse of Aelgar and her betrothed, waiting inside the gate with one of the sentries. Golde quickened her pace. A happy reunion was soon effected.

Introduced to Forne by her sister, Golde deluged them with questions while taking stock of the young man who would soon become her brother-in-law. Forne was a sturdy character with pleasant rather than handsome features. The receding fair hair revealed a high forehead and his eyes sparkled with devotion. Golde was content. Though she wished that he trimmed his beard more closely, she could see his essential goodness reflected in his face. He loved her sister and she, in turn, was patently enthralled by him. It was enough.

'How long have you been here?' asked Aelgar, looking around the bailey with awe. 'I am so proud that my sister can be invited to stay in such a place.'

'It has its drawbacks,' said Golde. 'I've been here a couple of days and I'm already finding out what they are.'

'Too many Norman soldiers,' observed Forne drily.

'That is true of Hereford as well.'

'Yes, my lady.'

'No more of that,' ordered Golde with a laugh. 'If you are to marry my sister, I'll not be called "my lady". You will be Forne to me and I will be Golde to you. Is that a fair exchange?'

Forne brightened. 'Very fair.'

'What of Ralph?' said Aelgar.

'He will not stand on ceremony. But where are you staying?'

'In the town with Forne's kinsman.'

'Then let us go there so that we can have a proper talk. It seems such an age since we last met and I have a thousand questions for you.'

'I have a few for you, too, Golde,' said her sister.

'Then why do we dawdle here?' Yet when she tried to lead them out of the castle, they hesitated. 'What is wrong?'

'Are you going to *walk*?' said Forne.

'I have not lost the use of my legs.'

'The streets are filthy. That dress is too beautiful to soil.'

'Let me worry about that,' said Golde, standing between them to link arms with them both. 'What is a dirty hem beside the pleasure of seeing my only sister again? Not to mention the delight of meeting you, Forne. I would walk through a swamp to be with the pair of you. Come on. Tell me all about the journey from Hereford.'

And the three of them sauntered happily out through the gate.

Abbot Serlo surpassed himself. Conducting the burial service with due solemnity, he spoke so movingly in the abbey church that every eye was soon moist and every heart touched. The Precentor watched the service with growing admiration. When mass was sung, the abbot delivered a eulogy which was a master-piece of careful selection. By stressing the finer qualities of Brother Nicholas, he made the less attractive aspects of the dead man's character fade into temporary oblivion, and nobody listening would have guessed what dark secret had been unearthed by a search of his cell. Even those who disliked Nicholas the most – Kenelm and Elaf among them – found themselves consumed with genuine pity.

Since the church had no burial rights, part of the cemetery was set aside for the graves of deceased inhabitants of Gloucester, brought to the abbey by means of Lich Lane. Serlo led the solemn procession to the area reserved solely for the bodies of departed monks, a corner of the cemetery which was tended with loving care. The coffin was borne aloft on the shoulders of six monks before being lowered on ropes into the gaping slit in the earth. More prayers were said in unison then the abbot committed the body to its last resting place. Those who died of natural causes excited sorrow enough among the monks, but the nature of Brother Nicholas's death brought additional misery. Some of the older people around the grave had to be supported as that misery robbed them of strength and movement.

It was a long time before the assembled monks began to disperse in silence. Abbot Serlo went back to his lodging with Brother Frewine but most of the others adjourned to the church to pray once more for the salvation of the murder victim's soul and the speedy capture of his killer. Everyone was so caught up in their own anguish that they took little note of anyone else around them. Nobody lingered to see the solitary figure who hovered in the deserted cemetery.

Owen was torn between grief and remorse. As he looked down at the grave, his tears poured forth once more. When handfuls of earth had been tossed reverentially on to the coffin, spades had taken over to complete the burial and to leave a mound which would in time disappear as the earth slowly settled into the cavity. Owen glanced around to make sure that nobody was watching him, then he opened his hand to reveal something which had been burning a hole in his palm since the funeral began. It was a bright new coin from the Gloucester mint and he could no longer keep it. Scooping a hole in the mound of earth, he inserted the coin as deep as it would go then quickly covered it up.

Having paid his last respects, Owen trudged slowly away.

* * *

The horses moved at a steady trot through pleasant countryside towards Gloucester. Ralph and Gervase rode into a leafy arcade of trees and emerged to find that they could now see the River Severn on their left as it surged down the estuary. A small boat sailed past as Ralph watched.

'I hate water,' he said soulfully. 'It frightens me.'

'Nothing frightens you.'

'It does, Gervase. Crossing the Channel in rough weather was a nightmare. It made my stomach heave for days. I have no wish to return to Normandy if it entails trusting my life to a piece of wood that floats on the sea. One thing I've learned is that I'm no sailor.'

'Would you not like Golde to see where you were born?'

'Of course.'

'To show her the beauties of Normandy?'

'Nothing would please me more.'

'Nor her. Golde has more than once confided to me that she would love to cross the Channel with you to your homeland.'

'This is my homeland now, Gervase.'

'But you also have estates in Normandy.'

'Administered by trusty people,' said Ralph. 'I keep in touch with them by letter. They manage well enough without me. No, I will be more than happy if I never have to take to the water again.'

'Not even on a river?'

'Not even then, Gervase. Especially one as churlish as the Severn. Look at it,' he said, waving an arm. 'Even from here you can see the strength of the current. I'll remain on dry land.'

A stand of sycamores rose up on their left to obscure the river and allow their thoughts to turn once more to the murder that had brought them out to visit Osgot.

'Brother Nicholas was an odd character,' said Gervase. 'Everyone took a dislike to him yet they will not tell you exactly why.'

'We can guess Osgot's reason.'

'Not every tenant has a well-favoured son, Ralph. Why did the others turn away from him? Nobody likes to pay rent but they do not always despise the rent collector, especially if they inhabit abbey land. When I was at Eltham, our rent collector, Brother Saul, was one of the most popular monks in the abbey.'

'Perhaps he did not look at young boys in a peculiar way.'

'There's more to it than that.'

'Is there? Remember what those novices told you.'

'I do, Ralph, but they only gave part of the story. I cannot believe that Brother Nicholas was entirely without friends. An abbey is a haven of tolerance. There must be someone within its precincts who liked him enough to overlook his unfortunate manner.'

'What about the Precentor?'

'Brother Frewine defended him, it is true, but I suspect that he would defend anyone in a Benedictine cowl out of sheer loyalty. The abbot would probably do the same.'

'He did, Gervase. I probed him hard but he would admit to no faults in his rent collector. Serlo pretended to admire the man but I sensed no real affection. Brother Nicholas was an outsider at the abbey.'

'That brings us back to the sheriff's conviction that the victim was murdered by one of his fellow monks.'

'I refuse to believe that.'

'So do I.'

'Monks are more guileful. They would hide a dead body where it could never be found. No, it was not one of them, Gervase.'

'We may both be proved wrong.'

'If we are, it will not be by Durand. His investigation has so far achieved nothing beyond stirring up a lot of dust. We have already discovered things which completely eluded him and his officers. And if we *are* to be given the dubious honour of a royal visit,' said Ralph as they came out into open country once more, 'our peppery sheriff will have his hands full at the castle. He'll not be able to conduct this inquiry properly.'

'Will the King come?' asked Gervase.

'He may, he may not. You know how changeable he is.'

'I also know that he does nothing without a purpose, Ralph.'

'Granted.'

'So what purpose could bring him to Gloucester?'

'Affairs of state.'

'Can you guess what they might be?'

'No, Gervase,' said the other. 'It sounds like a decision made on the spur of the moment. Why send a messenger to forewarn Durand of a possible visit when we could have brought the same information from Winchester? The King knew when and where we travelled.'

'Some emergency may have arisen.'

'That's my fear.'

'What could it be?'

'Only time will tell, Gervase,' said Ralph as the city loomed up in the distance. 'As long as William does not interfere with our work at the shire hall. We have enough problems as it is. The last thing we need is someone looking over our shoulder. Even if it is a King.'

'Supposing it were the lady Emma?'

Ralph beamed. 'Ah, that's another matter.'

'I thought it might be.'

'The lady Emma can look over my shoulder any time she wishes. If I were not married to the most wonderful woman in England, I would harbour dark desires about that extraordinary creature we met at the shire hall today.'

'Querengar the Breton?' teased his friend.

'The lady Emma!'

'Oh, her.'

'Beauty incarnate.'

'A pleasing face, I agree.'

'Pleasing! It could sow lust in the heart of a pope. I tell you, there was a brief moment when I wished I was still young and unmarried.'

'But since you *do* have a wife?' Gervase reminded him.

'And such a wife!' said Ralph, kicking his horse into a canter. 'I'll count my blessings and hasten back to her.'

Gervase spent the last mile trying to catch up with him.

The pleasure of seeing her sister again seemed to increase rather than pall. Secure in the love of a good man, Aelgar looked radiant and Golde could not have been more happy for her, knowing how much distress she had endured in the past. Her younger sister had been blessed with a pale loveliness which Golde had envied as a child until she realised what a mixed blessing it was. Unwanted suitors had plagued Aelgar throughout her young life, and Golde would never forget the ardent Norman lord who tried to take by force what he could not win by courtship. Now, happily, having survived all that, her sister had found the man of her dreams. The doting Forne allowed her to blossom into full womanhood.

Golde quickly warmed towards Forne himself. Like the two sisters, he was born of noble stock with a wealthy father who had been largely dispossessed after the Conquest. Yet enough land remained in the possession of the family to ensure a relatively comfortable life, especially when added to the property in Archenfield which Aelgar herself had inherited from the man to whom she had been betrothed until his brutal murder. Present joy helped past tragedy to recede in her mind. If anyone deserved her share of marital bliss, Golde mused, watching the young lovers together, it was her sister. Happiness was long overdue.

'Where will you live?' she asked.

'Together,' said Forne with a fond grin.

'In Archenfield?'

'Where else?'

'Hereford.'

'No, Golde,' said her sister. 'It is time for me to make a

complete break from there. My life is with Forne now.'

'What will become of the house?'

'It will be sold along with that eternal smell of beer.'

'I learned to enjoy the odour.'

'You were always the genuine brewer. Those I employ now have none of your skills. There have been complaints from the castle.'

'Yes,' said Forne. 'I hear that your ale was incomparable, Golde.'

'Ralph does not think so.'

'Have you not won him over?'

'No, he will touch nothing but wine.'

'A true Norman!'

'In most things.'

'What sort of man is he?' asked Forne guardedly. 'Aelgar has talked much about your husband but she hardly knows him.'

'I know enough to speak well of him,' said his betrothed.

'But you were not at first overjoyed when you learned that he was going to marry your sister. You had qualms. You told me so.'

There was a sudden pause, the first since they had met, and they squirmed on their benches as the discordant note was struck. The three of them were bunched around the table in the house owned by Forne's kinsman, Hadwig, a burgess in the city and a man of moderate wealth. The house was large enough to accommodate the two visitors in separate bays and Golde suspected that it was the first time they had spent a night under the same roof. It explained the tingle of excitement whenever they exchanged a glance, though there was no excitement now. Aelgar stared guiltily at the bare table and Forne searched for words to heal the slight rift he had just opened.

'I am sorry to speak out of turn, Golde,' he said.

'But you didn't,' she replied, contriving a smile. 'If you are to join our little family, you must feel free to comment on all its members. And that includes Ralph. He will certainly not hold back any comments about you, I can promise you.'

'I offended you.'

'Not really.'

'Please forgive me.'

'What is there to forgive?' asked Golde brightly, trying to dispel the awkwardness. 'It's hardly surprising that Aelgar had qualms about me because I had several myself. The last thing in the world I expected to do was marry a Norman. To ally myself with an enemy, so to speak.' She gave a little laugh. 'It's just that Ralph is the friendliest enemy I ever met, and the kindest possible husband.'

'I hope to meet him very soon.'

'You will, Forne.'

But she could see that he still had doubts about her and Golde felt even more uncomfortable. She had stepped back into an old life but part of her remained immovably in her new world. It was not just the fine clothes she now wore which set her slightly apart from her sister. There was something deeper, some change of perception, some subtle shift of loyalty. Forne was an irretrievable Saxon. Ready to love his future sister-in-law, he would never be able to shake off a latent resentment against her husband and that saddened Golde. It would colour her relationship with her sister. Aelgar looked up and reached out to put a hand on Forne's arm. It was a telling gesture. She was his now.

Golde tried to move the conversation to more neutral ground.

'What news of Hereford?' she asked.

'Little has changed,' said her sister.

'And our old neighbours?'

'They send their love.'

'Take mine back to them. I miss Hereford.'

'I'm not sure that I will.'

'Why not?'

'Forne and I will be together.'

'We may need to visit the town on occasion,' he said. 'Indeed, we may even be compelled to do so. I hope that does not happen but I put Aelgar's safety before all else.'

'Safety?'

He nodded sadly. 'Our holdings are not far from the Welsh border. That has never worried me. I have Welsh neighbours and have always been on good terms with them. But there have been stirrings across the border. Raiding parties have been sighted.'

'I thought that peace had finally been imposed,' said Golde.

'It has,' he explained, 'but there are some hot-blooded Welsh-men who refuse to accept it. Rumours are spreading like wildfire.'

'Rumours?'

'Of a possible attack on Hereford.'

'Not again!' sighed Golde.

'It is one of the reasons I was glad to bring Aelgar here,' he said, putting a protective arm around her. 'I wanted her out of Hereford until the danger blows over. We are completely safe in Gloucester.'

Hooves clacking on the hard road, the horses thundered on through the darkness. There were a dozen men in all, most of them armed and every one a seasoned rider. Night had started to close in on them and they were not entirely sure at what point they actually crossed the border into Gloucestershire and left Gwent behind. It was of no concern to them. In their hearts, they did not accept that the border really existed. As they urged their horses on, they believed that they were still in Wales.

They were some miles short of their destination when the tall figure at the head of the column brought it to a halt with a loud yell. Iron bits were tugged in soft mouths and the horses slowed instantly. The leader of the band turned to his tall companion.

'Why have we stopped?'

'Because this is where we part, Madog.'

'There is still some way to go.'

'We will ride on alone.'

'But we are your escort.'

'And I'm most grateful to you,' said the other, raising his voice so that all could hear. 'It is easier to ride faster in a pack.'

'Why dispense with us then?'

'You are no longer needed, Madog.'

'Danger may lurk on the road ahead.'

'We will be careful.'

'You are both unarmed.'

'We have God to protect us.'

'You'll need more than Him at your side when you meet those Normans,' said Madog bitterly. 'They're treacherous. Look what they've done to Wales.'

'I am never likely to forget that. Now, turn back.'

'Let us at least get you within reach of Gloucester.'

'We are within reach,' soothed the other, 'and if the two of us arrive alone, they might even let us into the city at this hour. Ride there with your men at our back and we would certainly be spurned.'

'We will not be far away.'

'That is reassuring.'

'You know where to find us.'

'I do, Madog.' They exchanged a wave. 'Goodbye, my friend.'

'*Yn iach!*'

The other riders gathered around to offer their own respectful farewells then the tall man was joined by the monk who had been at the rear of the column. Watched by their escort, the two of them set off at a more gentle pace and were soon swallowed up by the night. Unlike his companion, the monk was apprehensive.

'Will we be safe on our own?' he asked querulously.

'Of course,' said Abraham the Priest. 'This should, by rights, be Welsh territory. We are travelling on home ground.'

Chapter Seven

Ralph Delchard and his wife talked long into the night. It was the only opportunity they had to be alone together and to exchange details of how they had spent their respective days. Over the delicious meal served in the hall that evening, they had been too busy talking to their hosts to pay much attention to each other and they were determined to make up for it. When they were finally alone, conversation was preceded by an act of spontaneous passion, always their most pleasurable and effective means of communication. As they made love with uninhibited vigour in the privacy of their bed, the warm night brought them out in beads of perspiration and left them in a state of joyful exhaustion. When Ralph eventually rolled over on to his back, his face and chest were glistening.

'Thank you,' he whispered, cradling her in his arms.

'And thank *you*, Ralph.'

'Have I pleased you?'

'Delightfully.'

'Does that mean you will keep me on for a while?'

'A week or two more,' she joked, nestling into him. 'If you think that you can last that long.'

'Watch me!' They shared a laugh. 'I strive to be a satisfactory husband. Do I succeed?'

'Every time.'

'Good.'

'Not that I am keeping score, mark you.'

'I hope not! That would be calculation in every sense.' He kissed her on the temple and drew her closer. 'Well, my love, I think that we can be sure of one thing.'

'What is that?'

'The sheriff and his wife are not lying in each other's arms.'

'How do you know?'

'They have long gone past that stage.'

'I am not so sure.'

'I am,' said Ralph. 'My guess is that the lady Maud keeps a cold bed. Durand may not even share it with her any more.'

'That is idle comment,' she replied. 'And why blame her for any coldness between them? It is far more likely to arise from the sheriff's neglect of his wife.'

'Is that what she told you?'

'It's what I have gathered, Ralph. He is very attentive to her in public but that may be consolation for his disregard of her in private. What I do know is this. His work totally eclipses his wife. When his duties call him, she might just as well not exist.'

'You could make the same complaint about me.'

'I do,' she returned, 'but you never hear it.'

'I listen to everything you say, Golde.'

'Eventually.'

'Look at me now. I'm a captive audience.'

'Only because you are too weary for anything else.'

'Is that a challenge?' he said, easing his leg over hers.

'No, Ralph, merely an observation. Now take your rest and tell me what you have been doing all day.'

'Being thoroughly bored in the shire hall.'

'Gervase didn't seem bored and he spent as much time there as you. He told me that it had been a stimulating session.'

'Well, yes,' conceded Ralph as he remembered the encounter with the lady Emma, 'there were stimulating moments, it's true, but it was largely dross. Only Gervase Bret can get inspired by the fine detail of a charter or by the tedium of debate.'

'What about Canon Hubert?'

'Golde!' he protested. 'I refuse to talk about Hubert at a time like this. He has no place whatsoever in the marital couch. If he did, there would not be room for either of us, I can assure you. Leave him to his chaste mattress at the abbey. Tell me about your day. I am dying to hear about Aelgar and this new suitor of hers. Forne, is he called?'

'Yes. And he does not possess an ounce of Welsh blood.'

'Thank heaven for that!'

'He and my sister seem very well matched.'

'Like us, you mean?'

'Nobody is like us, Ralph.'

'No, we are quite unique.'

'Unusual, that is all.'

'We are a model for all young lovers.'

'Hardly!' she argued. 'Who would emulate us? Let's be honest here. We're much more likely to excite curiosity than imitation.'

'In what way?'

'Not every woman in my position would consider marrying you.'

'None of them would get the chance!'

'I'm serious, Ralph. You belong in here, in the castle and all that it stands for, while I come from out there with the other citizens. A lot of people would say that I betrayed my nation when I became your wife. There was a time when my own sister might have believed that, and I know that Forne has grave doubts on the subject.'

He bridled. 'What business is it of his!'

'Forne is to be my brother-in-law.'

'Then he will have to learn to respect you.'

'He does, I am sure.'

'So what are these grave doubts of his?'

'He let slip a remark that put into words what I could already see in his face. He has severe qualms about us. It's only natural.'

'I can see that I will have to talk to this Forne.'

'No, Ralph. Not in any spirit of anger.'

'I'll not have him criticising my wife!'

'He was not doing that,' she said, putting her face closer to his. 'Why not let me tell you exactly what happened before you rush to judgement? That is what you do in the shire hall, isn't it? Hear all the evidence before deciding on your verdict. Do the same here. Pretend that you're in the shire hall now, Ralph.'

'I daren't. I will fall asleep.'

'Not with me beside you,' she said, giving him a sharp dig in the ribs. His grunt of pain made her smile. 'That's better. Now, listen.'

Golde described her reunion with Aelgar and the subsequent visit to the house in the city. She tried to sing Forne's praises but she was conscious of having to invent much of her enthusiasm. Ideal as a husband for her sister, she feared that he might not turn out to be a perfect brother-in-law. Golde knew that everything would depend on what he and Ralph felt about each other. At the end of her account, her husband was slightly more well-disposed towards Forne, but he was far from expressing outright approval. Ralph wanted to reserve his opinion until he actually met the young man.

'Do you think they will be happy together?' he asked.

'Very happy.'

'That is all that matters.'

'I know,' she said, stroking his arm. 'Aelgar has chosen well. And they are like us in one thing, if in nothing else.'

'What is that?'

'Their truthfulness. They are completely honest with each other.'

'So they should be.'

'It is not always so in marriage.'

'It ought to be, Golde. True love permits no secrecy.'

'Not every union is blessed with true love,' she sighed. 'And even if it is at the start, circumstances can change. Take our host and his wife. The lady Maud adored him when they first met and he courted her with as much ardour as any lover. But now?'

'His responsibilities divert his attention.'

'His wife expects that. What rankles with her is that he refuses to say anything about his work. It is a closed book to the lady Maud and she would dearly like to flick through the pages. When I told her about us, she was very envious.'

'Envious?'

'Of my good fortune in having a husband who trusted me.'

'Implicitly.'

'I assured her that there was nothing you held back from me. It would hurt me deeply if there was. You confide in me as your wife and I confide freely in you. That way we spring no unpleasant surprises on each other, do we?'

'No, my love.'

'Holding something back is a form of lying, really. A deception. A concealment of truth. I told the lady Maud that you were very honest. Whatever the situation, you'd never lie to me. Would you, Ralph?'

Ralph thought about the possible arrival of King William in Gloucester and ran a tongue over dry lips. He had still not raised the subject with her and felt it unwise to do so now, even though he was breaking the vow they had once made to each other.

'Well?' she said, prodding him. 'Would you?'

'Of course not.'

'Why did you hesitate?'

'I'm tired, Golde.'

'Then let us get some sleep,' she said, snuggling into him with a purring contentment. 'You have to make an early start tomorrow.' She was about to doze off when she remembered something. 'I almost forgot, Ralph. They brought worrying news from Hereford.'

'Oh?'

'There has been more trouble on the Welsh border.'

'Not again!'

'Raiding parties have been sighted.'

'The Welsh are a bellicose nation.'

'I hope they do not strike this far south.'

Ralph quivered. 'As long as they do not contain Archdeacon Idwal,' he moaned. 'Renegade bands can easily be repelled but no fortifications are proof against Idwal. He is an invasion army in himself.'

'Do not get so agitated. I merely pass on rumours.'

'Well, I hope that they are proved false, Golde. But we're far too close to the Welsh border to be able to relax. Forne lives in Archenfield, well placed to catch the first whiff of revolt.'

'There's no serious danger, surely?' she said. 'If there were, the sheriff would be marshalling his men in readiness, yet there is no sign of that. Besides, if there was any hint of a real invasion, would not the King himself ride from Winchester with an army?'

Ralph fell silent. Long after his wife had drifted off to sleep, he brooded on what she had said. He had even more reason to wish that King William would not descend on the city now.

As far as their duties would permit, Canon Hubert and Brother Simon tried to enter into the life of the abbey. Like the other monks, they rose early to attend Matins and shuffled towards the church with heads bowed and hands tucked into their sleeves. When the service was over, they slipped quietly out to prepare for the day ahead while the rest of the holy brothers remained in church for Lauds. They were about to cross the cloister garth when Abbot Serlo hailed them. Stopping at once, they waited for him to catch them up.

'I wanted a quiet word with you,' began Serlo.

'As many as you wish, Father Abbot,' said Hubert.

'First, let me say how pleased I was to see both you and Brother Simon at the funeral service yesterday. I know that you have pressing duties in the shire hall, yet you found time to pay your respects to poor Brother Nicholas.'

'We were honoured to be part of the congregation and, though it is hardly a subject for congratulation, I must commend you on the way you conducted the service. It was most impressive.'

'And very moving,' said Brother Simon.

'You handled a difficult situation with the utmost tact,' continued Hubert. 'Your whole treatment of this wretched business has been quite exemplary.'

'Thank you, Canon Hubert,' said the abbot, 'but I do not feel that I have behaved in an exemplary manner. It is a novel predicament for me and I am not entirely sure how to cope with it. But prayer and meditation have taught me this. We must explore every possible means of tracking down the man who killed Brother Nicholas.'

'I agree, Father Abbot.'

'That is why I value a moment with you now. Something has come to light, something so disturbing that my first instinct was to keep it from you because it reflects badly on the abbey and hence on me.'

'I refuse to believe that.'

'So do I, Father Abbot,' endorsed Simon.

'Hear me out.' Serlo cleared his throat then spoke rapidly. 'Brother Frewine, our Precentor, as wise a man as any here, felt that the sheriff's officers may have missed something in their search of Brother Nicholas's cell and, prompted by some inner conviction, he requested permission to carry out his own search. Certain that he would find nothing, I was proved horribly wrong. Concealed behind a stone in the wall was a bag of coins, amounting to a substantial amount.'

'Saints preserve us!' murmured Simon.

'This is a grim discovery,' said Hubert. 'Do you or the Precentor have any idea where the money came from?'

'None, Canon Hubert. I need hardly tell you that personal wealth is anathema within the enclave. And before you ask me,' said Serlo as a question formed on the other's lips, 'we do not believe that it was a stolen portion of the abbey rents. The leather pouch contained new coins, all minted here in Gloucester. Our tenants would not pay with such money. It came from another source, I fear, but what could that source be?'

'And is it in any way connected to Brother Nicholas's death?'

'That is the question with which I have been wrestling.'

'Quite rightly, Abbot Serlo. But you must acquit yourself of any blame here. It is wrong to hold yourself responsible.'

'The fault lies with Brother Nicholas,' suggested Simon.

'Answerable to you, of course,' said Hubert, 'but capable of independent action over which you had no control. The nature of his work is crucial here. Spending so much time outside the abbey, he was beyond your ken, vulnerable to unholy impulses, drawn into some kind of corrupt practice. Thank you for confiding in us, Father Abbot. Though it is disturbing news, it is also an invaluable clue and I will pass it on to the lord Ralph as soon as I may.'

'This mystery grows murkier by the day,' said Serlo with a hand to his brow. 'I do hope that someone can solve it before too long.'

'So do we,' said Hubert solemnly. 'But tell us more about Brother Nicholas's work as a rent collector. How far afield did he go and was he absent from the abbey for any length of time? Why was he assigned to the work in the first place? It is a position of such trust . . .'

It was a dull morning when Ralph Delchard and Gervase Bret set off from the castle, the overcast sky reflecting the former's mood. He was churlish and preoccupied and Gervase knew better than to attempt any conversation on their ride. Hoping to take out his irritation on the posturing reeve, Ralph was annoyed to see that he had sent a deputy in his place, a polite young man, too obliging to merit any reproach and too eager to deserve the torrent of abuse Ralph intended to unleash on his master. The bell for Prime was ringing as the commissioners took their places in the shire hall beside Canon Hubert and Brother Simon. Ralph ordered that Abraham the Priest be summoned before them, deciding to release his bile upon the Archdeacon of Gwent instead.

As soon as the archdeacon and the monk who accompanied him entered the shire hall, Ralph began his attack.

'You were instructed to be here yesterday!' he accused.

'We know, my lord,' said Abraham gently. 'We regret the delay.'

'Regret is not enough. I demand an explanation.'

'Then you will have one as soon as you have the grace to explain to whom the explanation is being given.'

'To royal commissioners.'

'Do they possess names?'

'Damnation! Tell us your paltry excuse.'

'Are we allowed to sit while we do so, my lord?'

'Sit, stand or turn somersaults. But stop prevaricating.'

'There is no prevarication here, my lord,' intervened Hubert, 'and I do think it best that the archdeacon and his companion take a seat.'

He waved them to the front bench, performed the introductions and imposed a calmer note on the proceedings. Abraham was a tall, dignified man in his fifties, with a head supremely suited to a tonsure and a manner which combined spirituality and worldliness in the correct proportions. Brother Tomos was younger, plumper and distinctly more anxious. He had none of the archdeacon's composure. Lacking his master's command of Norman French, he was struggling to understand what was being said.

Impressed by the archdeacon's bearing, Gervase sought to make him feel more welcome and to prevent further browbeating from Ralph.

'We are pleased to see you here at last,' he said with a smile, 'and we are sure that only a serious mishap could have held you up.'

'It was more of a blessing than a mishap,' said Abraham.

'Was it?'

'Yes, Master Bret. We set off in plenty of time but our journey took us through a village where a young woman was with child. No sooner had we arrived than she went into labour. We could hardly leave her.'

'Did you linger in order to baptise the child?' said Ralph.

'No, my lord. In order to deliver it.'

Ralph was startled into silence, Hubert paled with embarrassment and Brother Simon began to gibber incoherently. The very notion of childbirth was deeply upsetting to the scribe. To have it raised so easily by the archdeacon caught him completely off guard.

Gervase was fascinated. 'You delivered the child?'

'Of course. Who else would take on the office?'

'Was there no doctor? No midwife?'

'None within call,' said Abraham. 'The child came slightly ahead of time and took them all unawares. As Tomos will tell you, the mother was in great distress. We heard her cries as we entered the village.' Simon added to them with an involuntary howl. 'I could hardly abandon her in her hour of need. She lives in my diocese. That means I must turn doctor, midwife, nurse or anything else on occasion, even if it means putting my shoulder to a plough.'

Hubert gaped. 'A *plough* was involved in this delivery?'

'No, Canon Hubert. I was simply trying to explain that I will become what is needed at any particular moment to relieve those in my care. A midwife was called for and that is what I became.'

'Was it a safe delivery?' wondered Gervase.

'Do not tell us!' cried Simon.

'Why not?' asked Abraham. 'Is it not always a moment of joy when we bring a new Christian into the world?'

'Yes, Archdeacon, but we need not dwell on the means by which that joy is achieved. It does not bear thinking about.'

'But it was such a privilege to be involved in the process.'

Simon emitted another yell and lapsed into open-mouthed horror.

'Was it a boy or girl?' said Gervase.

'A lusty boy, so anxious to come into the world that he would not bide his time. Mother and baby are both well, Master Bret, but it was a difficult labour. We had to tarry. When I realised that we would not reach Gloucester to answer your summons, I sent an apology ahead of me.'

'It was duly received,' said Hubert, 'so perhaps we can put aside your eccentric habit of delivering babies and turn our minds to the question of certain hides in the Westbury Hundred?'

'Of course, Canon Hubert.'

'Do you have a justifiable claim?' said Ralph.

'Yes, my lord. It begins with a moral right.'

'You Welshmen will preach about morality!'

'But it is grounded in legality.'

'Then why did you not advance it to the earlier commissioners?' said Ralph. 'Were you too busy bringing other children into the world?'

'Fortunately, no. I was visiting the Bishop of St David's. I did not even know about this Great Survey until I returned.'

'St David's?' said Gervase with interest. 'In that case, you may have met—'

'That is not germane to this inquiry,' interrupted Ralph savagely before another archdeacon could be named. 'We have Welshmen enough under this roof, Gervase, without adding more. Most especially that one.'

Abraham was puzzled. 'Why do you have a prejudice against us?'

'I do not.'

'Forgive me, my lord, but I feel hostility. Tomos?'

His companion gave a nervous nod of agreement.

'The lord Ralph is not hostile to anyone,' said Gervase, shooting him a look of reproof. 'He strives to be impartial and objective, as

129

do we all. That is why we can assure you of a fair hearing Archdeacon, be you Welsh, Irish, Dane or Breton. You talk of a legal claim. Have you documentary proof of it?'

'Of course. Tomos.'

The monk produced a charter from his satchel and handed it to his master. After unrolling it to remind himself of its contents, Abraham rose to pass it over before resuming his seat on the bench. Gervase glanced at the document and noted the seal at its base.

'This was issued by King Edward,' he observed.

'It ratifies a right to property long-held by my predecessors.'

'Strang the Dane also has a charter from King Edward.'

'Set one against the other.'

'It is not as simple as that,' explained Gervase. 'The lord Hamelin bases his claim on a charter from King William, as does Querengar the Breton. Each seems to have validity.'

'I am well acquainted with both men.'

'And with Strang the Dane, I expect.'

Abraham's face darkened. 'I know him best of all.'

'But like him the least, by the sound of it.'

'We have had our differences, I will admit, but they touch on other matters and do not belong here in this hall.'

'Are you familiar with Strang's reeve?'

'Balki? Oh yes! We all know Balki, alas.'

'He is certainly aware of you, Archdeacon,' said Gervase, recalling the discomfort shown by the reeve at the mention of Abraham's name. 'And not at all happy to be ranged against you here.'

'With cause. I intend to take his master's land from him.'

'Strang alleges that it has already been taken away by Hamelin of Lisieux and, given the chance, Querengar the Breton will seize it from all three of you. Which one of you are we to favour?'

'The one with the most legitimate claim,' said Hubert.

Abraham smiled. 'Then that will be me.'

'Tell us why, Archdeacon.'

'Without any mention of childbirth,' begged Simon.

'Very well,' said the Welshman calmly. 'Let us go back to the reign of King Edward for that is when the problem first arose . . .'

When the others dispersed after choir practice, Elaf lingered to speak to Brother Owl. The Precentor knew why. He sat on a bench with the boy and turned a sympathetic ear to his concerns.

'Are you still worried about Kenelm?'

'Yes, Brother Frewine.'

'He will recover in time.'

'That is what I thought but he seems to get worse. Fearful thoughts haunt him day and night. Can you not tell by his face?'

'Yes, Elaf. I can and did. Kenelm looks harrowed.'

'He will not survive much longer.'

'What do you mean?'

'He has talked of putting an end to it.'

'How?' asked Frewine with sudden alarm. 'He is surely not contemplating suicide? That would be an unforgivable sin.'

'Kenelm feels that he has already committed an unforgivable sin.'

'And he plans to take his own life?'

'No, Brother Frewine. His thoughts do not tend that way.'

'Thank the Lord!'

'He knows the penalty for such an act.'

'To lie forever in unconsecrated ground,' warned the other. 'To be turned away from the kingdom of heaven. Nobody should pay such a hideous price. In a young boy, it would be doubly tragic.'

'Kenelm realises that.'

'So whence comes this talk of ending it?'

Elaf gave a shrug and tussled with his conscience. Kenelm was his friend and he did not wish to betray a confidence. At the same time, he did not want to lose the one person who made his own life at the abbey more bearable. Seeing his dilemma, the Precentor tried to help him out of it. He put a hand on the boy's shoulder.

'You were right to come to me, Elaf,' he said. 'Whatever you tell me will go no further. I have helped you both in the past and, I like to think, pulled the pair of you out from beneath Brother Paul's avenging arm more than once. Let me help you again.'

'I'm not sure that you can.'

'Simply talking to me will bring its own reward for it will ease your mind. Unburden yourself of the load you carry.'

'It's such a heavy load,' confessed the novice. 'I have remorse of my own, Brother Frewine, as you can imagine. During the funeral yesterday, I thought that I would faint. But Kenelm suffers something far worse than remorse. It pursues him every hour of the day.'

'So what does he intend to do about it?'

'Leave the abbey.'

'Abandon his novitiate?'

'Yes, Brother Frewine.'

'But that would be such a waste.'

'So I told him.'

'His parents would never condone it.'

'I know.'

'Then why does he indulge in such futile talk?'

'If only it were futile!'

'Kenelm would not disobey his parents.'

'I fear that he may, Brother Frewine.'

The old man's face was at its most owlish. 'What are you telling me, Elaf?' he said in alarm. 'Kenelm is planning to run away?'

'I'm afraid so.'

'That would be a scandal.'

'I told him that.'

'A scandal for the abbey and a bitter blow for his dear parents. Nobody ever flees from here. It is unheard of, Elaf.'

'What about Siward?'

Frewine was checked. 'That was different,' he muttered.

'He disappeared one day. So did Dena. Those were the names that Kenelm cited. He said he'd follow their example.'

'I pray to God that he doesn't do that!'

'Why? What happened to them?'

'If only we knew!'

'What drove them to quit the abbey in the first place?'

'We are not even sure if that is what they did, Elaf.'

'But they vanished.'

'Sadly, they did.'

'So they must have run away because they hated it here.'

'Dena did not hate it,' said the Precentor. 'He had a beautiful voice and loved singing. Dena was always the first to come to choir practice and the last to leave. He liked it here. It was his natural home.'

'Then why did he want to escape?'

'I have no idea, Elaf. Nor do his parents. It is baffling. And Siward's disappearance was equally mysterious. He was more wayward, perhaps, more accustomed to feel the wrath of Brother Paul, but that would not have been enough to drive him away.'

The boy was apprehensive. His heart was starting to pound.

'I am not sure what you are telling me,' he said slowly.

'We do not know if Siward or Dena fled the abbey.'

'How else did they vanish?'

Brother Frewine winced. 'They may have been taken.'

Abraham the Priest was a revelation. On the face of it, he had by far the weakest claim, and yet he advanced it most convincingly. He needed no bullying manner like Strang the Dane and no beautiful wife like Hamelin of Lisieux. Nor did he trade on the unvarnished directness of Querengar the Breton. Advocacy was his weapon. Arguments were cleverly arranged before being presented in a lilting voice which seemed to lull his hearers into agreement. Resolved to dislike him, Ralph slowly warmed to the archdeacon. When the latter strayed briefly into the realms of canon law, he was challenged immediately by Hubert but he held his ground with equanimity and beat off the attack. Even Gervase's probing questions could not find a chink. Abraham was confounding them all.

'Let us end there,' announced Ralph, slapping the table, 'before we become entirely bemused. Thank you, Archdeacon. I am sorry to give you such a sour welcome. I had no idea that your delay was caused by your compassion for a young mother. If your skill in midwifery matches your ability in a courtroom, the lady was indeed fortunate.'

'She came bravely through the ordeal.'

'Do not put us through it again!' implored Simon.

'There is no time,' said Ralph. 'We have spent the whole morning listening to you. If nothing else, I hope that absolves me of the charge of prejudice. What we now need is a recess so that we may study your charter alongside the others in our possession. We also need to weigh your arguments in the balance and decide if there is need for any further examination.'

'I will await your summons, my lord,' said Abraham.

'Keep well away from pregnant women in the meantime.'

'This is not my diocese.'

'One last thing,' said Ralph as the two men rose to go. 'I expected to speak to you through an interpreter. How is it that you know our language so well?'

'I took the trouble to learn it, my lord.'

'Patently. But why?'

'It is very useful to speak in the tongue of our neighbours. In my experience, it is the best way to avoid misunderstandings. Also, my lord, simple necessity came into play.' He gave a tolerant smile. 'I learned your language because I had a strong feeling that you would never deign to learn mine. Am I right?'

'Absolutely.'

They parted on good terms and the two visitors left the room.

Ralph turned first to Canon Hubert and invited his comment with a raised eyebrow. The latter needed a moment to gather his thoughts.

'Our archdeacon has a beguiling tongue,' he said at length, 'but I was not entirely persuaded by it.'

'What about you, Gervase?' asked Ralph.

'I found his arguments very cogent.'

'More so than those of the other claimants?'

'Yes,' said Gervase, 'but he did not resolve the basic contradiction. All four of them have shown us royal charters relating to land in the Westbury Hundred. The problem is that they may not all refer to the hides in question. All the charters lack definition. As things stand, we could do no worse than to quarter the whole property and parcel it out between them.'

'That is a mischievous suggestion,' said Hubert.

'Then let me offer a better one. Why not see for ourselves?'

'I do not follow, Gervase.'

'It is simple, Canon Hubert. Let us suspend our work here and ride out to the Westbury Hundred. We may well find that the twenty hides claimed by the lord Hamelin are quite separate from the eight to which Strang would seem to have the right. And where do Querengar's lie?'

'In the control of Hamelin of Lisieux,' said Ralph.

'And his wife,' added Hubert pointedly.

'And, as you remind us, his charming wife.'

'I was less charmed and more critical of him, my lord.'

'Be that as it may, Hubert, I think that Gervase has a point. There is confusion here. The only way to plumb the depth of this controversy is to visit the disputed property in person.'

'Is that really necessary?'

'I believe it is, though we do not all have to go.'

'Thank goodness for that!' said Brother Simon.

'No, Hubert,' taunted Ralph. 'You and Simon can go alone. Who knows? On your way, you may come across a woman in labour and discover that you have the medical talents of Abraham the Priest.'

'Never!' exclaimed Simon.

Hubert shuddered. 'The very thought makes me go numb.'

'Ralph is only jesting,' said Gervase, shooting his friend an admonitory glance. 'I will volunteer to make the journey. Alone, if need be. You and Brother Simon will certainly be spared, Canon Hubert.'

The two of them nodded their gratitude in unison.

'That only leaves me,' said Ralph. 'What can I say?'

'That you will bear me company.'

'If I must, Gervase.'

'It is agreed. In the course of our travels, we may be able to kill two birds with one stone. Our journey should take us past other portions of abbey land. We can speak to the sub-tenants about their rent collector.'

'I am glad you mention Brother Nicholas,' said Hubert, 'because we bring news from the abbey about him. Abbot Serlo divulged it to us only this morning and it casts the rent collector in a new light.'

'Go on,' urged Ralph.

He and Gervase listened to a description of what was found in Brother Nicholas's cell. They were intrigued. Ralph scratched his head.

'Who has the pouch with the coins in it?' he asked.

'Brother Frewine, the Precentor,' said Hubert.

'I will need to speak to him.'

'Is there any message we can convey, my lord?'

'Simply that we are one step closer to identifying the murderer,' said Ralph confidently. 'Come, Gervase. We have a long ride ahead of us. And a great deal to discuss as we go.'

Leaving their satchels with Brother Simon, the two of them set off at once. Outside the shire hall, Ralph gave instructions to the reeve's deputy then asked him for directions to the Westbury

Hundred. He and Gervase mounted, gathered their escort then kicked their horses into action. As they turned the first corner, they were confronted by a sight which made Ralph gurgle in despair. Riding towards them at the head of his own escort was a small, wizened figure in a black cowl over which was worn a lambskin cloak frayed by age and stained with filth.

'He's here after all!' said Ralph, aghast. 'It's Archdeacon Idwal!'

Gervase laughed. 'Look more carefully,' he suggested. 'Since when would Idwal have an armed escort of Norman soldiers? And since when has he been promoted to the Bishopric of Worcester?'

'Is that who it is?' asked Ralph, giggling with relief.

'Yes. It is Bishop Wulfstan. I recognise him clearly.'

'This is excellent news, Gervase!'

'I would not say that.'

'Why?'

'Wulfstan is a royal counsellor. My guess is that he is not only here because Gloucester is part of his diocese. He has come from Worcester on a more temporal errand.'

'What do you mean?'

'His presence here confirms it, Ralph. The King is indeed coming.'

Ralph squirmed in the saddle as he foresaw a prickly discussion ahead with his wife. It made him ride out of the city with eagerness.

Durand the Sheriff conducted his guest to the hall in the castle. Wine awaited them and a servant poured two cups before he retired. When it was offered to him, the bishop waved the cup politely away but Durand felt the need of sustenance. He gulped down his own wine with undue haste and undisguised relish.

'That's better!' he said, licking his lips. 'I needed that.'

'Wine is a mocker, my lord. Put it aside.'

'I prefer to be mocked.' He indicated a chair and his visitor sat down. 'It is good to see you again, Bishop, though I would be grateful to know precisely why we are meeting like this.'

'So would I, my lord sheriff.'

'Do you have no notion what this portends?'

'None. I was hoping you might enlighten me.'

'All I know is that King William is on his way.'

'When is he due to arrive?'

'By nightfall today.'

'That is more than I was told.'

'A message to that effect arrived this morning.'

'I am glad I reached Gloucester before him,' said Wulfstan. 'The King does not like to be kept waiting. Who else has been summoned? If others descend on you, we may have some clue as to the size and nature of the crisis.'

'If, that is, a crisis actually exists.'

'Why else would he come here? Much as he appreciates us, I do not believe that King William would ride all this way to enquire after our health. Something is afoot. I smell an emergency.'

Durand took a step away from him. What he could smell was the noxious stink which came from the lambskin cloak. The garment looked even more ragged at close quarters, as wrinkled with age as its wearer and far more blotched. Wulfstan seemed sublimely unaware of the reek. He was a small man with a huge reputation, the only surviving Saxon bishop in England, ready to serve Archbishop Lanfranc as steadfastly as he had served Stigand, the previous primate. Well into his seventies, Wulfstan still had remarkable vitality and an extraordinary range of interests. His learning was matched by his political skills, making him one of the King's most able counsellors. Durand distrusted him as much as the bishop distrusted the sheriff, but he could not deny the prelate's expertise in affairs of state. Wulfstan was the Great Survivor. That, in itself, entitled him to a respectful hearing.

'I wonder if it may concern Wales,' ventured Wulfstan.

'Possibly.'

'Disturbing reports have reached me from Bishop Robert. He

ells me that Hereford is reinforcing itself against the possibility of attack.'

'We have also had worrying intelligence about activity on our western border,' confided Durand. 'Sporadic raids have taken place. They are on a very small scale but I wonder if they presage a larger assault.'

'I hope not.'

'So do we all, Bishop.'

'But if not Wales, what, then, brings the King to Gloucester again?'

'We will have to wait until he tells us but I begin to doubt that it is a real emergency. I know of nobody else who has been summoned. You and I are the sum total of his advisors, unless we count Hamelin of Lisieux, that is.'

'Is he in Gloucester as well?'

'On his own account. Commissioners have descended on us.'

'I thought they came and went.'

'The first ones did,' said Durand petulantly. 'After they had caused several flutters, I may say. When the returns for this county were examined in Winchester, irregularities appeared. Serious discrepancies. The new commissioners have come to investigate them.'

'That might explain the King's need to be here.'

'Might it?'

'Yes, my lord sheriff. The King needs money to raise an army to fight the Danes. That is the main purpose of this Great Survey, is it not?'

Durand was rueful. 'To see who owns what and how much can be wrung from them by way of tax or knight-service. I do not like tax collectors at the best of times, but these have been the worst who have ever afflicted my county.'

'And mine,' said Wulfstan philosophically. 'Letters of complaint flooded in to me, asking me to use my influence with the King to relieve the burden of taxation. What influence, I cry? If I had any,

I would employ it to seek relief for myself. The church of Worcester suffers as much as anyone.'

'Why grant us land if he then bleeds us dry with taxes?'

'Take the matter up with him,' suggested Wulfstan with a chuckle. 'I am not sure that I have the courage to do so. You saw how determined he was to push this Great Survey through when he first mooted the idea at the Christmas council here in Gloucester. The King would hear no whisper of criticism.'

'I admire that aspect of him.'

'So do I, my lord bishop. From a safe distance.'

'But to answer your original question, I doubt very much if he is coming on the heels of his commissioners. Apart from anything else, they knew nothing about his imminent visit. Other teams are visiting other counties to unravel peculiarities in the returns. Why should the King pick Gloucester when he has so many other counties to choose from?'

'A telling point.'

'All I know is that it is a most inconvenient time to receive a royal visit. Still less to host a meeting of the whole council, if that is what is in the wind. Not only are the commissioners here, I have had another problem dropped into my lap.'

'Another problem?'

'A murder, Bishop Wulfstan.'

'Where?'

'At the abbey.'

The bishop was on his feet. 'Who was the victim?'

'One of the monks, Brother Nicholas.'

'This is dire news,' said the other. 'Has any arrest been made?'

'Not yet,' admitted Durand, 'nor is there likely to be one in the near future. My officers are hunting high and low for clues but they are very scarce. It is a most vexing case in every way. Abbot Serlo refuses even to consider the possibility, but I feel more and more that the killer lives within the abbey itself.'

'A Benedictine monk? Out of the question!'

'The evidence points that way.'

'But you just told me how flimsy it is. Do not accuse a monk, my lord sheriff. I have spent a whole lifetime within the enclave, first in the abbeys of Evesham and Peterborough, then in my beloved Worcester. In well over half a century inside a cowl, I have never once met a monk who would dare to contemplate murder, let alone actually commit it. This has upset me more than I can say,' he confessed, starting to pant slightly. 'I must go to the abbey at once to learn the full details of this crime.'

'I expected that you would stay here at the castle.'

'In these circumstances?'

'But I have an apartment prepared for you, Bishop.'

'Thank you,' said Wulfstan, pulling his cloak around him so tightly that bits of it were shaken off to float aromatically to the floor. 'But I must decline your kind invitation. When the King calls me, I will return at once. Meanwhile, I will be at the abbey,' he asserted, hurrying towards the door. 'Look for me there. That is where I am needed.'

Chapter Eight

Caradoc made them think again. Having heard so much about Brother Nicholas from a variety of sources, Ralph Delchard and Gervase Bret had formed a very clear idea of his character. The deceased monk was a loner, deliberately kept away from an abbey where he never earned general acceptance, who had a suspect interest in attractive boys. The cache found by the Precentor confirmed that there was a darker side to the murder victim, one which he had cunningly hidden from his Benedictine brothers and which might in time provide the motive for his death. Caradoc talked about another Brother Nicholas, however, but he did so at such breathtaking speed that Ralph was only able to catch one word in three and sensibly left the questioning to Gervase.

'How long have you known him?'

'Some years now,' said Caradoc.

'And you say that you liked him?'

'Very much. Brother Nicholas was such a jolly fellow.'

Gervase looked at Ralph. '*Jolly?*' he repeated.

'For a monk. They are often such solemn individuals.'

'Jollity does not sit easily inside a monastery,' said Gervase. 'I was reared in one so I know it to be a fact. Yet a certain amount of merriment did break out even there from time to time. However, I would not have thought that your rent collector would ever be party to harmless fun.'

'He made me laugh, Master Bret.'

'That is extraordinary.'

'And my wife. Ask her.'

'Do you have a family, Caradoc?'

'Four boys. If you ride across my land, you are sure to see them.'

'How did they get on with Brother Nicholas?'

'Very well. They poked fun at him, but you expect that from lads of that age. Underneath, they thought him a likeable fellow.'

'This description does not match other reports of him.'

'I care nothing about that,' said Caradoc cheerily. 'All that I can talk about is our own experience. Brother Nicholas could not have been more pleasant while doing an unpleasant task. Nobody likes to part with money but it was far less painful to part with rent when he called.'

'Would you call him trustworthy?'

'I'd stake my life on it.'

Gervase translated the last remark so that Ralph understood its full force. Caradoc was a friendly man. Born of a Welsh mother and a Saxon father, he spoke the guttural language of the latter with the melodious voice of the former. Dark, bearded and swarthy, he had a face of appealing ugliness with twinkling eyes set too far apart and a nose which inclined first one way and then the other with almost grotesque uncertainty. His affable manner more than compensated for his facial deficiencies. On guard when he first saw them approach with an armed escort, Caradoc relaxed when he realised that they merely wished to talk about the rent collector.

'When did you last see him?' asked Gervase.

'Three or four weeks ago.'

'And was he in a jolly mood then?'

'He always was, Master Bret.'

'Where did he go when he left here?'

'Towards the river. It's only a couple of miles away.'

'Why there?'

'I have no idea,' said Caradoc, his face crumpling. 'And it is too late to ask him now. I cannot believe that he has been murdered in the way that you tell me. My wife will be very upset.'

'What about your sons?'

'They will shed a tear or two.'

Gervase was puzzled. Caradoc's remarks were at variance with everything he had ever heard about the monk. He probed deeper.

'Did they find nothing odd about Brother Nicholas?' he said.

'Odd?'

'Strange. Unusual. Unsettling in some way.'

'No, Master Bret. We farm abbey lands. That means we are bound to pay rent to the monk assigned to the task. It's in our interests to befriend the man so that he'll give a good report of us to the abbot. We would certainly give him a good report of Brother Nicholas.'

Gervase translated again and Ralph nodded his head pensively.

'Ask him about the others, Gervase.'

'I was about to,' said his friend, turning back to Caradoc. 'This is one of the abbey's outliers. You are not far from Westbury Hundred.'

'Not if you have a swift horse.'

'Who holds that land?'

'Everyone knows that. The lord Hamelin.'

'Hamelin of Lisieux?'

'Yes,' said Caradoc, choosing his words with more care. 'He is a mighty man in these parts and much respected by all of us. Respected and envied, I may say, for he has the most beautiful wife. Or so it is rumoured, for I have not had the pleasure of seeing her.'

'We have,' said Ralph, understanding him this time.

'And is she the angel of report, my lord?'

'I think so. Gervase?'

'The lady Emma is indeed well favoured,' he agreed, 'but that is not the point at issue. You say that her husband holds the land, Caradoc. Has it always been so?'

'Oh, no. Strang the Dane used to hold sway over it.'

'Did you ever meet him?'

'Several times.'

'What opinion did you form?'

'Not a very high one, Master Bret. He was too bellicose.'

'That's what we found.'

'Nobody dared to trespass on his land when Strang was there. He guarded it jealously and employed a creeping reeve called Balki. I only came across the fellow once but that was enough. He treated us like dirt and I'll not let any man do that to me.'

'How did he come to lose the land?'

'You will have to ask the lord Hamelin,' he said evasively.

'Was it taken away from him?'

'It is not for me to say.'

'But you must have heard rumours.'

'My whole life consists of hearing rumours,' said Caradoc with a grin. 'Rumours and snores, to be exact. For my wife works as hard as we do and she is so tired that she snores her way to heaven every night.'

'Tell me about these rumours.'

'I pay no heed to them.'

'Do they paint the lord Hamelin in a favourable light?'

'No, Master Bret.'

'How does he deal with trespassers?'

'Harshly, I think.'

'Have you ever heard of one Querengar the Breton?'

'Yes,' replied the other. 'A decent man, by all accounts. He holds land near a kinsman of mine in one of the commotes. Unlike most of the others, he has tried to adapt to Welsh customs.'

'Did you know that he has an interest in the Westbury Hundred?'

'No, Master Bret.'

'So he has never held land there?'

'Not to my knowledge, but that is very limited. Querengar may have held it in the past but I doubt that he does so now.'

'Why?'

'Because of the lord Hamelin. He rules the roost.'

'By force of arms?'

'There have been stories. How true they are, I have no notion. For my own part, I will not say a word against the lord Hamelin.' Another grin. 'And certainly not against this fabled wife of his. She came from France, they tell me. Her beauty holds everyone in thrall.'

'I see that you do pay heed to rumours, after all.'

'Only pleasant ones.'

'Are all the others unpleasant, Caradoc?'

'We must move on,' said Ralph with a nudge. 'Hurry, Gervase.'

'A last question, then. Tell me, my friend, is the name of Abraham the Priest known to you?'

'Why, yes. Known and respected. A wonderful man.'

'Yet you are not part of his diocese here.'

'That does not stop him visiting this area. Abraham is a kind man. I have met him a number of times and always enjoyed his company.'

'What brings him this far afield?'

'The spirit of friendship.'

'There must be something else.'

'Not to my mind.'

'Does he ever talk about the others I've mentioned? Hamelin of Lisieux? Querengar the Breton?'

'Neither, but Strang's name sometimes passes his lips.'

'With some distaste, I fancy.'

'Yes, Master Bret, though I cannot say why.'

'Gervase,' called Ralph. 'We must away.'

'One second, please.'

'You've asked a dozen last questions already.'

'It must take the archdeacon a long time to get here,' said Gervase, ignoring Ralph's impatience. 'He would have to ride in a loop around lord Hamelin's holdings. Unless, of course, he rides across them.'

'He would be a brave man if he did that.'

'Too hazardous?'

'According to the rumours,' said Caradoc. 'I am also sure that neither Strang nor Querengar would dare to venture on to that land. In fact, there is only one man I know who rode into Westbury Hundred without the slightest sign of fear.'

'Who was that?' asked Gervase.

'The man you've been asking me about.'

'Your rent collector?'

'Yes. Brother Nicholas.'

It was impossible not to notice the commotion. From the window of their chamber, Golde could see the activity down in the bailey. Soldiers were being mustered, orders given, visible attempts at smartening up made. Provisions began arriving in large quantities; butchers, bakers and other tradesmen delivered their wares to waiting servants who hurried away to the kitchens. Inside the keep itself, the sound of bustle and urgency drifted up to Golde. She guessed its meaning at once. A pattern of behaviour which she had seen so many times at Hereford Castle was repeating itself here. Important visitors were coming. The mild panic down below gave her an idea of the scale of their importance.

When Golde went down to join her hostess, Maud was not in her customary position with her embroidery. Instead, she was issuing shrill orders to a bevy of female servants before shooing them out with fluttering hands. She gave Golde a strained smile of welcome.

'We are having more guests,' she explained.

'I gathered that.'

'Durand has only just told me. That's so typical of him. We have no time to prepare, no time to make the castle look its best. Why on earth didn't you warn me, Golde?' she scolded, waving a finger. 'You must have known that this was in the wind.'

'Must I?'

'Of course. Durand told your husband when the message first came. And since the lord Ralph hides nothing from you, he must have confided the tidings.'

'What tidings, my lady?'

'The possibility of a royal visit.'

Golde was surprised. 'The King is coming here?'

'He should arrive by nightfall.'

'I see.'

'Bishop Wulfstan has already ridden into Gloucester and there may be other counsellors due before long. They will find us in disarray.'

'Not at all, my lady,' said Golde, trying to adjust her mind to the news. 'It's a great honour to be given a royal visit. I am sure that King William will find nothing about which he can complain.'

'Durand has already found a hundred things. He left my ears buzzing. That is why I am rushing around in such a frenzy.'

'Then I will not get under your feet, my lady.'

Seeing the chance to withdraw, Golde took it gratefully and moved towards the door. Maud hurried across to intercept her.

'Answer my question first,' she demanded.

'What question?'

'Are we not friends, Golde?'

'Of course, my lady.'

'Then why did you not have the kindness to warn your friend? It is embarrassing to be the last person to know. How can I play the hostess if I am not told that guests are descending on me?'

'It was unfair of your husband to keep it from you.'

'Forget my husband. Talk about yours.'

'Ralph?'

'Yes,' said Maud tartly. 'When did he tell you?'

'Well . . .'

'Come on. You pretended to be surprised at tidings you already know. How long have you been keeping this secret from me?'

'I have kept nothing from you, my lady.'

'Then why remain silent?' She saw the dismay in Golde's face and her anger mellowed into sarcasm. 'So? The lord Ralph is not the paragon you imagined. He is not the soul of honesty, after all. You have been deceived as cruelly as I have, Golde. The wonderful husband who tells you everything has this time held his tongue.'

'With good reason, I am sure,' said Golde loyally.

'An excellent reason. It is the one used by Durand. I am a wife. A mere woman. I have to wait my turn in the queue before I learn what is going on.' She gave a cold smile. 'It's comforting to know that there is at least one person standing *behind* me in the queue.'

Golde reddened. 'You have much to do, my lady. Excuse me.'

'The lord Ralph did not tell you because he did not think it fit.'

'That is a matter between the two of us.'

'I wish that I could be there when you raise it.'

Golde dropped a curtsey then went quickly out through the door. Bitter recrimination took her all the way back up the stairs. Her hostess had crowed over her. It was galling to be put in such a position and the fault lay squarely with Ralph. She vowed to tax him on the subject at the earliest opportunity. Sweeping into the room, she gave vent to her humiliation by slamming the door behind her and emitting a yell of rage.

They had ridden only a short distance across the Westbury Hundred before they were challenged. A horseman approached, waved them to a halt then demanded to know their names and their business. Ralph Delchard gave him a dusty answer and sent him on his way, peeved that anyone should dare to obstruct his way. He rode on with Gervase and his escort, stopping only when they met some of the sub-tenants who worked the land nominally held by Hamelin of Lisieux. It was an area of rich pastures and gurgling streams, undulating gently and dotted with woodland. They could see why it was sought after so eagerly by all four claimants.

The sub-tenants refused to a man to discuss the competing

claims. As far as they were concerned, Hamelin of Lisieux was their overlord and they accepted him without protest. The commissioners realised why.

'Fear!' said Ralph as they cantered on. 'That's why they're all so tight-lipped, Gervase. Naked fear. The stink of it is unmistakable.'

'The lord Hamelin knows how to instil loyalty.'

'With a sharp sword. Not one of them has the courage to speak up for Strang or Querengar yet they clearly know both men. What's happened to Saxon bravery? Is it extinct in these parts?'

'Apparently.'

'There must be someone who will tell the truth.'

'Under oath, perhaps. And guaranteed indemnity.'

'Then that is how it must be,' decided Ralph. 'I'll summon every man in the Westbury Hundred before us if I have to. Get them in the shire hall and I'll make the rogues talk.'

'Do not blame them, Ralph. They are frightened.'

'Then I will frighten them even more!'

'Turn your terror on the lord Hamelin.'

'If we find he is at fault, I certainly will.'

'Why not mention it to him?'

'What's that?'

'You have a chance to do it right now,' said Gervase, gazing off to the left. 'If I am not mistaken, he is coming to meet us in person.'

'God's tits!'

Ralph's bellow was prompted by the sight of Hamelin of Lisieux riding towards them on a destrier with a dozen armed men at his back. Coming around a stand of trees in an orderly column, they galloped the visitors and came to a noisy halt in front of them, fanning out so that a wall of armour blocked their path. Hamelin gave them a quizzical smile of welcome.

'What are you doing on my land?' he asked politely.

'Finding out if it is really yours,' said Ralph.

'Can there be any doubt about that? Speak to the sub-tenants.'

'We have,' said Ralph. 'They are too scared to talk.'

'Too scared?' mocked the other. 'Scared of what? Of whom?'

'Overlords who ride around with their men-at-arms.'

'But that is exactly what you are doing.'

'I am fulfilling the King's command,' said Ralph sternly, 'and that means that nobody, however many swords at his beck and call, can stand in my way.'

'We are not standing in your way, my lord. Ride where you will, ask what you wish. We merely came out to see what brought you here.'

'We might ask you the same thing, my lord,' said Gervase. 'Your manor house is several miles from here, as are the bulk of your holdings. Why come to the Westbury Hundred?'

'To check that all was well, Master Bret.'

'Could not your reeve have done that?'

'Of course,' said the other airily, 'but I wanted to remind myself what beautiful land this is. Well worth fighting for in the shire hall.'

'Is that the only place fighting has taken place?' asked Ralph.

'You tell me, my lord.'

'Your armed escort speaks for itself.'

'The roads are dangerous. I need protection.'

'So do your sub-tenants.'

'That is perilously close to an insult.'

'No offence was intended, my lord,' said Gervase, anxious to keep the exchange on a moderate note. 'Our real purpose is to determine exactly which land you actually hold. Your charter would seem to suggest that Strang's eight hides are contiguous with, but separate from, the twenty hides granted to you. Querengar's ten hides overlap with both of you but also seem to contain land which is distinct from yours and Strang's. The only way for us to resolve the confusion was to rely on the evidence of our own eyes and ears.'

'I admire your conscientiousness, Master Bret.'

'Thoroughness is the only path to justice.'

'Quite so.'

'Then perhaps you will stand aside while we ride on,' said Ralph.

'With pleasure, my lord,' said Hamelin obligingly. 'I must get back to Gloucester. I want to be in the city well before the King arrives.'

Ralph was stung. 'You know about his visit?'

'Of course.'

'How?'

'I told you. I am well informed.'

'Nigel the Reeve again?'

'Excuse us. We must bid you farewell.'

'Before you go, my lord,' said Gervase, recalling what Caradoc had told them. 'I believe that you know a Brother Nicholas?'

'I know of him. The abbey's rent collector.'

'Is he a friend of yours?'

'My taste does not turn to Benedictine monks, Master Bret.'

'Then why is he granted privileges?'

'Privileges?'

'Yes,' said Gervase. 'Safe conduct across your land. Nobody can trespass here without impunity, that is clear. Yet Brother Nicholas, we hear, was able to traverse your holdings at will. Why was that?'

'He represented the abbey. I respected him.'

'Even though you would spurn him as a friend?'

'I do not persecute monks,' said Hamelin suavely. 'Why should I? They are not trying to seize lawful property from me. A black cowl will always guarantee a man safe passage across my land.'

'Abraham the Priest wears a black cowl.'

Hamelin of Lisieux tried to force a smile but it refused to come.

* * *

He was an accomplished horseman. Being an archdeacon was no sedentary occupation; Abraham conducted services before many altars throughout Gwent and the peripatetic nature of his work obliged him to spend a fair amount of time in the saddle. He made virtue of a necessity and learned to ride well. The copse was a few miles away but he covered the distance at a steady canter. There was no sign of habitation among the trees, no telltale column of smoke rising above them. Yet he knew they would be there. Leaving the winding track, he headed for the copse and plunged in between the trunks of some stout elms.

The men were on their feet, alerted by the sound of approaching hoofbeats. Hands rested on weapons. When they saw who it was, they relaxed and gave him a cheerful welcome. Abraham dismounted and went across to Madog who was holding a piece of half-eaten chicken.

'We didn't expect you so soon,' said Madog.

'I know.'

'Is it settled already?'

'Not yet.'

'Then why have you come?'

'To warn you of the delay,' said Abraham, lowering himself on to a fallen log. 'After hearing my evidence, the commissioners decided to ride out to the Westbury Hundred to view the property for themselves. There will be no more work at the shire hall today. I will have to stay in the city for another night at least.'

Madog waited. 'We will remain here.'

'Have you enough to eat?'

'More than enough. Thanks to a kind man who keeps chickens.'

'You stole them?' chided the archdeacon.

'He had more than enough to spare. But what news of Gloucester? Are these commissioners honourable men? Is there any hope at all that you may carry the day?'

'If justice exists, I will carry it but it is only a faint hope.'

'Those hides are part of Wales!'

'That argument did not impress in the shire hall.'

'It's not an argument but a fact of life.'

'There are other facts of life which we must accept, Madog,' said the other softly. 'The main one is that power lies in the hands of the commissioners. Their verdict is final. They are decent men, more honest and reasonable than I dared to expect, but that does not mean they will find in our favour.'

'They must!'

'We shall see. Meanwhile, you'll have to be patient.' Madog gave a nod and took another bite from the chicken. 'But there's other news, my friend. The King is due to arrive in Gloucester.'

'The King!'

Madog was so startled that he spat the chicken straight out. His exclamation brought the rest of the band around them in a circle. They craned their necks to hear the tidings.

'When?' asked one of them.

'Soon,' said Abraham, 'judging by the preparations. I saw them taking provisions to the castle. I stopped a butcher and asked him why he had just delivered so many carcasses to the gate.'

'I know which carcass I'd like to deliver!' said Madog and gained a patriotic cheer. 'The King, is it? Well, he's no King of ours.'

'Why is he here?' asked someone else.

'I have no idea,' admitted the archdeacon.

Madog was thoughtful. 'Bring word as soon as he arrives.'

'I will.'

'This may be an accident that heaven provides. King William. Coming to Gloucester.' He gave a grim laugh. 'Within reach at last.'

Canon Hubert was delighted when he was summoned by Abbot Serlo, and that delight increased when he saw that the latter already had a visitor. The venerable Bishop Wulfstan was waiting to greet him. Educated in a Norman abbey, Hubert took a lordly view of

Saxon prelates and held them in low esteem. Wulfstan was the signal exception. Hubert admired him for his intellect and revered him for his spiritual commitment. He just wished that the Bishop of Worcester would divest himself of the filthy lambskin cloak which was already filling the room with a smell of decay.

'Bishop Wulfstan brings interesting news,' said Serlo.

Wulfstan hunched his shoulders. 'Hubert may already know it.'

'Know what?'

'That the King is riding towards us.'

'Coming to Gloucester?' said Hubert in surprise.

'There,' said Serlo. 'He is as astonished as I was.'

'Was the fact of this visit kept from you, Hubert?'

'It appears so, Bishop Wulfstan,' said the latter, annoyed to learn something so important in this way. 'What is the nature of the visit?'

'Nobody knows until King William actually gets here.'

'I would value time alone with him myself,' said Serlo hopefully. 'Do urge him to visit the abbey. We can discuss my plans for rebuilding the church. That will surely arouse his interest.'

'I will speak up on your behalf, Abbot Serlo.'

'Thank you.'

'When the time calls.' He turned to Hubert. 'It is good to renew our acquaintance, Canon Hubert, if only by accident, so to speak. I hear that you are doing valuable work as a royal commissioner.'

'It is a responsibility I shoulder willingly.'

'That is characteristic of you. But let us turn to the reason why I wished to see you,' said Wulfstan, sucking air in noisily through his few remaining teeth. 'This appalling crime in the abbey.'

'A sickening event, Bishop Wulfstan.'

'It falls to the sheriff to apprehend the culprit but he, it seems, is convinced that the guilty man is actually a monk at the abbey.'

'A ludicrous notion!'

'That is what I told Durand,' said the abbot.

'You have my endorsement,' promised Wulfstan. 'I would not listen to such nonsense from the sheriff. It is why I turn to you for I believe that you and your colleagues have instituted an inquiry on your own account. Is that true?'

'Up to a point, Bishop Wulfstan.'

'What point is that?'

'We have other demands on our time.'

'Accepted. But you still manage to turn your gaze upon this disgusting act of murder and Abbot Serlo is rightly grateful. Until the crime is solved, the unpleasant atmosphere here will continue.'

Hubert believed that much of the unpleasantness could be dispelled if the bishop's cloak was either set alight or sprinkled with frankincense but he tactfully suppressed the observation. Instead, he tried to raise all their spirits while parading his own virtues before them.

'There is a hideous symbolism in the murder of a Benedictine monk,' he declared, 'and nobody appreciates that more than I do. Limited as my time is, I will devote as much as I can to the pursuit of the killer. I have already examined the two boys who actually stumbled upon the corpse and, I feel, drawn information out of them which Durand the Sheriff failed to elicit. I know the mind of a novice, he does not.'

'Your colleagues, too, have been active,' remarked Serlo.

'That is so, Abbot Serlo. Under my direction, the lord Ralph and Gervase Bret have been diligent officers. They have searched for clues in the abbey and, at my suggestion, they will look further afield.'

'Most encouraging,' said Wulfstan. 'Has progress been made?'

'We believe so.'

'Then you are to be congratulated, Canon Hubert.'

'Yes,' agreed Serlo, exuding approval. 'It was a happy coincidence that you came among us at this time. The sheriff is an industrious man but he lacks your insight. Also, of course, he will be rather preoccupied with a royal visitor in his household. My fear is that the murder inquiry will lose impetus. The trail will go cold.'

'Not as long as I am here!' boasted Hubert.

'The abbey is indebted to you.'

'We all are,' said Wulfstan. 'Tell me. What conclusions have you so far reached? Where do you think the killer will be found?'

Hubert inhaled deeply and enjoyed his moment in the sun.

On the long ride back to the castle, Ralph Delchard and Gervase Bret had ample time to review their visit to the Westbury Hundred. Though largely inconclusive, it had given them some valuable information.

'We saw the lord Hamelin in his true light,' said Ralph. 'He is a different person with armed men at his back.'

'And without his wife.'

Ralph grinned. 'I did note her absence.'

'If only his sub-tenants had been more forthcoming.'

'They are frightened rabbits, hardly daring to peep out of their burrows while the lord Hamelin is about.'

'He certainly likes to make his presence felt.'

'I'll do the same when I have him in the shire hall again.'

'With his wife.'

'With, as you predict, the gorgeous lady Emma. How can someone so beautiful be taken in by someone so perfidious?'

'His perfidy has yet to be proven, Ralph.'

'More's the pity!'

'All that we have established is that the lord Hamelin cleverly blurred the boundaries between the various hides. It enabled him to snatch Strang's land from under his very nose.'

'I suspect that he did the same to Querengar.'

'We need to question them all much more closely.'

Gloucester appeared on the horizon and they rode on in silence for a few minutes, grateful when a light drizzle fell to cool their warm brows. After a period of meditation, Gervase turned to his friend once more.

'I am surprised he has not come to your attention before, Ralph.'

'The lord Hamelin?'

'Yes. If he hails from Lisieux, his estates cannot be far from your own. Has he never been mentioned in reports from Normandy?'

'Only in passing.'

'Yet he spends much time there, it seems,' said Gervase. 'That is where he met the lady Emma no doubt. He would certainly not encounter such a woman here.'

'It is the one thing the French can do well.'

'What is?'

'Produce glorious creatures like that.'

'Hereford has its own crop, remember.'

'I do,' said Ralph guiltily, 'and Golde is a prime example. In praising the lady Emma, I do not disparise my own wife. Not to mention yours, Gervase. Alys is living proof that Winchester also has its share of remarkable beauties.'

'I think so.'

'Do you miss her?'

'Sorely.'

'And so you should.'

'I still believe I did right to leave her behind. Alys does not care to travel. She has none of Golde's vitality, I fear. That is the difference between us, Ralph. While I ride back to the castle to pine for my wife, you can look forward to seeing yours.'

'Yes,' said Ralph.

But the word was a burning cinder in his throat. He knew that he would face stern questions from Golde.

When they reached their destination, it was clear that the King and his entourage had not yet arrived. There was an increased vigilance about the sentries and a general nervousness pervaded the castle. Gervase was keen to retire to his apartment but Ralph detained him for a while, reluctant to engage in the stormy confrontation he feared. Left alone at last, he put on his most engaging smile and returned to his chamber. Golde was waiting with icy calm. She knew.

'I'm sorry to be so late, my love,' he said, depositing a token kiss on her forehead. 'Gervase and I had to ride out to the Westbury Hundred to solve a tricky problem.'

'And did you solve it?'

'We had only partial success.'

'I'm glad that you feel able to confide the fact to me.'

'What do you mean?'

'It is refreshing to be given a taste of honesty again.'

'Golde!'

'Yes?' she said with laboured sweetness.

'Is this all the welcome I get?'

'I am saving my welcome for King William.'

'So that's it,' he sighed.

'Yes, Ralph. That is it. The trivial matter of a royal visit which you heard about from the sheriff but which you somehow forgot to mention to your wife. Do you know how much that hurts me?'

'Hurting you is the last thing I want to do.'

'Then why didn't you warn me?'

'Because there was no certainty that the King would come.'

'Could you not have explained that to me?'

'I could,' he admitted, 'but I didn't. It was a grave mistake.'

'It was more than that,' she said, her temper flaring. 'It was a betrayal. After all you promised! Only last night I lay in your arms and told you how much I loved you because you were so open with me. Now – *this*!'

'It is not as bad as you think,' he said, reaching out for her.

'Don't touch me,' she warned, stepping back to elude him. 'And don't try to palm me off with an apology because I'm too furious even to listen to it. King William is coming and you failed to tell me. Imagine how foolish I felt when I learned the news from the lady Maud. Learned it and suffered it,' she said ruefully, 'for she was so delighted to see that I had been kept in ignorance just like her. How she rubbed my nose in it! It was degrading, Ralph. You were cruel to subject me to it.'

'Not deliberately, Golde.'

'I've hardly stirred outside this chamber since.'

'Come here,' he said gently, offering his arms again.

'No – stay away.'

'Golde!'

'This is not something which can be kissed away, Ralph. You took a deliberate decision not to tell me something I ought to have known.'

'The sheriff swore me to secrecy.'

'Did that mean your wife had to be excluded?'

'I thought so.'

'And do you think so now?'

'No, I was wrong. I confess it frankly. As for the lady Maud,' he said vengefully, 'I'll not have her mocking my wife. I'll speak to her sharply on the subject and it will not happen again, I assure you.'

Golde was livid. 'I don't need you to fight my battles for me and I certainly don't want you to go charging in to make a bad situation far worse with your heavy-handed interference. No, Ralph,' she said, shaking with rage, 'I can take care of myself. But I would rather fight battles of my own making than be landed in them by you. Especially when you've taken away the one weapon I need to defend myself.'

Ralph was distraught. Unable to comfort her, he sought a means of atonement but he had no idea what it might be. Gesturing his apology to her, he made one last attempt to enfold her in an embrace. Her hostile stare made him freeze. Reconciliation was still too far off. Golde moved to sit on the bed, her back to him, and Ralph decided to give her time to calm down and let himself quietly out of the room. After the unexpected venom of her attack, he needed a chance to recuperate.

His host was in no mood to give it to him. When they met on the stairs, Durand the Sheriff was at his most wrathful. He let out a growl.

'I was looking for you, my lord!' he said menacingly.

'Has the King arrived yet?'

'Forget him. We need to talk about the abbey. Bishop Wulfstan has just come from there and I could not believe what he told me.'

'I never believe bishops myself,' said Ralph. 'On principle.'

'According to him, you have been going behind my back. You and Master Bret and that bloated Canon Hubert are trying to discharge my office for me by holding your own murder inquiry.'

'That is not strictly true, my lord.'

'I had it from Wulfstan himself. He told me how Canon Hubert ridiculed my efforts and bragged about your own. Apparently, you have discovered clues which I am too bone-headed to find. Is this so, my lord?' he demanded, eyes alight. 'Must we address you as Ralph the Sheriff from now on? Am I to quit the castle and let you be constable in my stead?'

'Of course not.'

'Then why do you presume to interfere?'

'Help, my lord. We are only trying to help.'

'Well, it is the strangest kind of help I have ever received and it is neither wanted nor tolerated. How dare you! If anyone else tried to "help" me in this way, I'd cut him in two. If anyone else concealed evidence from me in a murder investigation, I'd throw him in my dungeon. This is unworthy of you, my lord!' he railed. 'You're a guest here and deserve the consideration due to a guest. But there are courtesies due to a host and you have completely failed to show them.'

'Will you at least let me explain?' asked Ralph.

'Your behaviour explains itself.'

'We are not your competitors, my lord, but your auxiliaries.'

'Auxiliaries obey their master! You maim his reputation.'

'No, my lord.'

'Be warned,' shouted Durand, his temples throbbing. 'I rule here. Life and death are at my command. Only the King has more power in this county. If there is any more interference from you, I will be forced to bring the full weight of the law down upon you.'

'We simply wish to solve a crime!'

But his plea went unheard. Turning on his heel, Durand charged off to the hall and left his guest alone. Ralph was dazed by the force of the assault. His first impulse was to retreat to the privacy of his room but there was no solace there. He was more likely to walk into another ambush. Upstairs and downstairs, there was no escape. Caught between an irate wife and an enraged sheriff, Ralph did the only thing he felt able to do. He sat down on the step and occupied a position between the two. It was lonely but there was at least a measure of safety.

The daily routine at the abbey left the novices little opportunity to be on their own, and the few moments that Kenelm was able to steal never seemed to last long. Elaf was always prowling in his wake, seeking to reassure him, fearing that his friend might do something impetuous, hardly daring to let him out of his sight. Kenelm was pleased, therefore, when he finally shook off his shadow. Instead of going to his usual refuge in the garden, he found a quiet spot near the Infirmary and lurked unseen beside a holly bush. Precious minutes alone were devoted to more recrimination. Kenelm was convinced that his only means of escape lay in quitting the abbey completely.

A quiet voice interrupted him with an almost deafening impact.

'What are you doing here?' asked Owen, crouching by the bush.

'Go away!' snarled the other.

'I followed you, Kenelm.'

'Well, I don't want to be followed.'

'I know. I saw you dodge over here to shake off Elaf.'

'Have you been spying on me, Owen?'

'No, no!' replied the other, backing away from the brandished fist. 'I'll go, if you wish. I just thought you might want to talk about Brother Nicholas, that's all.'

'Not to you.'

Owen sagged. 'No, I suppose not. You never liked him.'

'He was loathsome.'

'Brother Nicholas was murdered,' said the smaller boy with wild passion. 'Can't you find any sympathy in your heart?'

Kenelm was immediately chastened. 'Yes, I can,' he said, chin falling to his chest. 'I never liked him but I regret what happened to him. I could not regret it more, Owen. His death has ruined my life.'

'How?'

'That's no business of yours.'

'But it is, Kenelm. We are taught to help each other.'

'Leaving me alone is the only way to help me.'

'Very well.' A studied pause. 'Did he give *you* anything?'

'Who?'

'Brother Nicholas.'

'Why should he give me anything?'

'That means he didn't.'

'What are you talking about?'

'Friendship. Brother Nicholas was my friend.'

'He had no friends.'

'Yes, he did,' said the other staunchly. 'Me.'

Kenelm's curiosity was stirred. 'Is that what he told you?'

'Of course.'

'When?'

'Whenever he saw me.'

'But he was hardly ever in the abbey.'

'That's what you think. He slipped back sometimes when he

was supposed to be out collecting rents. At night, usually. To see me.'

'Why ever should he want to see you?'

'We were friends.'

'What sort of friends?'

'Good ones.'

Kenelm studied the innocent young face before him. Owen had neither the skill nor the experience to deceive him. It was much more likely that he had deceived himself.

'And did Brother Nicholas ever give *you* anything, Owen?'

'Oh yes.'

'What was it?'

'A token.'

'Of what?'

'Our friendship, of course.'

An uneasy sensation coursed through Kenelm. He moved closer.

'Did you have to do anything to get this token, Owen?'

'Do anything?'

'Yes, for Brother Nicholas. Did you?'

Owen nodded. 'I had to promise to tell nobody.'

'About what?'

'What happened. What we talked about. What we did.'

'Go on,' pressed Kenelm, desperate to hear more.

But Owen's face suddenly clouded as he remembered the taunts and beatings he had suffered at Kenelm's hands in the past. He drew away at once. There was nobody with whom he could share his secret, least of all a novice who disliked Owen's one true friend.

'Tell me,' urged Kenelm. 'What did you and Brother Nicholas do?'

Owen gave an enigmatic smile.

'You wouldn't understand,' he said.

Chapter Nine

Gervase Bret was so tired on his return from their ride that he took a short nap in his chamber. Awaking refreshed, he went out to see what arrangements had been made for a meal that evening and was alarmed to find Ralph Delchard sitting motionless higher up on the staircase with his head in his hands.

'Are you hurt?' he said anxiously, rushing up to him. 'What happened, Ralph? Did you have an accident?'

'Yes, Gervase.'

'A fall down the steps?'

'A bad collision with our host,' said Ralph, waving him away and hoisting himself to his feet. 'You won't see the bruises. They're all on the inside. The sheriff knows how to deliver a hard punch.'

Gervase was astonished. 'Durand actually struck you?'

'Only with his tongue, though he would have been happy to use the flat of his sword against me. And against you, Gervase,' he added, 'for you are as guilty as I am.'

'Guilty of what?'

'Trying to do the sheriff's work for him at the abbey.'

'Ah! He's found out.'

'Bishop Wulfstan told him, apparently. Not the first time the Church has landed us in trouble. Durand was beside himself and who can blame him? In his place, I'd have been just as furious.'

'What did he say?'

'That we were to stop interfering with his duties.'

'We are too far into this investigation to pull out now, Ralph.'

'I know, but I felt it wise not to mention that.'

'Is he aware of what we managed to find out?'

'Yes,' sighed Ralph. 'We were accused of withholding evidence. But for our positions, that offence would land us in serious trouble. As it is, our punishment was no worse than having our ears chewed off. Well,' he said on reflection, 'my ears, anyway. Is there anything left of them?'

Gervase nodded. 'I'm sorry that you had to bear the brunt of his displeasure, Ralph. I'll make a personal apology to him and see if I can calm him down a bit.'

'Take your time. At the moment it would be like putting your head into a lion's mouth. Wait until the sheriff has stopped roaring. But I'm glad you've appeared at last,' he said, touching his friend's arm. 'The steward was here a while ago with a message for us.'

'Are we to dine in the hall again?'

'No, Gervase. A banquet is being prepared for the King and we are not bidden. The steward told us to order what we desired and it will be served in the anteroom.'

'In the circumstances, that may be just as well.'

'Yes, it will keep us clear of Durand.'

'Have you placed an order yet?'

'I'm still composing it in my mind, Gervase,' said Ralph with a grin. 'It's a choice between sheriff's head on a plate or bishop's tongue in a rich sauce. It was Bishop Wulfstan who informed against us. He ought to be silenced in perpetuity.'

'Who discussed our involvement in the case with him?'

'Canon Hubert. He probably preached a sermon.'

'But he is so discreet as a rule.'

'Not when he has an abbot and a bishop to impress,' noted Ralph. 'All discretion goes out of the window then. Hubert seeks preferment. He'd strip naked and dance a jig for them if he thought it would gain their approval. Still,' he said, shaking himself, 'enough bleating. I got no more than I deserved. And I'm not unaccustomed to being shouted at by irate sheriffs. On to other matters.'

'You haven't told me what undertakings you gave.'

'None, Gervase.'

'Didn't the sheriff demand a promise from you?'

'He tried to put the fear of death into me and assumed that would be enough. Durand doesn't believe that we would have the gall and the stupidity to continue with our enquiries into the murder.'

'Do we?'

'What do you think?'

'I still have the gall.'

'Well, I can provide the stupidity.' They laughed quietly. 'But we must proceed more cautiously than ever. Without the blabbing mouth of Canon Hubert to land us in the dung heap.' He looked up the stairs with some trepidation. 'I'd better tell Golde where we are to dine.'

'Before you do, answer me this.'

'Make the question simple. I am quite befuddled.'

'Something has been preying on my mind since our journey this afternoon. It was that remark of the lord Hamelin's about needing to get back to Gloucester.'

'What of it?'

'How did he know of the King's visit?'

'From that pompous, puffed-up reeve, I expect.'

'But how did Nigel himself find out? He is hardly an intimate of the sheriff's. Nigel resents his power. My guess is that Durand told nobody apart from us. Not even the lady Maud, probably.'

Ralph quailed. 'Let's not discuss the question of wives.'

'But you take my point?'

'I do, Gervase.'

'The lord Hamelin is concealing something from us.'

'While distracting our attention with the lady Emma. If a general meeting of the Council has been summoned, he might have a legitimate reason to come to the castle. But that does not seem to be the case. Apart from Bishop Wulfstan, I know of nobody else who has been called here. The lord Hamelin will

repay careful watching.' His eyes rolled. 'So, of course, will hi
wife. On which rather sensitive topic,' he said with another glanc
up the stairs, 'you'll have to excuse me.'

'I will see you both in the anteroom.'

'I hope so.'

While his friend descended the stairs, Ralph went slowly u
them, praying that the interval of time had helped to soothe Golde
Instead of entering the chamber, he knocked tentatively on th
door and awaited her response. It was immediate.

'Who is it?' she called.

'Me,' he said with contrition.

The door opened at once and she pulled him gently inside.

'You're my husband, Ralph. There's no need to knock.'

'I didn't wish to intrude.'

'On what?'

'Nothing,' he said, brightening at her friendly manner.

'Where have you been?'

'Suffering at the hands of Durand, my love. And please don'
ask me why because it's too painful to relate again.' He shut th
door and gave a shrug. 'I came to say how sorry I was.'

'I, too, am sorry, Ralph. I spoke out of turn.'

'No, Golde. Your rebuke was well deserved.'

'It gave me no pleasure to administer it.'

A sheepish grin. 'I certainly had none in receiving it, I can tel
you.'

'Can we put it behind us?'

'Only if you forgive me.'

'In time, perhaps.'

'I'll settle for that.' He took her in his arms and sealed thei
reconciliation with a kiss. 'It will not happen again,' he said. 'A
proof of which, I can tell you that the King is not expected unti
after nightfall.'

'Why so late?'

'He wishes to slip into the city unobserved, Golde. Whateve

business brings him needs to be cloaked in secrecy for some reason. When I say that, I have said all that I know myself.'

'I believe you.'

'Beyond the fact that it affects us. A royal guest will naturally take precedence and a feast is being prepared in the hall. We three have been asked to eat separately in the anteroom.' He indicated the door but Golde did not move. 'Are you not hungry, my love?'

'Yes, but I want proof of your penitence first.'

'Must I don sackcloth and ashes?'

'A simpler form of atonement will suffice,'

'Name it, my love, and I will agree to it.'

'Good,' she said briskly. 'Let us first eat with Gervase then visit them straight afterwards. They are half-expecting us.'

'Who are?'

'My sister and her betrothed. I want you to meet Forne.'

Ralph stiffened. 'The arrogant young fool who dares to have serious qualms about your marriage to me?'

'I knew that you'd like him,' said Golde with a laugh.

Before the bell for Compline drew them to the abbey church for the last service of the day, Canon Hubert and Brother Simon walked side by side around the cloisters. Both were at peace. Unaware of the sheriff's reaction to their search for the killer, Hubert was still preening himself after his performance in front of Abbot Serlo and Bishop Wulfstan. He had made a profound impression on both of them and it would stand him in good stead. Both men had influence. It would be used in his favour.

Simon's tranquillity had returned the moment he set foot back inside the comforting walls of the abbey and shook off the horrid memories of the archdeacon's venture into midwifery, an escapade which had appalled Simon and made him glad that he did not live in the diocese of Gwent. Abbey life was all to him. There was no danger of meeting any young Welsh mothers shrieking in labour there.

'What is your opinion, Brother Simon?' asked Hubert.

'Of what, pray?'

'This dispute we have spent so much time trying to resolve.'

'I am only your scribe, Canon Hubert. I have no opinion.'

'In the shire hall, perhaps not. In the privacy of the cloister, it is a different matter. You heard all that we did. What is your conclusion?'

'Hamelin of Lisieux has prior claim.'

'That is what I have come to accept.'

'Only the Breton can mount a serious challenge.'

'Not the Welshman?'

'I found it too distressing to listen to all his evidence.'

'A pity, Brother Simon. His arguments were sound and forcefully put. They had a certain glibness but you expect that from the Welsh. Credit where it is due. Abraham the Priest gave a good account of himself.' His brow furrowed. 'Though I could have done without the lurid description of his journey here.'

'So could I, Canon Hubert!'

They turned a corner to perambulate along another side of the garth and found a diminutive figure waiting for them. Elaf stood there with a look of quiet apprehension. The monks stopped in front of him.

'You wish to speak to me?' said Hubert loftily.

'If I may, Canon Hubert,' replied the boy nervously. 'You and Master Bret were asking me about Brother Nicholas.'

'And?'

'I remembered something else about him.'

'Is it significant?'

'I think so.'

'Well? Be quick. Compline is at hand.'

'A week before Brother Nicholas's death, I saw him talking to someone outside the abbey. A well-dressed man. I have never seen him before. All that I remember is that they seemed to be having some kind of argument.'

'What made you decide that?'

'The way the man was waving his arms about.'

'In anger, you mean?'

'Yes. Brother Nicholas was trying to calm him down. When he turned to point at the abbey he caught sight of me by the gate and scowled. I ran back inside.'

'And that was all?'

'Yes, Canon Hubert.'

'Brother Nicholas did not come after you to scold you?'

'No, I hardly saw him after that. Then, with the shock of what we discovered in the church, it went out of my head, this meeting he had with the stranger.'

'Did he appear to be a stranger to Brother Nicholas?'

'Oh no. I think they knew each other.'

'How could you tell?'

'By the way they stood and talked.'

'Can you describe this other man?'

'Not really. They were some distance away.'

'Was the fellow old or young?'

'Old, I think. He had a beard.'

'That tells us little. Almost every man in Gloucester seems to have a beard. Yet another deplorable habit of the Saxons. But you said earlier he was well dressed. A man of wealth?'

'Yes.'

Hubert patted him on the head. 'You did well to bring this to me, Elaf. Have you told any of this to Brother Frewine?'

'As soon as I remembered it.'

'What did he say?'

'That I was to come to you or to Master Bret.'

The bell began to toll and monks headed towards the church from all directions. Hubert and Simon were about to join them when they became aware that the boy was hovering. He had more to tell.

'This may have nothing to do with it,' he said tentatively, 'but

I talked to Brother Owl . . . er, Brother Frewine, that is, about something else. Earlier this year, two novices disappeared from the abbey.'

'Disappeared?'

'So I thought. Their names were Siward and Dena. I believed that they must have run away.'

'And didn't they?'

'Nobody knows for sure, Canon Hubert. They have never been found. Their parents still grieve for them.'

'How tragic!' said Simon.

'Very tragic,' added Hubert. 'When you spoke to Brother Frewine, did he throw any light on their departure?'

Elaf's lower lip began to tremble with dismay. A disturbing idea had been implanted in him by the Precentor. Hubert put a steadying hand on his shoulder and knelt down in front of him.

'Does he know why they left, Elaf?'

'He thinks they may have been kidnapped.'

The visit got off to a quiet start. Schooled by his betrothed, Forne was polite and engaging. Ralph, too, was on his best behaviour, pleased to see his sister-in-law once more and anxious not to upset her. Aelgar and Forne were astonished by his grasp of their language and it did much to smooth out some of the inevitable social wrinkles. They were in the parlour of the house where the guests from Hereford were staying; Golde felt completely at home there but Ralph was uneasy in what were her natural surroundings. Even in the friendly atmosphere, he was never quite able to relax. However, the visit had one unexpected bonus.

'You *know* Querengar the Breton?' said Ralph in surprise.

'He has holdings in Archenfield.'

'Have you met him?'

'Once or twice,' said Forne. 'He struck me as a forthright man. With a pleasant manner. I could not say that of many of them.'

'Them?' echoed Ralph.

'Invaders.'

'Forne!' said Aelgar warningly.

'The lord Ralph did ask.'

'And I got a fair answer,' said Ralph. 'So you think of Querengar as an invader, do you? Even though he has lived in this country for over twenty years. That is almost as long as you, Forne.'

'I was born here.'

'Why is the Breton so unusual?'

'Because most of the others who took our land from us revel in their conquest,' said Forne bitterly. 'They live in their fortified manor houses and treat us with disdain. In Archenfield, where I live, but especially in lowland Gwent, there are dozens of them, Normans, Bretons and, worst of all, the hated Flemings.'

'They are not easy to love,' agreed Ralph.

'If they fought at Hastings, they were given our land.'

'The spoils of war, Forne.'

'Need we talk about this subject now?' said Golde meaningfully.

'No,' added Aelgar.

'But I must just point something out to this argumentative young man of yours,' said Ralph easily. 'You call it your land, Forne, but your ancestors stole it from the people who were settled here before them. So, in a sense, you, too, are enjoying the fruits of conquest, albeit at several removes. As for Querengar and the rest, they give valuable service by settling in less desirable parts of the kingdom like Wales and the Welsh borders. Most of their estates are held by military tenure, I'm sure you know what that means.'

'Only too well!'

'Can we change this topic now?' pleaded Aelgar.

'But I find it interesting.'

'We do not,' said Golde.

'Stop it before you start to get angry,' said Aelgar.

'I'm not at all angry.'

'Forne!'

'Talk to your sister while we have our discussion.'

'No!'

'Aelgar will do nothing of the kind,' said Golde, smarting at his dismissive tone. 'Ralph and I came to visit both of you so that all four of us could get to know each other better. Aelgar and I will not be swept aside like a couple of children being sent out to play.'

Ralph grinned. 'I'd like to meet the man who can sweep you aside, my love. But you are quite right. This is not a fit subject.'

'We must return to it another time, my lord,' said Forne with tenacity. 'Then I can put my side of the argument.'

'It has already been put at the Battle of Hastings.'

'Ralph!' snapped his wife.

'That was an unworthy comment,' he conceded. 'I take it back. And I would like to thank Forne for his comments on Querengar. They were very useful. So tell me, Aelgar,' he said, trying to introduce a more jocular note. 'Where will this amorous young man take you off to when he marries you and throws you over his shoulder?'

'We will live in Archenfield.'

'Does that idea appeal to you?'

'Very much.'

'I know the area well. It holds pleasant memories for me.' He winked at Golde. 'It's where your sister and I first got to know each other properly. If it were not so close to Wales, I could find Archenfield rather appealing myself.'

'I hope you will visit us there,' said Aelgar.

'Gladly,' replied Golde. 'When time serves.'

'And when the King sees fit to release me from these onerous duties,' said Ralph with a sigh. 'I long for the day when I can actually start to enjoy my own estates again. If it ever comes, both of you will be invited to visit us in Hampshire.'

Aelgar was touched. 'That would be wonderful! Forne?'

'Yes,' he said without relish.

'We would love to see you there,' said Golde.

'Almost as much as we'd love to see ourselves there,' added Ralph.

Talk turned to the preparations for the wedding and a contentment settled on the room. Forne was disappointed that he was unable to argue at will with Ralph, but he made himself amenable and his devotion to Aelgar once again shone through. The two sisters were in their element, each feeling more complete now that they were sharing their lives with a man they loved. It was a far cry from the days when they both worked in the brewhouse in Hereford. Ralph looked on with interest but took progressively less part in the conversation. He was back in Golde's world now and still a relative stranger. He liked Aelgar, not only on her own account but because she mirrored so many of Golde's qualities. About Forne he was undecided. Beneath the obliging manner was a resentment and pugnacity which he found irritating.

At the end of the evening, he and Golde took their leave and mounted their horses. It was not far to the castle but a walk through dark and dirty streets was not advisable. With Golde to protect, Ralph had taken the additional precaution of wearing his sword. The horses walked slowly along the lane, their hoofbeats amplified in the hollow night.

'What did you think of Forne?' asked Golde.

'It is as you said, my love. He and your sister are well matched.'

'Did you like him?'

'When he made himself likeable.'

'What do you mean?'

'I could have done with more respect from him,' said Ralph. 'He never quite recovered from the fact that I arrived with a sword. It upset him. I could see that.'

'You shouldn't have goaded him, Ralph.'

'I did nothing of the kind.'

'Yes, you did.'

'He needed no goading, my love. Forne was well and truly goaded before we even got there. My very existence goads him.'

'You could have been more tactful.'

'I'll not let anyone shout me down, Golde.'

'There was provocation, I know,' she accepted. 'All in all, it passed off well and I'm so grateful that you agreed to come with me.'

'Did I have any choice?'

She laughed.

'I have *some* sympathy with the fellow,' he said. 'Seen through his eyes, I must appear like something of an ogre. Is that how I appear to you?'

'Now and then.'

It was his turn to laugh. Their horses swung into a narrow street and ambled slowly on. Ralph and Golde rode in silence and savoured the night air. It was the first time since they had been in Gloucester that they felt truly alone. The sensation was liberating.

'Let's escape,' said Ralph on impulse.

'From what?'

'This city. Let's ride off now, Golde.'

'Where would we go?'

'Anywhere to get away from it. I'm fed up with the endless round of responsibilities. I just want to be with you. Let's go!'

'Are you serious?'

'Never more so, my love.'

'But you turn your back on everything,' she said reasonably. 'It's unthinkable. What about Gervase? Would you really desert him?'

'I was forgetting Gervase.'

'There's Canon Hubert and Brother Simon as well.'

'They don't matter quite so much.'

'Your duties matter, Ralph. That's why you always discharge them so zealously. People depend on you and you never let them down. I know you too well. You'd never run away from anything. Ralph Delchard is the sort of man who will stand and fight.'

'Unfortunately,' he sighed, giving up. 'Ah well, it was a nice idea while it lasted. To start anew. To ride off in the moonlight with the woman of my dreams.'

'The woman of your dreams is too tired. She needs her sleep.'

'Don't be so unromantic!'

'Then choose a better time.'

Before he could answer, a drumming sound was heard in the middle distance. Many hooves were dancing their way into Gloucester. They nudged their own horses into a trot until the castle loomed up ahead of them. The noise grew louder, then the cavalcade appeared. Twenty or more riders surged across the Bearland, the open space in front of the castle where troops could be mustered or where the defending garrison could have clear sight of any besieging army. In the gloom, Ralph and Golde had no clear sight of the visitors but Ralph identified them at once. As they slowed down to clatter across the drawbridge, he turned to his wife.

'King William!'

'He has come late.'

'By design.'

'And with a sizeable entourage.'

'I'll be interested to see who rides with him.'

'And will you tell me when you find out?' she teased.

'Immediately.'

Ralph's smile congealed as soon as it was formed. Something had aroused his suspicion. When the last of the horsemen had ridden through the castle gate, a tall figure emerged from the shadows and strode swiftly across the Bearland. The man had been watching the arrival of the royal party. Ralph only saw the man in silhouette but his gait and bearing were distinctive. He had witnessed both at the shire hall.

Golde noticed that he now sat bolt upright in the saddle.

'What's wrong?' she asked.

'I'm not sure.'

'You've gone tense, Ralph.'

'It was that man who walked in front of the castle.'

'Do you know him?'

'I think so.'

'Who is he?'

'Abraham the Priest.'

The long tables were bedecked with dishes of all kinds and wine flowed freely in the light of a hundred candles. A magnificent repast awaited the visitors. Though he had complained about the royal visit, Durand the Sheriff was also pleased by it because it was an indication of his own status in the King's counsels. Sitting with his guests, the sheriff was at his most affable and his wife at her most charming. The long wait had left the hosts themselves feeling the pangs of hunger and they could now allay them in the best possible way. Yet there was no air of celebration in the hall. The delicious fare was consumed with thanks rather than with any jollity. The King was there on serious business. It showed.

Durand waited until the end of the meal before he broached the topic which had occupied his mind since he first heard of the possibility of a royal visit. He leaned respectfully across to his guest of honour.

'Is there anything else you require, my liege?'

'A soft bed and a quiet night.'

'We all need those.'

'Not all of us, Durand,' said William, casting an eye over some of the members of his entourage. 'There are a few here who would prefer a warm woman in that soft bed, then the night would be far from quiet.'

'Hot blood runs in young veins.'

'I should know. I have spilled it often enough.'

William the Conqueror, King of England and Duke of Normandy, spoke with gruff regret. He was a big, broad-shouldered man with extremely long arms. The aura of majesty was unmistakable but so was the fatigue of warfare. He was approaching his sixtieth year now and the cares of office showed in the craggy face, already lined by the succession of betrayals, reversals and disappointments he had suffered, and scored most deeply by the death of his wife, Matilda, a tiny woman for such a portly warrior but a true queen in every sense. William was a bundle of contradictions, peremptory yet pious, uncultured yet intelligent, harsh yet capable of great gentleness, a belligerent man who desired nothing more than the peace which constantly eluded him.

'You have not told me the purpose of this visit,' said Durand.

'Do I need a purpose before I can come to Gloucester?'

'Of course not, my liege.'

'Is friendship not excuse enough, Durand?'

'More than enough. But I am bound to observe that two members of your Council have arrived with you, and Bishop Wulfstan was already here at your request. May we expect others to join us?'

'No,' said William, sitting back in his chair. 'With your own good self, I have four sage counsellors around me. That will suffice.'

'To discuss what?'

'Whatever we choose.'

'I will press you no more on the matter,' said Durand, backing off at the sign of evasion. 'I just felt that I should point out that another of your erstwhile counsellors is in Gloucester at this time.'

'Who is that?'

'Hamelin of Lisieux.'

'His opinion will not be sought,' said William sharply. 'I heard that he spends most of his time in Normandy with that pretty wife of his. What brings him here?'

'A dispute over his holdings, my liege.'

'But of course. I was forgetting that the second commissioners were sent to the county. Are they still here?'

'Under this very roof. Except for Canon Hubert and their scribe They prefer to lodge at the abbey.'

'A fortuitous decision,' said Wulfstan, sitting on the other side of the King and easing himself into the conversation. 'A foul murder was recently committed there. They have been able to assist in tracking down the fiend responsible.'

Durand crackled. 'Their help is quite unnecessary.'

'But Canon Hubert has such a quick mind.'

'Too quick, Bishop Wulfstan.'

'I have met the man,' said William thoughtfully. 'And I know Ralph Delchard and Gervase Bret even better. All three are very able or I would not have given them such high office. Make use of them while they are here, Durand. You could not ask for more efficient deputies.'

'I do not ask for any deputies at all.'

'The crime must be solved swiftly,' urged Wulfstan. 'You should be grateful that these men are taking the trouble to help you.'

'I am grateful,' lied Durand.

'So you should be,' said William firmly. 'Seek assistance from those best suited to give it to you. That is what I always do. I ask, I discuss, I consult. As a result, my decisions are the sounder and I do not feel that my authority has in any way been undermined. Is that your fear?' he asked shrewdly. 'A loss of control?'

'Only a sheriff can investigate a homicide.'

'Not when he is sitting in council with his king. We will spend a lot of time in this hall over the next day or two, Durand, because we have much to discuss. My needs have priority over those of the abbey. Even the bishop will acknowledge that.'

'Freely, my liege,' said Wulfstan.

'I am sure that you have capable officers but they will lack the perseverance of Ralph Delchard and the others. Put your trust in them,' he said, resting a hand on the sheriff's arm. 'They are not untried in such matters. If anyone can apprehend the killer, it is them.'

Durand's food was organising an armed rebellion in his tomach.

Kenelm was in a quandary. Too tired to stay awake, he was too afraid to sleep lest it render him vulnerable to more of the hideous nightmares that afflicted him. As he lay on his mattress in the dormitory, he inhabited a kind of limbo between the two, dozing off, shaking himself instantly awake, then feeling the drowsiness creep over him once again. He had jerked himself out of his slumber for the third time when he heard the sound. Someone was moving stealthily across the floor. The creak of a board caused them to stop and wait before inching their way forward again. At first Kenelm thought it might be Elaf, but his friend was still on the mattress next to him, sleeping soundly, impervious to all around him. Who, then, was creeping out of the dormitory?

Raising himself on his elbows, Kenelm saw the figure flit through the doorway. He was bewildered. Owen was the last novice he expected to sneak out in the middle of the night. He was the most timid and well-behaved boy in the abbey, and nocturnal wandering was strictly forbidden. Kenelm wondered what could possibly make Owen court a beating from the Master of the Novices. He had to find out. Rising to his feet, he made for the door with greater speed than Owen, cleverly negotiating the floorboards which creaked. Kenelm caught up with him near the cloister garth. The other boy was patently frightened, darting nervously from one hiding place to another, but something impelled him to go on.

Kenelm followed until he saw where Owen was going. He stopped immediately. Nothing could make him venture into the cemetery at night. It held the accusing presence of Brother Nicholas. Watching the other boy pick his way nimbly between the gravestones, Kenelm lost his nerve and turned tail. He ran all the way back to the dormitory but it was no refuge. New horrors assaulted him. Sleep of any kind was impossible.

Owen, meanwhile, was filled with a strange confidence. When he reached the mound of fresh earth, he gazed down at it without any sign of fear. Even in death, Brother Nicholas was still his friend. The only way to reach him now was by means of prayer and Owen knelt on the damp grass with his palms together. His prayer was long and fervent. He was convinced that Brother Nicholas heard every word. When he opened his eyes and clambered to his feet again, he was smiling. He had talked a night to his friend as he had done so many times before. It was thrilling. Waving a farewell, he turned to scamper away but someone was waiting for him, a stout figure in a monastic cowl barely visible in the darkness. Pale moonlight gave him a ghostly air.

Owen was unperturbed. He went hopefully towards the man.

'Brother Nicholas?' he asked.

Occupying a chamber near the base of the keep, Gervase Bret retired early to bed and fell swiftly asleep. Even the heavy murmur of voices from the hall did not disturb him. It took the fist and voice of Canon Hubert to pluck him from his dreams.

'Gervase!' called Hubert. 'Wake up, Gervase!'

'What?' muttered the other, opening an eye. 'Who's there?'

'Canon Hubert!'

'Here at the castle?'

'I must speak to you!'

'One moment.'

Forcing himself awake, Gervase got out of bed and crossed to unbolt the door. Brother Hubert was supporting himself against the wall with one hand. He was covered in sweat and panting stertorously. Gervase beckoned him in and shut the door behind them. When he opened the window, the first rays of sun were streaking across the sky. They enabled him to see his visitor's face.

'Canon Hubert, are you all right?'

'I've been running.'

'I can see that. Sit down. Get your breath back.'

'Thank you, Gervase.'

Gulping in air, Hubert lowered himself precariously on to a small stool and put a palm across his heart. A man who rarely moved at more than a stately waddle had broken into an undignified sprint. Gervase knew that only an emergency could have made him do that. He waited until his caller had a semblance of control over his breathing.

'What is the matter?' he asked.

'Another disaster has befallen the abbey.'

'Murder?'

'We are not sure, Gervase. We pray that is not the case.'

'So what happened?'

'One of the novices was abducted in the night.'

'Are you sure?'

'No other explanation fits the facts,' said Hubert, wiping an arm across his brow. 'The boy's name is Owen. His absence was noted at Matins and a search instituted. He is nowhere to be found in the abbey.'

'Calm down,' advised Gervase. 'You may yet be mistaken. The boy may be playing a prank and hiding from you.'

'Owen never plays pranks. Brother Paul, the Master of the Novices, tells me he is the most obedient of them all. Besides, where would he hide? They have looked everywhere.'

'They looked everywhere for Brother Nicholas, if you remember, and he was concealed among them all the time. But you say he was abducted. Assuming that this Owen did leave the abbey, could he not have gone of his own accord?'

'No, Gervase.'

'Why not?'

'To start with, he would not have been able to get out. All the doors are locked at night. Only the porter could have let him leave. And we are talking about a dedicated young boy here. He

thrives on monastic life. Owen had no reason to go and eve
reason to stay.' His jowls wobbled with consternation. 'But the
is much more disturbing intelligence, Gervase. He may not be t
first.'

'The first what?'

'Victim. Two other novices disappeared in the past.'

'Under what circumstances?'

'Similar ones, from what I can gather. There at night but go
the next morning. Again, with no just cause to flee the abb
Everyone is convinced that all three boys were kidnapped.'

'Why?'

'I dare not even contemplate that.'

'But didn't you tell me that all the doors were locked?'

'They are, Gervase. By the porter.'

'Then how did someone get in to abduct them?'

'How did someone get in to murder Brother Nicholas?' sa
Hubert, shifting dangerously on the stool. 'Abbot Serlo believ
the crimes may be connected and I am bound to agree. That's w
I took to my heels to rouse you. I hope that you do not mind.'

'Of course not, Canon Hubert. You did the right thing.'

'I thought to speak first to the lord Ralph but I hesitated
knock at the door of a married man. It seemed improper. I cou
hardly be invited into his chamber as I have been here.'

'Nevertheless, Ralph must be woken,' said Gervase. 'Have
fear. I'll take the office upon me. Stay here and recover while I a
about it.'

'Do you think we are right?'

'About what?'

'A link between the murder and the abductions?'

'There is only one way to find out. What I do know is th
you've told me more than enough to get me out of bed. When he
stopped cursing me for waking him, Ralph will say the sam
Hold fast.'

Still in his night attire, Gervase ran swiftly out on bare feet.

The Owls of Gloucester

* * *

Abbot Serlo, Bishop Wulfstan and Brother Frewine stood in a line and stared balefully down at the ground like three ancient owls with only one mouse between them. They were outside the church, lost in thought, weighed down with a new grief, drawn together by suffering. Serlo's pain was keenest. He was *in loco parentis* and one of his beloved children had been snatched away. The Precentor felt numb. Owen was the last boy he would have wanted to lose and he feared that the novice's trusting nature might have been his downfall. Older and wiser than either of them, the bishop tried to put fear aside so that he could think more clearly. Child abductions were not unique events in his long life. He did not dwell on how most usually ended.

The return of Canon Hubert brought all three of them out of their reveries. Ralph Delchard and Gervase Bret had been given full details by their colleague but they wanted to hear them afresh. After greetings had been exchanged, they let the abbot give his account. The evidence from Kenelm was what intrigued Ralph.

'He followed Owen to the cemetery?' he said.

'So he told us, my lord,' replied Serlo.

'Whatever was the boy doing there?'

'Only he would know that.'

'Most lads of that age would not go near such a place in the dead of night. Especially on their own. Well, this Kenelm was too frightened to stay, it seems. I can understand that. Owen must be very brave.'

'Hardly,' said Frewine. 'I have never met such a timid creature.'

'Timid?'

'Shy, modest and reticent.'

'Yet he walks among the gravestones in the dark. An unusual boy, this Owen, clearly.' He rubbed his chin. 'Hubert tells us that all the abbey doors are locked at night.'

'Yes, my lord,' said Serlo. 'But the porter is always at the gate.'

'Who holds the keys to the other doors?'

'He does.'

'Are there no duplicates?'

'I have one to the rear entrance but rarely use it.'

'Is it kept somewhere safe, Abbot Serlo?'

'Extremely safe. It has never gone missing.'

'And it is still where it should be?'

'Yes, my lord. I checked.'

'In that case, we are faced with only one conclusion. Someone had a means of getting into the abbey at night. He let himself in, seized the boy, then left by the same door.'

'That, alas, is what we have decided.'

'May I add another possibility?' asked Gervase.

'Please do,' encouraged Wulfstan. 'Your opinion is valued. Canon Hubert has told us how much you have helped him with his investigation into the murder.'

Ralph choked. '*His* investigation!'

'What is this possibility, Gervase?' asked Hubert, eager to move attention away from himself. 'We do not see it.'

'Suppose that the man we seek did not let himself into the abbey at all?' suggested Gervase. 'Because he was already inside it.'

Serlo was affronted. 'You accuse one of my monks?'

'No, Abbot Serlo.'

'The sheriff did. In plain terms.'

'An outrageous allegation!' said Wulfstan.

'Let him finish,' said Frewine quietly. 'I do not think that Master Bret is pointing the finger at any of us. Are you?'

'No, Brother Frewine. The person I suspect is an interloper. If you steal a tree,' said Gervase, 'the best place to hide it is in a forest. If you steal a cowl, the one place it will never be detected is in a monastery.'

'We have a bogus monk in our midst!' gasped Serlo.

'Gervase may be on to something,' said Ralph.

'He would surely have been exposed,' contended Frewine. 'Each of us knows all the others.'

'By day, perhaps,' said Gervase, 'which is why the interloper ould not have mingled with you then. But if he let himself into ᵉ abbey just before the doors were locked, he could bide his me until an opportunity arose. An opportunity to kill Brother ᴺicholas, for instance. An opportunity to abduct Owen and, in all robability, the earlier boys who disappeared. It is mere suppo-tion, of course,' he continued, spreading his arms, 'but I feel that deserves consideration.'

'Serious consideration,' declared Hubert.

'There, Gervase!' said Ralph with light sarcasm. 'You have the pproval of the leader of the murder inquiry. Sheriff Hubert imself.' The canon took an uncomfortable step backwards. 'I gree with your reasoning about the disguise and will even accept at the man in question was inside the enclave before the doors ere locked. But one thing is still unexplained. How did he get ut of the abbey again?'

'With a key.'

'The only two in existence are accounted for.'

'Then there must be a third.'

'How was it obtained?'

'A duplicate was taken from one of the others.' He turned to erlo. 'Is there a locksmith in the city, Abbot Serlo?'

'Two. We have employed both here in the past.'

'Give us their names. We will need to speak to them.'

'Both are entirely trustworthy.'

'I'm sure that they are,' said Ralph, 'but how are they to know vhere a key comes from when a customer requests a duplicate? A ocksmith is acting in good faith. He is no accomplice here.'

'I am sorry to disagree,' said Frewine softly, 'because Master ᵣet has been so plausible. But we are very particular about the ecurity of this abbey. With such valuable items and holy relics to uard, we have to be. All the keys are kept on a single ring. Day or ight, it never leaves the hand of the porter who is on duty. How, hen, could it have been copied by a locksmith?'

'It was not,' said Gervase. 'Nobody would try to borrow a key from a bunch when a single one existed. The duplicate must have been made from the other key.'

'But you heard Abbot Serlo tell you that it rarely leaves his lodging. And then it is only for personal use.'

All eyes turned to the abbot. A distant memory troubled him.

'That is not strictly true, Brother Frewine.'

'Others have borrowed the key?' asked Ralph.

'Once or twice.'

'Recently?'

'Oh no, my lord. Some time ago.'

'When was the last time? A year ago?'

'More like two.'

'And who borrowed your key on that occasion?'

Abbot Serlo's voice dropped to an embarrassed whisper.

'I do believe it may have been Brother Nicholas.'

Chapter Ten

It was an entirely new experience for Ralph Delchard. He would never have believed that it was possible for him to enjoy himself within the confines of an abbey, especially when plucked unceremoniously from the arms of his wife in the early hours of the morning, but that was what was happening. Pleasure was coursing through him. It was not because he had discovered a hitherto unacknowledged spiritual dimension in his life, still less an affinity with the three Benedictine monks who greeted him at the abbey. What excited him was the thrill of the chase. Another crime had been committed, but more clues lay in its wake this time. His blood was up. Simultaneously, an innocent boy might be saved and a cruel murder solved. He was glad that Gervase Bret had hauled him out of bed.

Controlling his exhilaration, he spoke gently to Kenelm.

'Tell your story once more,' he invited.

'Yes, my lord.'

'Begin from the moment you heard Owen leave. Had he ever crept out of the dormitory at night before?'

'Never!' said Kenelm.

'How can you be so sure?'

'He was not bold enough, my lord.'

'Unlike you and Elaf.'

'Those days are gone.'

Kenelm was feeling sorry for himself. A sleepless night had left him sagging with weariness but the new day brought nothing but endless interrogation. Shocked by Owen's disappearance and anxious to help, he was finding that his concentration wandered

191

and his memory played tricks on him. He pulled himself togeth
and went through it all again with plodding slowness. It w
painful.

The five of them were in the Precentor's lodging. Abbot Ser
had been shed along with Canon Hubert, the putative leader
the murder inquiry. Only the bishop followed Ralph and Gerva
to the new venue. Brother Frewine summoned the novice a
they were able to hear the boy's account at first hand. It gave the
priceless new facts with which to work. Seeing Kenelm's obvio
exhaustion, Ralph took pity on him and released him after anoth
bout of questioning. When the boy had gone, Ralph turned
Brother Frewine.

'That's the second time he's broken the rules to wander about
night and the second time he's had a nasty surprise. I have
feeling that the lad will stay in his bed from now on.'

'If only that were true, my lord,' said Frewine.

'You have cause to doubt it?'

'Grave cause. Kenelm is planning to leave us.'

Wulfstan was upset. 'Abandon his novitiate?'

'So I understand, Bishop Wulfstan. As you saw for yourselve
the boy is in a state of high anxiety. Brother Nicholas's dea
made a deep impression on him. He thinks that the only way
can deal with the situation is to run away.'

'Owen's fate may make him reconsider,' observed Gervase.

'Possibly.'

'Let us have his friend in,' said Ralph.

The Precentor nodded and opened the door to summon th
other novice. Elaf was morose, rocked by what might hav
happened to Owen and desperate to do all that he could to try
find him. At Ralph's behest, he described the argument he ha
seen outside the abbey gate between Brother Nicholas and th
well-dressed stranger. When they had probed him on every deta
Elaf, too, was set free and ran off to confer with Kenelm. The
was another bond between them now. Both had seen thing

which might have a bearing on the serious crimes committed at the abbey. Each had witnessed elements in a continuing catastrophe.

Bishop Wulfstan was impressed by their undoubted honesty.

'Worthy novices, both,' he said. 'The Order must not lose them.'

'We will do all we can to keep them,' promised Frewine.

'I will speak with them alone myself, if that would help.'

'Greatly, Bishop Wulfstan. They worship you.'

'God needs no competition from me.' He looked at Ralph. 'You are deep in thought, my lord. May we know what you have decided?'

'I am still trying to piece it together. Gervase?'

'So am I,' said the other, 'but this much I will vouchsafe. Brother Nicholas strayed ruinously from his monastic vows. I know that it is a painful notion to accept,' he continued as the bishop winced, 'but it can scarcely be denied. Money was found in his cell by Brother Frewine and there are other indications which lead me to a conclusion which you will find incredible. But it must be confronted.'

'Brace yourselves,' warned Ralph. 'Tell them, Gervase.'

'I will be brief. Brother Nicholas was paid to provide young boys to someone who came here in disguise to collect them. The same man was probably seen by Elaf having an argument with Brother Nicholas outside the gate and it led in time to murder. Wearing a cowl and using the key provided by his accomplice, the man let himself in once more last night and chanced upon Owen in the cemetery.'

'No!' protested Wulfstan. 'A Benedictine monk engaged in such a business? I cannot accept that. I will not.'

'I will,' said Frewine simply.

'So will I,' agreed Ralph. 'My thoughts move in the same direction. I would make only one comment, Gervase.'

'What's that?' he asked.

'I do not think that this man "chanced upon" the boy.'

'How else could he know where and when to find him?'

'I have no idea. But he did. He must have.'

'The very idea of such a monster prowling on consecrate ground is abhorrent to me,' said Wulfstan. 'He must be stoppe Locks on every door must be changed. Patrols set up. Speci protection offered to the novices. They are mere children. The deserve to be watched over as closely as any holy relics.'

'From now on they will be, Bishop Wulfstan,' said Frewine.

'Too late in the day for those already abducted,' said Ralp 'We must act fast. One of them at least may be recovered befor any real harm befalls him.'

'Where will you begin your search, my lord?' asked Wulfstan

'At the two locksmiths.'

'Abbot Serlo is mortified that he might unwittingly have helpe to further this dreadful event. For his sake, and for the sake of hi abbey's reputation, these crimes must be answered.'

'They will be, Bishop Wulfstan.'

'You and Master Bret will earn our undying thanks.'

'Do not forget Canon Hubert,' said Ralph mischievously. 'Ou self-appointed master. He will be a crucial figure.'

'There will be consequences,' Gervase reminded him. 'If w are to devote our full attention to this matter, we will have t forgo our work in the shire hall. That will not make us popula with the claimants.'

Ralph was dismissive. 'I care nothing for popularity.'

'It is just as well, Ralph, for the sheriff will also hurl abuse us. My fear is that he'll do far more than that and actually prevent us lending our assistance.'

'No question of that!' insisted Wulfstan.

'You have the power to stop him?' said Gervase.

'The King does, Master Bret, and he has already used it or your behalf. When I told him of your splendid efforts thus far, h was so impressed that he more or less ordered Durand to allow ou to continue. The sheriff has been muzzled. Ignore him.'

'This is excellent news,' said Ralph genially. 'Come, Gervase. t's time to batter on a couple of doors. One of those locksmiths must provide another key for us. The one that unlocks this mystery.'

'Aren't you forgetting something?' said Gervase.

'What?'

'Brother Frewine still has that money.'

'Of course!' said Ralph, slapping his thigh by way of self-reproach. 'How remiss of me! That leather pouch.' He smiled at the Precentor. 'Could I trouble you to show it to us?'

'With pleasure, my lord.'

Opening the door of a cupboard, Frewine took out the pouch and handed it to Ralph. He weighed it in his palm. When he opened the neck of the pouch, Ralph tipped the coins on to the table beside the flickering candle. Wulfstan was shocked by the amount of money and Gervase fascinated by its glinting newness. Ralph's interest was in the pouch. He took out the strip of leather he had found in the bell tower and held it against the thongs which threaded their way through the pouch.

It was a perfect match. Ralph grinned with satisfaction.

'What you found was only part of his hoard, Brother Frewine,' he explained. 'The rest was hidden behind a beam in the bell tower and, if my guess is correct, snatched away by the man who killed him. I've got his scent in my nostrils now, Gervase. Let's after him!'

Seated in a chair, Abbot Serlo stared ahead of him with an expression of remorse on his face. Canon Hubert stood beside him to offer consolation.

'It was my fault,' said Serlo quietly. 'I am to blame, Canon Hubert.'

'Nothing could be further from the truth, Abbot Serlo.'

'But I gave that key to Brother Nicholas.'

'Unwittingly.'

'That is how it all started.'

'We do not know that for certain.'

'I provided the key which allowed three of my novices to taken from the abbey against their will. What dreadful fate awai them when they left here? What obscenities were they subject to? What agonies did they endure?' His whole body convulsed. will never forgive myself.'

'There is nothing to forgive, Abbot Serlo. How were you know to what use that key would be put? When you loaned it Brother Nicholas, it was, presumably, for another purpose.'

'Yes,' explained Serlo. 'He was due back late one night fro his travels with a satchel full of the rent he collected. He ask if he could let himself in by the back gate so that he cou deposit the money here at my lodging. At least, that was t reason he gave but I surmised that there was another mo benevolent one.'

'Benevolent?'

'Brother Nicholas had his detractors but he was, at heart, kind man. At the time of which we speak, almost two years a now, we had an ancient porter, Brother Andrew, too old discharge the office at night but too proud to admit it. Calle are rare after dark so he was able to sleep most of the time.' looked up at Hubert. 'I thought that Brother Nicholas w showing consideration to an old man, asking to be let in by t back gate so that Brother Andrew was not roused from h slumber.'

'Did Brother Nicholas ever borrow the key again?'

'Never. Shortly after the first occasion, our dear porter fell in an eternal sleep. If he came back late after that, Brother Nichol had no qualms about ringing the bell at the main gate for h successor.' He rose to his feet. 'It never occurred to me that he h no more need of my key because a duplicate had already be made.'

'That is only supposition.'

'The lord Ralph seemed convinced. So did Master Bret.'

'Their theory is plausible but still unproven.'

'It has the awful ring of truth about it.'

'Even if that is the case,' said Hubert gently, 'you are beyond censure. Brother Nicholas had his throat cut. Is the man who made the knife culpable because he sold it unknowingly to a murderer?'

'No, of course not.'

'The same holds for you.'

'But it does not, Canon Hubert.'

'Why not?'

'Because the cutler who provided the knife has not been directly confronted with its gruesome handiwork. I have. In supplying that key, I gave Brother Nicholas and his accomplice a means of access to this abbey. That access made possible a murder and three abductions.'

'I am unpersuaded,' said Hubert, shaking his head. 'My colleagues may be a little too hasty in their judgement. Let us take these supposed abductions. How do we know that is what they are, and where is the evidence that the same man was involved?'

'Three novices have been seized from this abbey.'

'Three have disappeared, it is true. But were they seized?'

'They must have been, Canon Hubert.'

'When did the first boy go astray?'

'It must have been all of eighteen months or two years ago.' His despair intensified. 'Yes, almost two years ago. I recall it now. Soon after I lent that key to Brother Nicholas. That is when Siward was taken.'

'It could be an unfortunate coincidence.'

'No, Canon Hubert. The link is undeniable.'

'What of the second boy?'

'Dena vanished from our midst some time last year.'

'A considerable time after Siward, then?'

'Yes.'

'If someone really did have designs on them, why not abduct both together? It does not make sense to delay the second visit so long. No, Abbot Serlo,' said Hubert, 'I begin to have reservations about this.'

'I wish that I could share them.'

'At least absolve yourself of any criticism.'

'Impossible!' said the abbot, wringing his hands as he paced the room. 'And even if I do not accuse myself, they will.'

'They?'

'Owen's parents.'

'I was forgetting them.'

'They will be utterly heartbroken when I tell them. They are good Christians, Canon Hubert. God-fearing people who placed their only child here in the abbey in the confident belief that he would be nurtured and protected. What am I to say to them?' he asked, arms flailing. 'No words of comfort exist for parents in such a situation. I have been through it twice before, remember. First, when Siward left. Then with Dena's parents. I have never been through such harrowing interviews.' He clasped his hands in prayer. 'Dear God in heaven, do not inflict the ordeal on me again. Help us to find him, Lord. We humbly beg you to return your young servant safely to the abbey.'

'Amen,' said Hubert.

'They will have to be told,' said Serlo through clenched teeth. 'It is their right. Owen's parents must be informed.'

'But not just yet, Abbot Serlo.'

'It is a cruelty to keep it from them.'

'Is it not more cruel to put them through a torture which may yet be avoided. Hold off a while, I implore you. Give us a little time to look more closely into this crime. With God's blessing, we may be able to give Owen's parents some good news.'

'That depends on your colleagues.'

'Hold faith with them.'

'Can they really solve these crimes, Canon Hubert?'

'The lord Ralph and Gervase Bret are remarkable individuals.'

'But you said earlier that you had doubts about their theory.'

'I do,' admitted Hubert readily. 'But in matters like this, they have a curious habit of proving me wrong.'

By the time they left the abbey precincts, Gloucester had already stirred. Tradesmen were open for business and people were milling in the streets. Ralph and Gervase called on the first of the two locksmiths but drew a complete blank. The man neither recognised the key which they showed him nor remembered having made one quite so large. Everything hinged on the second locksmith. Ralph had misgivings.

'What if the duplicate was not made in Gloucester?'

'Where else?'

'Brother Nicholas travelled far and wide.'

'Only into the country,' said Gervase, 'and locksmiths are thin on the ground there. I daresay that Tewkesbury has one, Winchcombe, too, but the abbey holdings do not lie in that direction. The rent collector would have no cause to visit either town.'

'His accomplice might,' suggested Ralph. 'What better way to cover his tracks than to employ a locksmith far away from here?'

'But there was no need to cover his tracks.'

'Why not?'

'Because he never expected anyone to discover that the duplicate had been fashioned. For two whole years, nobody did. Brother Nicholas and his accomplice made one fatal mistake, Ralph.'

'What was that?'

'They never expected us.'

Ralph was reassured enough to give a hearty laugh. When they found the second locksmith, the street in which his shop lay was quite busy. Two customers were calling on the tradesman himself.

Ralph wanted to push to the front of the queue but Gervase advised patience so that they could study the locksmith and gauge his character. Palli was a short, fussy, fidgety man with shoulders hunched by a lifetime of bending over his work. Thick veins stood out on the backs of unwashed hands. Ralph noted the dirt under his fingernails.

'I'm glad the fellow does not cook my food,' he said.

'He seems proficient enough at his trade,' noted Gervase, looking around. 'His shop is larger than the other one and these customers clearly trust him. He may well be our man, Ralph.'

'And if he isn't?'

The question hung unanswered in the air. When both customers departed, Ralph and Gervase stepped up to the counter. Palli appraised them with a keen eye. It did not approve of Ralph Delchard. The little locksmith turned instead to Gervase Bret.

'Can I help you?' he grunted.

'I hope so,' said Gervase, showing him the key borrowed from the abbey. 'Did you make this?'

'No,' said Palli at once.

'How do you know? You have not looked at it properly.'

'I don't need to. I can see at a glance that it doesn't bear my mark. Here,' he explained, taking a large key from a hook and pointing to a crude pattern stamped into it. 'All my work bears my signature.'

'Forget this particular key,' said Gervase, wishing that the man would stop twitching. 'I borrowed it from the porter at the abbey. What I want to know is whether or not you made a duplicate of it.'

'Why didn't you say so?'

'Take it, man,' ordered Ralph irritably. 'And be quick about it.'

Giving him a hurt look, Palli accepted the key, weighed it in his hand then subjected it to thorough scrutiny. He ran a finger gently over it as if stroking a cat. Ralph's irritation grew.

'Well?' he demanded.

'I may have done,' said the other uncertainly, 'but I couldn't be certain. So many keys pass through my hands, my lord.'

'But surely not as large as this one,' argued Gervase. 'Apart from the abbey, only the castle and the churches would have something this size.'

'I know. I make keys for both.'

'So you are used to this kind of work.'

'It is my trade, sir.'

'There is another locksmith in Gloucester. If someone wanted a duplicate of that key, where would they go? To him or to you?'

'To me, if they had any sense. He is a poor workman.'

'Stop boasting about yourself,' ordered Ralph. 'It's very important that we know if a duplicate was made. Now, have you seen this key before or one identical to it?'

'I've seen a number like it, my lord,' said Palli, turning it over in his hand. 'Whether they were identical is another matter. I've certainly made no duplicate in recent months.'

'This would not have been a recent commission,' said Gervase.

'Oh.'

'We can't give an exact date but it might be up to two years ago.'

'Two years!'

'Think back.'

'You're asking a lot there,' said Palli, fidgeting with the key before handing it back. 'Two years! Several keys have passed through my hands in two years.'

'This one will pass through your innards if you don't try harder,' warned Ralph. 'Cudgel your brain, man. A key from the abbey. Two years ago. A duplicate is wanted. That sort of thing doesn't happen every day.'

'No, my lord,' conceded the man. 'You have jogged my memory. It's not often that a monk walks into my shop. Especially one who pays me so well. Yes,' he said, groping in his mind for detail. 'I'd have thought it was only a year ago but it could

well be two, even more. And he did ask for a duplicate to b
made. Quickly, for he could not leave the key with me for an
length of time. The one I sold him must still be at the abbe
You'll know it by my mark.'

'You'll know me by *my* mark, if you're not careful!' warne
Ralph.

'This monk you mention,' said Gervase. 'Can you describ
him?'

'They all look the same to me.'

'But he was definitely from the abbey?'

'Oh yes. He left the key with me first thing in the morning an
came back after nightfall. My wife and I had gone to bed. Sh
was not best pleased when he came knocking on our door.'

'You said that he paid you well.'

'More than I asked.'

'Why was that?'

'Because he was so delighted with my work,' said Palli. 'H
had this satchel over his shoulder and he took the money out o
that. I could hear the coins jingling. That satchel sounded as if i
was full.'

Ralph and Gervase had the identification they needed. Brother
Nicholas had bought the duplicate key himself. The one which he
had given to Palli had been borrowed from Abbot Serlo. It was
not needed by the rent collector again. Gervase thanked the
locksmith and they went out. Ralph's annoyance gave way to a
surge of excitement.

'I knew it, Gervase! We're on the right track.'

'It's going to be a long and winding one.'

'No matter. We'll follow it.'

'Where next?'

'To the odious Nigel the Reeve,' said Ralph. 'Our work at the
shire hall is suspended indefinitely. He'll need to inform everyone
of that. And while we're at it, we can ask him how he knew that
King William was due in the city last night.'

'There is someone else to whom I'd like to put that question.'
'Who's that?'
'The Archdeacon of Gwent.'

'No, Madog. Put it from your mind at once. I will not listen to such talk.'

'The others have listened,' said Madog, indicating his men. 'And they agree with me. It's too good a chance to miss.'

'This is madness.'

'It's revenge.'

'You would have no hope of success.'

'Let us worry about that.'

'I forbid you even to discuss it.'

'You are too late. It's settled.'

'Does my opinion count for nothing?'

Madog looked shifty and declined to answer.

Abraham the Priest had found them in the same copse. They were bored with the encampment, weary with the long wait and desperate for action to relieve the tedium. The news he brought from Gloucester would not be welcome.

'There has been a further delay,' he told them.

'Again!' said Madog over the general murmurs of complaint.

'I fear so.'

'But why? We all hoped that we would have ridden back to Wales by now with a piece of our territory restored to us. What is wrong with these commissioners? Can they not make a simple decision between the four of you?'

'This dispute is far from simple, Madog.'

'Is that why it is being dragged out?'

'I have no idea,' admitted Abraham. 'All I can tell is what Nigel the Reeve told me. Judgement is suspended. I must wait to be called.'

'How long?'

'As long as it takes.'

'This is villainy on their part, Archdeacon. They mean to keep you until you tire of waiting and ride away, thus forfeiting your right to be heard. Demand a speedier resolution.'

'It is the same for the others as for me, Madog. They, too, must sit on their hands while the commissioners are otherwise engaged.'

'I care not for them. Yours is the only claim that matters.'

'God willing!'

'Make them see that.'

'I have put our case as eloquently as I could,' said Abraham with quiet dignity. 'They recognised its strength. I could see it in their eyes. But they will not make a judgement until they are ready. I will stay in Gloucester with Tomos until we are called again but there is no need for you to tarry,' he said, raising his voice for all to hear. 'I was grateful for your company on the ride here but we can make our own way back. Go home, friends. Your wives and children miss you. Why spend another night under the stars when you could be back in Wales?'

'We'll stay,' said Madog firmly.

'But we have no need of an escort.'

'We rode with you to make sure that you were not ambushed on the way and because we have a vested interest in the land you are trying to restore to us. That in itself is reason enough to linger.'

'It might take days.'

'What I have in mind would take only a second. And that's the real reason we won't go from here. We have business in Gloucester.'

'No, Madog. Keep away from there.'

'It was you who told us where King William was.'

'I begin to wish that I hadn't.'

'Then why did you confirm it by watching him arrive?' said Madog with a knowing smile. 'I see your position, Archdeacon. As a priest, you can never condone violence; as a Welshman, you long for his death as fervently as the rest of us.'

'That's untrue!' denied Abraham over the shouts of approval. 'I would not condone this under any circumstances, Madog. It is sinful. It is criminal. And what is more, it is doomed to failure.'

'Not if it is carefully planned.'

'You would never be allowed near the King. He is protected by an entire garrison. What can a handful of men do against them? You are up against impossible odds, Madog.'

'That's why you must help us.'

'Never!'

'It's your duty. Think what this monster has done to our country. That land in the Westbury Hundred is only a fraction of the territory which has been stolen from us and occupied by foreigners. Why fight in the shire hall for a few hides of land when you can help to reclaim the whole of Wales?' A cheer went up from the men. 'It's no coincidence that we are here at the same time as the King. It is destiny.'

'Then it is one I reject,' said Abraham firmly.

Madog tapped his chest. 'One man is all that it will take.'

'Go home. Forget this nonsense.'

'One man, Archdeacon. Inside the castle at night. All I need to know is where the King will be sleeping.' He saw the question which formed in the other's eyes. 'How can you find out? It is easy. The commissioners lodge at the castle. They will know which apartment the King occupies. Talk to them. Then find a means to look inside the castle in order to make a plan of it. Send the information to me.'

'It would be pointless.'

'Let me worry about that.'

'The King is guarded day and night.'

'Find out where he sleeps.'

'No, Madog,' said Abraham staunchly. 'I will not do this.'

The others converged on him to form a menacing circle.

'Do you have any choice?' said Madog.

* * *

Strang the Dane was in as fiery a mood as ever at the shire hall. With Balki at his side, he directed his anger at Nigel the Reeve.

'A delay?' said Strang. 'A further delay?'

'How many times must I tell you?' asked Nigel.

'I want a resolution today.'

'We all do, Strang. I want the commissioners out of my city so that I can get on with running it properly. They have caused far too much commotion here and I want them on their way.'

'Then order them to do their appointed duty.'

'I wish that I could.'

'Make them, Nigel. Force them to come back here.'

'They do not recognise my authority,' said the reeve frostily.

'Then petition the sheriff. Let him call them to account.'

'Royal commissioners answer solely to the King, I fear. They will only sit in session when they are good and ready, Strang. It is annoying, I know, but there's no remedy. You must wait.'

'But I can't. I have a shipment of iron ore leaving soon.'

'That is irrelevant.'

'Not to me,' said Strang hotly, 'so don't be high and mighty with me. This is my livelihood. I must be aboard that boat.'

'Then leave Balki to deal with the commissioners.'

'I want to see justice done with my own eyes. Besides, I will need Balki to sail with me. We cannot cool our heels here because the royal commissioners are too lazy to do their job.'

Nigel tried to silence him but the reeve's supercilious tone only enraged the Dane further. He was yelling at the top of his voice when one of his rivals rode up on his horse. Hamelin of Lisieux was mildly amused.

'Oh!' he said. 'It is Strang the Dane. I mistook you for a fishwife, haggling over her prices. Good day, Nigel.'

'Good day, my lord,' returned the other politely.

'Have you heard the news?' growled Strang.

'Heard it and accepted it,' said Hamelin. 'The law is a snail, my friend. It crawls very slowly. I would have preferred this business to have been resolved by now but the snail has a little distance to go it seems.'

'I'd like to crush its shell under my foot.'

'Be patient.'

'How can I be? I must leave Gloucester very soon.'

'Take my advice and depart right now,' said Hamelin easily, 'for you will avoid humiliation that way. My claim obliterates all others. You are wasting your time by challenging it.'

'We do not think so, my lord,' said Balki.

'Your opinion has no validity.'

'Yes, it does. As the commissioners will show.'

'If and when we ever see them again!' grumbled Strang. 'There's no sense in staying here. You know where to find me, Nigel. Make it soon.'

With his reeve in attendance, Strang stalked off down the street.

'A pleasant fellow!' said Hamelin.

'I am glad to see the back of him, my lord.'

'Did you tell him the cause of the delay?'

'Of course not,' said Nigel. 'It would only have fed his anger the more to learn that the commissioners had put his concerns aside to turn their attention elsewhere. Besides, I only confide in friends, my lord.'

'I am glad that I am one of them.'

'The best.'

'Thank you. How did the others receive the news?'

'Neither was pleased but none were as malevolent as Strang. I wish they could all have accepted the delay with the good grace you showed.'

'Unlike them, I am in no hurry.'

Nigel grinned. 'Unlike them, you foresee the verdict.'

'There is that,' said Hamelin casually. 'What word from the castle? The King arrived last night, I hear. Do we know to what purpose?'

'Not yet, my lord.'

'Let me know what you learn.'

'Instantly.'

'And what about these public-spirited commissioners? Are they really looking for a missing boy instead of sitting in judgement here? What is wrong with Abbot Serlo?' he said artlessly. 'He used to have such a strong grip. Not any more. First he loses a monk. Now a novice. If he is not careful, the whole abbey will float away from him.'

After returning the borrowed key to the porter, Ralph and Gervase hoped to speak to the abbot but the latter was otherwise engaged. Canon Hubert explained to them why Serlo could not be disturbed.

'He is in the chapter-house,' he said sonorously. 'Chapter is normally the time when the temporal business of the abbey is discussed but, for obvious reasons, that has been postponed. Abbot Serlo is addressing the monks about the worrying disappearance of Owen.'

'We have some news for him on that score,' said Gervase. 'Ralph and I visited a locksmith in the city. He recalls making a duplicate key for a man who sounds very much like Brother Nicholas.'

'But you never met Brother Nicholas.'

'I did,' said Ralph. 'Unfortunately, he was lying naked on a slab in the mortuary so his conversation was limited. But we're certain it was him. He paid the locksmith out of a satchel filled with the rent he'd collected. And this happened at precisely the time when he had the abbot's key in his possession.'

'So far, our guesswork is accurate,' said Gervase.

'That will reassure Abbot Serlo greatly,' said Hubert, 'and I fear that he is in need of reassurance. In a private moment with me, he confessed how this latest crime had wounded him to the heart. It was lucky that I was there to offer succour.'

'Yes,' teased Ralph, 'it must have been very comforting for him to know that he had the leader of the murder investigation at his side.'

'A misunderstanding, my lord.'

'I wonder how it arose?'

'Not from anything I said, I assure you.'

They were standing near the abbey gatehouse in bright sunshine but they were far too preoccupied either to note or enjoy the fine weather. The fate of an innocent young boy was at the forefront of their minds. Ralph did not pursue the taunting of his adipose colleague.

'There's something else you may tell the abbot,' he said seriously. 'We believe that the lad may still be in the city.'

'What makes you think that?' asked Hubert.

'We spoke to the sentries at the gates. Nobody left Gloucester during the night. Owen must have been kept here. If his captor tries to smuggle him out, he will not find it easy. Eyes are peeled at every gate.'

'That is good to hear, my lord.'

'I have deployed my own men in a thorough search for the boy. It will be a difficult task in a place this size but they will knock on as many doors as they can. Someone may have seen something in the night.'

'Could not the sheriff's officers help?'

'I prefer to work independently of Durand,' said Ralph. 'He does not take kindly to unsolicited help.'

'But it has been solicited. By the abbot and by Bishop Wulfstan.'

'Have the boy's parents been told yet?' asked Gervase.

'No,' said Hubert. 'I counselled against it.'

'Very wise. It might only inflict unnecessary suffering on them. Do they live in Gloucester itself?'

'A few miles away, Gervase.'

'Then they will not pick up any gossip in the city.'

'That would be the worst possible way to find out,' said Ralph.

'Well, we know how the kidnapper got in and out of the abbey. But where is he hiding the boy? More to the point, is Owen still alive?'

'I hope so,' sighed Gervase.

Hubert was more positive. 'I'm certain of it. When I was alone with the abbot, he confessed something he had been too frightened to put into words before. The thought has haunted him ever since the first of the novices was taken from the abbey.'

'What thought is that, Canon Hubert?'

'Abbot Serlo tried to dismiss it from his mind when Siward went. He almost persuaded himself that the boy must have run away. It was a less disturbing interpretation to put on the facts. Dena's disappearance made that notion untenable.'

'What are you talking about?' pressed Ralph.

'The abduction of Owen. The abbot knows why he was taken.'

'Does he?'

'Bishop Wulfstan agrees with him. But, then, the bishop has been campaigning against it for many years.'

'Against what?'

'The kidnapping of young boys. It is not only this abbey which has suffered. All over this county there have been strange disappearances.'

'To what end, Hubert?'

'Monetary gain.'

'The boys are *sold?*'

'I fear so, my lord. We have stumbled upon a slave trade.'

Surprised to be told that she had another visitor, Golde was even more astonished when she found Abraham the Priest waiting for her at the castle gate. He introduced himself and explained his predicament.

'I am sorry to disturb you, my lady,' he said, 'but I need to speak with your husband as a matter of great urgency.'

'He is not here, I fear.'

'I know that but I hoped you could tell me where he was.'

'Could not the reeve do that? He is answerable to my husband.'

'Nigel the Reeve has been less than helpful. All he would say was that the commissioners had suspended their deliberations. No reason was given. We were simply informed of the decision.'

'Then my advice would be to accept it,' said Golde warily. 'My husband will not thank you for badgering him about your claim. The place to do that is in the shire hall.'

'This is nothing to do with my claim,' he said with passion. 'I must apprise him of something else. And quickly. Please tell me where he is. I have met the lord Ralph and I know that I can trust him.' He glanced towards the keep. 'I am not sure that I could say the same of the sheriff.'

Golde could hear the sincerity in his voice and knew that he would not come in search of her husband on a trifling matter. She tried to help.

'The truth is that I don't rightly know where he is,' she said.

His shoulders sagged. 'Oh, I see.'

'What I can tell you is this. My husband was summoned to the abbey in the early hours of the morning. Some crisis has blown up there, it seems. If you really must track him down, the abbey would be the best place to start.'

'Thank you, my lady. Thank you very much.'

The Archdeacon of Gwent strode off through the gate and left her wondering what had put the arrowheads of concern in his brow. She was about to turn away when horses came trotting into the bailey. Four men-at-arms were escorting a woman of such beauty that every eye was immediately turned to her. When she saw Golde, she nudged her horse across to her and flashed a brilliant smile.

'Good morning,' she said brightly. 'I am calling on the lady Maud.'

'I am just about to return to her myself.'

'Then I will accompany you, if I may. You must be a guest here.'

'Yes, my lady. My husband is one of the royal commissioners visiting Gloucester. His name is Ralph Delchard.'

'Then I know him. I met him at the shire hall when my own husband appeared there to substantiate a claim. You are fortunate. Ralph Delchard is a proper man in every sense.' She beamed regally. 'I am the lady Emma, wife to Hamelin of Lisieux. I am sure that your husband must have mentioned me.'

'Of course,' said Golde with convincing honesty.

But it was a lie which smouldered at the back of her mind.

Brother Paul was lenient. Showing a compassion they did not know he possessed, the Master of the Novices released both Elaf and Kenelm from their lessons that morning in the belief that they needed time to recover from the horrors they had witnessed. It was a welcome change of heart. When he confessed that he had left the dormitory at night once more, Kenelm expected to be flogged by Brother Paul. Instead, he was free to wander in the garden with his friend but it gave him no discernible joy. He remained distrait. Elaf was concerned about him.

'You look ill, Kenelm.'

'I feel ill.'

'Go to the Infirmary. Seek a remedy.'

'My illness cannot be cured with a herbal compound, Elaf. It's not my body that is sick. It's my mind.'

'Do those terrible thoughts still come?'

'They are worse since last night. I fear so for Owen.'

'So do I, Kenelm.'

'I feel so guilty that I laughed at him now.'

Elaf nodded. 'What I cannot understand is why he went to the cemetery in the first place. And at night.'

'It was the only time when he wouldn't be seen.'

'Doing what?'

'Can't you guess? He was going to pay his respects.'

'To Brother Nicholas?' said Elaf in wonderment. 'Why?'

Kenelm stared at him to make sure that he could trust him, then he looked around to ensure that there were no eavesdroppers. With a hand on his friend's shoulder, he led him deeper into the garden.

'Nobody must know this, Elaf.'

'You can rely on me.'

'Can I?'

'Of course.'

'Swear it.'

'I do, Kenelm!'

'I didn't even tell this to Brother Owl and the others.'

'Not even to Bishop Wulfstan?'

'Most of all to him. He frightens me. He is so saintly.'

'Bishop Wulfstan inspires me,' said Elaf. 'But what's this secret you kept from them? Was it something that happened last night?'

'No, yesterday.'

'Go on.'

'I slipped away to be alone.'

'Yes, I know, Kenelm. I looked for you everywhere.'

'I was in no mood for company,' explained the other, 'so I sought a hiding place. Over by the Infirmary. But someone followed me.'

'Owen?'

'Yes, Elaf.'

'Why?'

'He wanted to talk about Brother Nicholas. Don't ask why he chose me but he did. If I'd known it was the last time I'd ever speak to him, I'd have listened more carefully.'

'What do you mean?'

'He was saying something important.'

'About what?'

'Why he liked Brother Nicholas. Yes, I know, we hated him and so did the other novices. I think the only one of the monks who could bear to be near him was Brother Owl.'

'He puts up with anybody.' A half-smile came. 'Even us.'

'Yes, even us. He's been a friend.'

'Tell me about Owen.'

'He and Brother Nicholas were closer than we thought.'

'Is that what Owen told you?'

'Not in so many words,' said Kenelm, 'but that's what it amounted to. How and when they met, I'm not sure, but they obviously did or they couldn't have developed a bond between them. That's what it was, Elaf. A bond. Like the one between us.'

'But we spend all day together.'

'It makes no difference.'

'It does, Kenelm. We're both novices. We're the same age, we have the same interests. It's, well . . . it's sort of natural. Brother Nicholas was a monk. He was much older than Owen. What could they possibly have in common?'

'That's what I've been thinking about.'

'Did Owen say what it was?'

'He hinted at it, Elaf. What he did last night proves it. I mean, it takes bravery to go in among those gravestones in the dark. I didn't have it. I ran away. But Owen had it. And I know who he got it from.'

'Who?'

'Brother Nicholas.'

Elaf frowned. 'From this bond they had between them?'

'Yes. If I'd heard this a few days ago, I'd have sniggered as loud as anyone, but not now. What happened to both of them has made me show a little more respect. Brother Nicholas was murdered. Owen was taken away by someone. They deserve respect, Elaf.'

'I know.'

'Well, don't laugh when I tell you why Owen went to the cemetery last night. Do you promise?'

'I promise.'

'It's very simple, really.'
'Is it?'
'Owen loved him.'

Chapter Eleven

Abraham the Priest was relieved to hear that Ralph Delchard and Gervase Bret were still at the abbey but he had some difficulty in finding them. The prolonged search gave him time to question his motives for wishing to see the commissioners. Competing loyalties tugged his mind first one way and then another, causing him to stop, press on, turn to leave, resume the search and hesitate all over again. When he finally caught up with them, they were in the cemetery, gazing down at the last resting place of Brother Nicholas and looking for signs of a struggle. There were none. Only a raven's beak had disturbed the earth in the mound. The feet of many mourners had already trampled the grass around the grave so it yielded up no useful clues.

The Archdeacon of Gwent called out to them and raised a hand in greeting. Ralph was not pleased to see him. Fearing that they were about to be petitioned by the newcomer about his claim to land in the Westbury Hundred, he was uncompromisingly firm.

'Good day to you,' he said briskly. 'You must excuse us.'

'But I have to speak to you, my lord.'

'Another time.'

'This will not wait.'

Ralph was blunt. 'It will have to, Archdeacon. The shire hall is the only place where we consider any dispute so you must save your breath until we return there. May I say, however, that this attempt to gain our ear in private does not become you? It will hardly advance your claim.'

'I did not come to talk about the dispute, my lord.'

'No matter. Whatever subject you wish to discuss, we are deaf to it. Our minds are engaged elsewhere. Stand aside, I pray, for we are on urgent business that must not be delayed.'

'Nothing is more urgent than my business, my lord.'

'More urgent than the murder of a monk and the abduction of a novice? Really, Archdeacon. Let us keep a sense of proportion here.'

Abraham was shaken. 'The abduction of a novice? When?'

'Last night. From this very cemetery.'

'But how? The abbey is surely locked.'

'That mystery at least is solved,' said Gervase, adopting a more friendly tone. 'A duplicate key was obtained. Someone was able to let themselves in and out of here at will.'

He gave a concise account of what had happened, observing, as he did so, how anxious and uncomfortable the archdeacon was. The poise and dignity he had shown in the shire hall were nowhere to be seen. The impulse which brought the Welshman after them seemed to involve a degree of soul-searching. His face was drawn, his eyes had a haunted look. Gervase's tale only served to deepen his anguish. Putting aside his own tidings, he pressed for more details about the missing boy. Ralph shifted his feet impatiently but Gervase answered every question, sensing that Abraham had a special interest in the subject.

'Unhappily, I may be able to help you,' he said.

'Where's the unhappiness in that?' protested Ralph. 'Help of any kind will be happily received. If you have none to give, move out of our way while we continue our investigations.'

'Forgive me, my lord. My comment was poorly phrased. What I meant was that I know why Owen was taken and where he is destined to go. It is that which causes my unhappiness, the fear that the boy will suffer the same fate as the others.'

'Others?'

'Siward and Dena?' suggested Gervase. 'The earlier novices.'

Abraham shook his head. 'I know nothing of any other novices, Master Bret. I was talking about young boys who vanished from the Welsh commotes. Over the years, there have been far too many cases for them to be explained away as unfortunate accidents. Grieving parents have come to me for help and comfort too often. It is horrifying. I have preached many sermons against it.'

'Against what?' said Ralph.

'The slave trade.'

'Abbot Serlo touched on that,' recalled Gervase. 'He confided to Canon Hubert that the disappearances from the abbey could be in some way connected with it.'

'I am certain of it,' said Abraham sadly, 'because I have set myself to stamp out this hideous trade. It is barbaric. I have written both to Archbishop Lanfranc and to Bishop Wulfstan because I know that they, too, are waging a war against these vile men.'

'How does this trade operate?'

'Cunningly, Master Bret.'

'But where are the boys taken?'

'To Bristol. They are then shipped to Ireland where they are sold for high prices. It is blood money. I have raised the alarm in the Welsh commotes and everyone has been on their guard. No abductions have been reported for some time. I began to hope that the trade was dying out but I am clearly wrong. They are looking elsewhere for their victims,' he said incredulously. 'Even inside the Abbey of St Peter!'

'What you have told us is very useful,' conceded Ralph. 'How would the boys be taken to Bristol? Overland?'

'No, my lord. That would be too risky even at night. I believe that they are hidden aboard boats which sail downriver to Bristol. They are then transferred to a larger vessel which heads for Ireland.'

'Has no effort been made to reclaim them?'

'None that has met with any success. We have no friends across the water. The Irish Vikings would never admit that they had bought slaves from here, still less hand them tamely back on request. I know of one distraught father from Archenfield who took to a ship himself to search for his two lost sons in Ireland.

'What happened to him?'

'He never returned.'

'Is no check put on this trade at Bristol?'

'Yes, my lord,' said Abraham, 'but the slave traders are devious men. Whether by bribes or by guile, they'll find a way to smuggle their cargo out somehow. That is why we must stop it at source by catching the perpetrators of this outrage.'

The Archdeacon of Gwent had regained much of his eloquence and controlled passion. As he described the extent of the trade and his persistent efforts to eradicate it, Ralph gained a new respect for him. What he was hearing were vital new facts which pointed them in the direction they had to take next. Irritated by the Welshman's arrival at first, he was now profoundly grateful for it.

'We think the boy may still be in Gloucester,' he said.

'I doubt that, my lord.'

'But I've alerted the sentries at the gates. They have instructions to stop and question everyone leaving the city. There is no way that Owen can be taken out by the man who abducted him.'

Abraham gave a melancholy smile. 'If only that were true.'

The coracle looked far too small and flimsy to brave the treacherous waters of the River Severn. As it bobbed and spun, it described crazy patterns and seemed to be on the verge of sinking at any moment. But it was handled by an expert, seasoned by a lifetime as a fisherman and able to manoeuvre the craft in the most daunting conditions. Where others might have been alarmed by the sudden lurches and random twists, he treated them as if they were the gentle rocking of a cradle.

Owen did not share his confidence. Trussed up in the bottom of the coracle, he was covered by a blanket which was in turn covered by the morning's liberal catch of fish. The boy was in terror, fearing for his life and wishing that he had never ventured out at night to pray beside the grave of his beloved Brother Nicholas. It was bad enough to be attacked, overpowered, tied up and dragged out of the safety of the abbey, but this new ordeal was unbearable. As the coracle was buffeted by the current into a bewildering series of circles and dips, Owen prayed that someone would remove the gag from his mouth.

He wanted to be sick.

'You must let me help,' implored Abraham the Priest. 'Please, my lord.'

'You have already been extremely helpful,' said Ralph.

'But I wish to join you in the hunt.'

'That will not be necessary.'

'Owen is not a member of your diocese,' said Gervase quietly. 'You have no responsibility for him.'

'I have a responsibility for any child who falls victim to slave traders. It is my personal crusade. In any case,' he said, looking from Gervase to Ralph, 'a missing novice hardly falls within the sphere of your responsibility. You are relative intruders here.'

Ralph was terse. 'Our assistance was sought by Abbot Serlo.'

'I am glad that it was, my lord. But I am sure that the abbot would be just as eager to seek my help if he knew of my familiarity with this particular crime. Take me with you.'

'No, Archdeacon.'

'Why not?'

'Because I say so.'

'Do not be offended,' said Gervase, trying to soothe him. 'There is no personal animus here. We admire you for what you have done in trying to put a stop to this trade but we are more accustomed to following the trails of ruthless criminals. A murder is also involved here, remember. If and when we catch up with the killer, he is not likely to surrender without a fight. We cannot risk injury to you, Archdeacon.'

'I would willingly take that risk.'

'Out of the question,' decided Ralph.

'Besides,' said Gervase with a polite smile, 'until you met us, you had no idea that this second crime had taken place. Another errand brought you here, a serious one, I suspect, judging by the way it seemed to trouble your mind.' Abraham gave a mild start. 'Would you care to tell us what the problem is?'

'Gervase, we cannot tarry,' said Ralph. 'This can wait.'

'I think not, Ralph.'

'It must. Owen's fate must be averted.'

'We can spare a few minutes. Unless I am mistaken, what we are about to hear is something of grave importance. Is that not true?' he said, turning to the archdeacon. 'Well?'

But the Welshman was caught up in a battle of loyalties once more, unable to speak yet horrified at the dire consequences of holding his tongue. Ralph became more restive. Seeing the archdeacon's obvious distress, Gervase tried to ease him out of it by speaking to him in Welsh.

'Why did you come to us?' he asked.

'Because I could not turn to the sheriff.'

'The sheriff?'

'Durand of Gloucester is not a man who inspires trust,' said Abraham, 'and he would be equally distrustful of me. If I took my warning to him, he would either refuse to believe a word I said or suspect me of being part of the plot.'

'Plot?'

'What on earth is he gabbling about, Gervase?' asked Ralph.

Gervase ignored him. 'What is this about a plot?'

'Master Bret,' began the other slowly, 'I have only come to you after a great deal of agonised thought. Please understand my position. I feel it my duty to alert you to something but there is a strict limit to the amount of information I can give.'

'In short, you need to protect someone.'

'It is you who must organise the protection.'

'Why?'

'King William is in Gloucester.'

'So?'

'He is in danger.'

'The King is always in danger. He lives under constant threat.'

'I talk of particular danger,' said Abraham, wanting to convey urgency without providing too much detail. 'Let us just say that news has come to my ears of an attempt on his life.'

Gervase tensed. 'When? Where?'

'Soon, Master Bret. At the castle.'

'But he is surrounded by guards.'

'The assassin will find ways to circumvent them.'

'Assassin. We are talking about one man?'

'I believe so.'

'Who is he?'

'I have told you all I can.'

'But you obviously know who he is.'

'Master Bret, I told you. There is a strict limit.'

'In other words, though you wish this assassination attempt to be thwarted, you will not reveal the assassin's name.'

'Questions of loyalty are entailed.'

'That means he's a fellow countryman.'

'Warn the King. Insist that he takes additional precautions.'

Ralph was about to burst. 'Will the pair of you stop jabbering away in that heathen tongue and tell me what on earth is going on!'

Gervase translated the gist of the archdeacon's remarks. The effect on Ralph was immediate. He reached out to grab the Welshman's arm.

'This is some ruse,' he accused. 'You are trying to deceive us.'

'No, my lord,' said Abraham, gently detaching his arm. 'I am bound to say that your manner disappoints me. I looked for understanding and you behave exactly as the sheriff would behave.'

'Durand would have you tortured until he got at the truth.'

'I have told you the truth. A plot is being devised.'

'Then tell us the details.'

'I don't know them, my lord. I swear.'

'But you are certain of its existence.'

'I am. It pains me to admit this.'

'Why did you bring this information?'

'Because I will not stand by when murder is planned. Even if it is the murder of a foreign king who has inflicted so much untold misery on my country. If steps are taken, this assassination can be prevented.'

'It will be in any case,' promised Ralph, 'as so many other attempts have been prevented before. What can one man do against a whole garrison? Only a mad Welshman would conceive such a wild scheme.' He fixed Abraham with a stare. 'What is his name?'

'Do not ask me, my lord.'

'We need to know.'

'Why? It will mean nothing to you.'

'Even contemplating the assassination of the King is a serious offence. The man must be apprehended at once. You spoke earlier about eliminating the slave trade at source by arresting those involved in it. Give us a name and we can stop this crime at source as well.' Abraham shook his head. 'You are withholding evidence from us.'

'I think that the archdeacon has shown bravery in coming to us in the first place,' said Gervase, taking a softer approach. 'He has faith in us, Ralph, and we must show a like faith in him. We must pass on the message to the castle. There is no need to say where it came from.'

'Then what *are* we to say, Gervase?'

'A warning came to us from an anonymous informer.' He looked at their companion. 'A warning which was only given after an immense amount of thought and recrimination.'

'I have been in torment,' confessed Abraham. 'There is no way out of this dilemma. Whatever I do will tax my conscience hereafter. If I remain silent and the assassination takes place, I could never forgive myself. But in revealing the very existence of the plot, I have to betray someone I hold dear and who may pay for my betrayal with his life.'

'No doubt of that!' said Ralph.

'Alert the King.'

'What will you do?' wondered Gervase.

'Pray that this whole business ends without bloodshed.'

'Not if I have anything to do with it,' said Ralph.

'Our task is to search for Owen,' said Gervase.

'Take me with you,' pleaded the archdeacon.

'If we do, it will only be to hand you over to the sheriff.' Ralph swiftly repented. 'No, that will serve nothing. Gervase is right. If they double the guard there is no way that any assassin would be able to get near the King. But there is another question you must answer and I'll take no more prevarication. I believe that you were first engaged in this plot then lost your nerve to see it through.'

Abraham was vehement. 'No, my lord!'

'You sought to help this assassin.'

'I resisted him. I'm a man of peace.'

'Then why were you lurking outside the castle on the night the King arrived?' Abraham swallowed hard. 'Do not deny it. I saw you with my own eyes. If you were not spying on behalf of your friend, what were you doing, Archdeacon?'

'I was curious.'

'Curious to see how large an escort he had? Curious to study the castle's fortifications? Curious to find out every detail which might be of value to an assassin?'

'My lord!' protested the other.

'How did you even know that the King was coming here?'

'By complete chance. I witnessed the sudden activity around the castle. It was clearly being victualled for important visitors.'

'They did not have to include King William.'

'I spoke to one of the butchers who delivered carcasses of beef to the castle. He overheard the guards talking about a royal visit. That confirmed what I expected.'

'So you hastened to pass on this intelligence to your friend?' He saw the flash of guilt in the other's eyes. 'Now, we have it. The whole plot stems from your information. But for you, this so-called friend would have been totally unaware of the King's presence here. True or untrue?'

'Horribly true.'

'You set this business in motion.'

'Inadvertently.'

'There is nothing inadvertent about an assassination!'

'I have rebuked myself ever since.'

'Not as sharply as you deserve to be rebuked.'

Gervase sought once more to cool the proceedings before Ralph worked himself up into a real temper. He was also anxious to resume their search for the missing boy, and that could not be done while they were distracted by a reported assassination attempt.

'Go on ahead of me, Ralph,' he advised. 'We have heard enough to be convinced that the danger might be real. Raise the alarm at the castle so that further measures may be taken to safeguard the King. I will be hot on your heels, I promise you.'

'Why not come with me?'

'Because I need to speak to Abraham on his own.'

'If it is in that incomprehensible language, I am off. The sound fills me with dread.' He glared at Abraham. 'As for King William inflicting untold misery on your country, Wales got ample revenge. They sent the Archdeacon of St David's to inflict even greater misery on *us*!'

'Archdeacon Idwal?' said the other in surprise. 'You know him?'

'To our cost!'

'Idwal is a remarkable man.'

'Yes,' said Ralph. 'Remarkably unlovable. If ever there was a worthy candidate for the assassin's dagger, it is Idwal of St

David's!' He turned on his heel and marched away. 'Be quick about it, Gervase!'

'Is that where the lord Ralph's prejudice against the Welsh comes from?' asked Abraham. 'An unfortunate encounter with Idwal?'

'Two unfortunate encounters.'

'I have always found him so friendly.'

'Leave him aside,' said Gervase. 'This matter must be resolved. As for the lord Ralph's attitude towards the Welsh, I have to point out that it has hardly been softened by the news you bring us of a Welsh plot against the King.'

'It does not really deserve the name of a plot, Master Bret.'

'Then what is it?'

'A wild notion of hot-headed patriots.'

'Patriots? So more than one person is involved?'

'Yes and no.'

'How many others?'

'That is irrelevant.'

'Not to me, Archdeacon. I'm glad you didn't mention this to the lord Ralph or he would certainly have taken you with him to the castle. And not with overmuch ceremony, I fear. Tell me all,' he urged, 'for I can see that you are no assassin. You're a devout Christian who abhors murder as the evil it is. That is why you rebelled against the idea. But you could only rebel against something you knew about and that makes you an accessory of sorts.' He watched the Welshman carefully. 'You told one or more friends about the King's visit here. Were you asked to provide any additional information to them?'

Abraham lowered his head. 'Yes, Master Bret.'

'But your conscience refused to let you do it. I see how it was. You unwittingly provided the spark which lit a fire and it flared up out of your control. But you refuse to gather more fuel for that fire. Is that it?'

'You are very perceptive.'

'May I counsel you, Archdeacon?'

'Please do.'

'The lord Ralph is right. It must be stopped at source and you are in the ideal position to do that. Go to this friend or friends. Be completely open. Admit that you have alerted the castle to the danger. And impress upon this *lone* assassin,' said Gervase with emphasis, 'that a garrison of armed soldiers is now lying in wait for him. Force him to abandon what is a futile bid. That way, you will save *his* life for he will surely sacrifice it if he tries to get near the King. Do you agree?'

'I'll leave Gloucester immediately.'

'In which direction?'

Abraham was enigmatic. 'That is for me to know. You and the lord Ralph are on one mission of mercy. I depart on another.'

Golde could not decide why she disliked her so much. The lady Emma was a lively and intelligent woman, unfailingly courteous to her hostess at the castle and unceasingly polite to Golde herself. There was no hint of condescension in the visitor's manner. She was relaxed and friendly.

'I should not have called upon you at such a time,' she apologised. 'Had I know whom you were entertaining, my lady, I would not have dreamed of trespassing upon you.'

'Nonsense!' said Maud. 'You are doubly welcome. It is true that the King's visit has placed an extra burden on us but it does not really fall on me. How could it when I am scarcely allowed near him? Durand excludes me completely from matters of state.'

'Is that why King William is here?'

'So I understand.'

'Has your husband given you no clearer indication?'

'None,' said Maud sourly. 'Since the visitors arrived last night, I have hardly seen my husband. He expects me to know my place. At the altar I swore to obey him, and that is what I will always do, but I will not pretend that I enjoy being kept on the outer fringes of his world. Is it so with the lord Hamelin?'

'Far from it, my lady. He discusses everything with me.'

'It is the same with Golde and the lord Ralph,' said Maud, trying to bring her other guest into the conversation. 'They do not keep secrets from each other. Well, most of the time, that is.'

Golde was reluctant to be drawn into a defence of Ralph at a point when she was feeling a distant sense of betrayal. When she studied the lady Emma's lovely features and gorgeous attire, she was honest enough to admit to herself that she was faintly jealous of her, but that was not the only reason why she wished to detach herself. Evidently, the others were well acquainted with each other, having a fund of news to exchange and endless reminiscences to share. Golde was in the way. When she made her excuse and quit the room, she knew that they would have a much more enjoyable time without her.

Desiring some fresh air, she elected to go for a walk around the perimeter of the bailey so that she could reflect on the true cause of her resentment of the lady Emma. No sooner had she descended the steps from the keep, however, than she saw Ralph hurrying towards her.

'Ah, there you are, my love!' he said, arriving to give her a peck on the cheek. 'I was looking for you.'

'Why?'

'To explain why I had to hop out of your bed with such indecent haste this morning. Hubert brought worrying news from the abbey. One of the novices has been abducted.'

'Oh,' she replied. 'It grieves me to hear that. I can see that Canon Hubert would be upset about it, but why did he need to involve you and Gervase? Surely, this is a problem for the abbey.'

'It spills out far beyond that, Golde. I have no time to recount all the details. Suffice it to say that the abduction is linked to the murder. The man who seized that boy last night is, in all probability, the same person who killed Brother Nicholas. We have picked up his trial. I had to come back here on other business,'

TRAIL

he said, 'so I thought I would tell you what is going on. Gervase and I may be away for some time.'

'What of your duties in the shire hall?'

'They must wait.'

'I see,' said Golde levelly, noting his eagerness to get away. 'In that case, I'll not hold you up. Thank you for warning me. I appreciate it.'

He peered at her. 'What is wrong?'

'Nothing, Ralph.'

'Then why this strange coldness?'

'Am I being cold?' she said, contriving a warm smile. 'I am sorry. It was not intentional. Be on your way. Gervase will be waiting.'

'Then he can wait,' said Ralph, taking a step towards her. 'You're upset with me again, Golde. I can tell. Are you still harbouring a grudge because I forgot to mention the King's arrival?'

'You didn't forget, Ralph. You chose not to remember.'

'It amounts to the same thing.'

'No, it doesn't. Deliberation was involved.'

'Ah, so that's my crime. Deliberate deception.'

'This has nothing to do with the King's visit,' she said. 'Well, only indirectly. But my concerns are paltry beside yours. A boy's life is in danger. Go in search of him at once.'

'Not until you tell me why you are so fretful.'

'Fretful?'

'Yes,' he said. 'You accuse me of holding things back from you but now you are the one guilty of deception. What is going on?'

'The lady Maud has a visitor.'

'Is that what has put your nose out of joint?'

'Lady Emma. The wife of Hamelin of Lisieux.' She watched his reaction. 'Yes, Ralph. You met her at the shire hall. She told me how much you impressed her. The lady Emma was sure that you would have mentioned her name to me.'

He winced. 'But I didn't.'

'May I know the reason?'

'Because she was not germane to our inquiry,' he argued weakly. The lord Hamelin brought her along to support him and distract us. Naturally, we spotted his device at once. To a man, we ignored the lady Emma completely.'

'Ralph!' she said with amused cynicism. 'I might accept that Canon Hubert ignored her and I'm sure that Brother Simon hid under the table, but you could never ignore a woman as beautiful as that. Undyingly faithful as he is to Alys, I daresay that even Gervase raised an eyebrow.'

The sheepish grin. 'The lady Emma does seize the attention.'

'Why not admit that at the start? I'm not complaining out of envy, though any woman would suffer that when confronted with her. Once again, you put me in an invidious position. The lady Emma told me something I should first have heard from you.'

'I accept that.'

'How many more times will this happen?'

'Never, my love.'

'You said that when we fell out earlier. Then this second lapse occurs. It made me feel so foolish. That's why I could not stay in the lady Maud's apartment with them,' she said. 'The lady Emma was asking about the King's reason for being here and the lady Maud was lamenting the fact that she had no idea what it was. When it became a discussion of what husbands tell their wives, I had to get out of there.'

'I can understand that.'

'If you had had the sense to tell me about your meeting with the lady Emma, none of this would have happened.'

'Exactly. I am duly shamed, Golde, and just wish we did not have to have this dispute at the one time when it cannot properly be resolved. But, as you see, I really have to go. However, with regard to the lady Emma, I will say one thing.'

'What's that?'

'No man could lead her astray. She dotes on her husband.'

'Is that so?'

'Yes,' he said with a grin. 'Almost as much as I dote on m⟨⟩ wife.'

It was Golde who kissed him this time.

Having parted on more amicable terms, Ralph hurried back ⟨⟩ the gatehouse. Gervase was waiting for him but so, he now sa⟨⟩ was Nigel the Reeve. The two were engaged in a mild argumen⟨⟩ Ralph swept up to bring it to a summary conclusion.

'What are you doing here?' he demanded of the reeve.

'Hoping to see you, my lord.'

'I cannot stay to be seen. Urgent business calls.'

'That is exactly what I was discussing with Master Bret,' sai⟨⟩ the other. 'This urgent business. I know what it is but, at you⟨⟩ direction, I have not mentioned it to the four claimants in th⟨⟩ dispute which you have been trying to resolve. But they ar⟨⟩ hounding me, my lord. They demand to know why there's been ⟨⟩ delay and how long it will last.'

'We do not know how long.'

'Can I at least explain the reason for your decision?'

'I am sure you've already done so to one of them,' said Ralph. eyeing him darkly. 'The well-informed Hamelin of Lisieux gets to hear everything from his lackey. As for the others, they could not all have been barking at your heels. We have just spoken to Abraham the Priest and he didn't even raise the subject of the shire hall.'

'He is not the problem, my lord,' admitted Nigel. 'Strang the Dane is the worst offender here. He and his creeping reeve have been trailing me relentlessly. They have commitments out of the city and cannot stay long. Yet they fear to go lest you sit in session during their absence and omit them from your considerations.' He sounded reasonable for once. 'Querengar has shown restraint but even he is pressing me. It's only fair to tell them something.'

'I agree,' said Gervase. 'Since the lord Hamelin knows, why

nceal it from the others? They must recognise the seriousness
' the crime.'

Mulling it over, Ralph put his foot in the stirrup of his horse
id hauled himself into the saddle. He kept Nigel the Reeve
aiting for his decision. When it came, it was abrupt.

'Tell them,' he said at length. 'Warn them that it might be days
efore we are able to reconvene. Tell them all. Beginning, of
ourse, with the lord Hamelin or he will be vexed with you.'

nxiety continued to peck away hard at Abraham the Priest. It
as no consolation to him that he had done what he believed was
he right thing. In obeying the impulse to reveal the existence of
n assassination plot, he had salved his conscience to some degree,
ut left it vulnerable to further attack. Riding alone out of the city,
e wondered if he should have invited Tomos to go with him so
hat he could take soundings from his companion. On reflection,
e was grateful that he had not, convinced that the young monk
night not approve of his actions and not wanting to forfeit the
nquestioning faith which the latter placed in him. There was also
nother side to his gratitude. In leaving Tomos in ignorance, he
vas sparing him any unpleasant repercussions. Abraham had to
confront Madog and his men on his own and take all their anger
upon him.

Brad. It was a short word in Welsh but it had a long meaning
for the archdeacon. Treason. Betrayal. Reneging on a bargain.
Violating a trust. Turning away from his country. Committing a
shameful act. Disloyalty. Treachery. Was that really a fair description of his behaviour? He had betrayed his friends, it was true, but
only because they were bent on a course of action he could never
support. It was they who planned to commit treason, and only his
treachery could stop them. And was it really treachery to deflect
Madog and the others from a course of action which was almost
certainly suicidal? Nothing could be achieved by the pointless
waste of lives on an ill-conceived venture.

Abraham told himself that he had not betrayed his count
Having proudly assisted at the birth of a baby boy, he had n
helped to keep several adults in the breathing world. That was
achievement which was worth the obloquy he would earn.
time, the child would grow up to hear how the Archdeacon
Gwent himself had delivered him into his Welsh heritage. Abraha
could only hope that Madog and his men would, in time, wei
commonsense against disappointment and realise that the arc
deacon had been their salvation. Such a resolution was a long w
off, he knew that. There would be much pain and recriminatic
before then, much abuse to withstand.

It could be lessened. If he told them a lie, Abraham cou
deflect the blame from himself and let them expend their rag
impotently on the King himself. He could tell them that Willia
had left Gloucester for an unknown destination. None the wise
Madog would lead his men back home to Wales. It was a
attractive idea but it was almost instantly dismissed. His frienc
might not know the truth but he would and it could not be he
back from them. Besides, he was their spiritual leader. They looke
to him as a Christian exemplar. He had acted in the way that Go
would want him to act. There was no need to apologise to them c
even to justify his actions. God had spoken through him.

Buoyed up by that thought, he nudged his horse into a cante
until the copse at last came in view. It was an ideal refuge, larg
enough to conceal them yet too small and isolated to be part o
the forest and thus subject to the savagery of forest law. No
verderers and foresters would patrol this outcrop of trees. They
were safe from scrutiny and could plot a hundred assassination
beneath the green leaves without being disturbed. But the arch
deacon would disturb them now. Instead of bringing them the
information they demanded, he would be announcing the demise
of their plan.

When he reached the copse, he slowed his horse to a trot and
picked his way through the trees, gritting his teeth and trying to

shake off vestigial doubts. These were his friends and countrymen. He had no cause to be afraid of them. Abraham came into the clearing with a welcome on his lips but it was stillborn. Madog and his men were not there and there was no sign that they ever had been. The words which he had been turning over in his mind remained unspoken. He had no idea where they could be. The Archdeacon of Gwent was all too aware of the implications. They were acting on their own now.

Whatever they decided, he was utterly powerless to stop them.

Ralph Delchard checked first with his men to see if their search had turned up anything of interest but there was nothing to report. When he and Gervase Bret rode to each of the city gates, they met with the same response. Nothing suspicious had been seen. No boy had been taken out through them since they had opened that morning. Recalling what Abraham had told them, the two friends turned their attention to the quayside, wondering if the river might be used as a means of spiriting Owen away. Once again, they were out of luck. Few craft had sailed downriver and none had been seen with a boy aboard who answered to the description of Owen. Ralph turned back to regard the city.

'He's still here, Gervase.'

'The archdeacon doubted that.'

'What does he know of a manhunt? Instinct is the crucial thing and mine tells me that the lad is hidden away somewhere. If we had more men, we could turn Gloucester inside out until we found him.'

'The sheriff has men enough.'

'Can you imagine him handing them over to us?'

'No, Ralph,' said the other. 'And they are needed at the castle. Now that you have passed on the word about a possible attempt on the King's life, the whole garrison is on its toes. Durand does not strike me as the kind of man who would be moved by the plight of a novice. Protecting a King will seem far more vital to

him than hunting for a boy who was foolish enough to wande
around the abbey at night.'

'That has been worrying me.'

'What has?'

'The sheer coincidence of it. Owen leaves the dormitory an
someone just happens to be lurking in readiness for him. Why?
does not make sense.'

'It does to anyone who has been in an abbey. Young boys ar
playful. It is only natural. Until they reach maturer years, ther
will always be one or two who risk a beating to slip out at nigh
Look at Kenelm and Elaf. They had many midnight escapades.'

'I do not follow your argument.'

'The man who lay in ambush was not waiting specifically fo
Owen. He may have had no idea who would appear. What he wa
counting on was that, sooner or later, some wilful novice woul
be out on the prowl. Brother Nicholas would probably have tol
him that.'

'I am still not convinced.'

'Then you have to side with the sheriff.'

'God forbid!'

'He still believes the killer lives in the abbey itself. An insider
who knows where to skulk in order to wait for his prey to emerge
from the novices' dormitory. If he was Brother Nicholas's accomplice, he would know how devoted Owen had been to the dead
man. Devoted enough to pay a secret visit to his grave.'

'Now that begins to make sense.'

'Another monk as the murderer?'

'Someone who was privy to the close relationship between
Brother Nicholas and Owen. Monk or not, such a person would
be able to anticipate a visit to the cemetery from the boy. Yes,
Gervase,' he said as the idea got a purchase on his mind, 'we can
rule out coincidence altogether. We are looking at careful planning
here. At calculation.'

'If he is calculating enough to get a boy out of an abbey, he will rely have the skill to smuggle him out of the city. Owen could ve been hidden away in any of those carts we saw trundling rough the gates. Or perhaps he was lowered over the wall at ght by ropes. He has gone, Ralph. The archdeacon felt that and agree.'

Before Ralph could reply, two familiar figures walked towards em. Strang the Dane had an arrogant strut, Balki a loping stride. either looked happy at the accidental meeting.

'I want to register a complaint!' said Strang aggressively.

'When do you do anything else?' returned Ralph.

'You have failed in your duty, my lord.'

'I have responded to a call for help.'

'So we have been told by Nigel the Reeve,' said the Dane, 'but nly after we battered at his eardrums. He has just told us what he ould have said this morning and saved us wasted time.'

'What are you doing here?' asked Gervase.

'What do you think? Some people may neglect their work but cannot afford to do that. Since you will not need me for some days at least, I am sailing to Bristol with a cargo of iron ore. It has een expected all week.' He pointed to a boat moored at the quayside. 'There it sits.'

'That is yours?' said Ralph.

'Yes, my lord. It has been here too long as it is. One thing about iron ore, though,' he added with a grim smile, 'nobody is tempted to steal it. They would have dirty hands and aching muscles if they did.'

Ralph looked at the boat more carefully. It was a large craft with a single sail. The deck had been reinforced to take the weight of its regular cargo. When he saw how low it was in the water, he realised how large a quantity of iron ore was being carried on board. Most of it was covered by a tattered tarpaulin.

'It will need to be searched,' he announced.

'Why?' said Strang defensively.

'So that we can be sure you are only taking what you claim to

be taking. Stay here while it is searched.' He was about to st
aboard when he noticed how much the boat was moving about
the water. 'Gervase will do the office for me.' His friend gave hi
a resigned look. 'Carry on, please. We must leave no sto
unturned and no tarpaulin unlifted.'

While Gervase climbed about, Strang was vociferous in h
protest. Balki insisted on taking part in the search, pulling bac
the tarpaulin helpfully and making it clear that there was nobod
and nothing else aboard apart from the designated cargo. Annoye
by the bellows of complaint, Ralph finally silenced the Dane wi
a yell and sent him on his way, glad that he would not have t
endure the man's troublesome company for a few days. As soon a
Gervase came ashore, the two men cast off. Oars were used t
guide them out into the middle of the river then Balki hoisted th
sail and it took a first smack from the wind. Ralph watched as
glided slowly downriver.

'You would not get me into that boat.'

'So I saw,' said Gervase.

'Someone had to search it. Every boat that comes downrive
must be inspected from now on. If this is their means of transport
we will block it off completely.'

'Unless we are already too late, Ralph.'

'Late?'

'They may have got him out during the night.'

'I hope not.'

'Owen may already be sailing to damnation.'

Sheer fatigue sent him off into a deep sleep. When he finally
awoke, his stomach was still queasy but he was no longer being
tossed helplessly around in the coracle. It was a small mercy.
Trying to move, Owen realised that he was still bound hand and
foot with a gag preventing any call for help. Wet, frightened and
aching all over, he forced his eyes open to take stock of his
surroundings. He was propped against a wall in some kind of

ined building. Water could be heard gushing past nearby. It was
small room with a rotting floor and a door that had fallen off its
nges. Since birds flew in and out at will, he surmised that there
ere holes in the wall at his back.

In the far corner was a pile of old sacks, whitened by their
ntents but blackened with age. Other clues slowly met his gaze.
wen was eventually able to work out where he must be. It was an
bandoned mill. His heart sank as he saw what it must mean. He
as some distance from Gloucester. The abbey he loved so much
nd the city which surrounded it were far away. He wondered if he
ould ever see them again. Whenever he moved even slightly,
opes chafed his wrists and his ankles. His muscles seemed to be
n fire. Wanting to cry, he could not even produce tears. It was
ustrating. Owen turned his mind once more to his departed
riend. His silent plea was charged with despair.

'Help me, Brother Nicholas! Where *are* you?'

King William sat at the table with the others ranged around him.
The two leading barons who had ridden with him said little,
having already had discussions with him on the journey to
Gloucester. Durand the Sheriff was unusually quite reticent,
agreeing with all that was suggested and concealing any reserva-
ions he had about the proposed course of action. It was Bishop
Wulfstan who provided most of the questions. The one prelate at
the table was not daunted by the presence of four soldiers.

'I am not entirely persuaded, my liege,' he said respectfully.

'Why not?' said William.

'Because your army is already stretched and your resources
pushed to the limit. Retrenchment is the order of the day.'

'That's foolish talk,' said Durand.

'Is it?'

'Yes, Bishop Wulfstan. In military situations, we cannot always
stop to count the cost. If we did, we would never do anything.'

'Armies must be paid, fed, moved here and there.'

'It is an expensive business,' said William heavily. 'Nobo[d]
denies that. Least of all me. I have spent my whole life paying [o]ne
set of men to fight another. I have fought in endless battles myse[lf].
Victory is the best source of revenue. We must never forget th[at].
What we spend now, we recoup when we win the field.'

Wulfstan was uncertain. 'Are we confident of winning t[his]
time?'

'Yes!' asserted Durand.

'But you will not be bearing arms yourself, my lord sheriff.[']

'No matter. I will be there in spirit.'

'And in the person of your knights,' added William approving[ly].
'Durand will pay more than his share towards this enterprise. Th[at]
is why I held this meeting in Gloucester before holding a larg[er]
council to announce my plans. I could be sure of complete loyal[ty]
here.'

'From the Church in particular,' Wulfstan reminded him.

'But you are the only one to oppose this invasion,' said Duran[d].
'Loyalty means unconditional support, Bishop Wulfstan, n[ot]
penny-pinching moans of dissent.'

'You'll hear no moans from me, my lord sheriff. I question th[is]
decision because it is only right that someone should. Call me
devil's advocate, if you wish, though I am sure you call me wors[e]
in private. King William does not employ me to agree with ever[y]
word he says.'

William grinned. 'It is just as well!'

'My task is to make you think of every aspect of a plan.'

'And you do it admirably, Bishop Wulfstan. But,' he said as h[e]
stretched his arms, 'we have been at it long enough, I fancy. Le[t]
us break off here and meet again this evening to finalise what w[e]
have agreed. Thank you all. Progress has been made.' The others
rose to leave. 'Stay, Durand,' he said. 'I want some private
conference.'

Wulfstan and the two barons bade them farewell and left the
hall. The bishop was anxious to return to the abbey for news of

he steps taken to track down the missing boy, and his companions
wanted to exchange with each other the doubts they had been too
tactful to raise during the discussion. All three of them left the
keep.

Still in the hall, King William rose to his feet with a cup of
wine in his hand. Old age had caused him to fill out and had put
something of a waddle into his walk. He strolled across to the
window.

'What do you think, Durand?'

'About the invasion? I have already told you.'

'Forget that,' said William. 'I refer to the information we
received earlier. To be honest, I am inclined to ignore it.'

'That would be reckless.'

'A certain amount of recklessness is always necessary.'

'But there is no point in taking chances, my liege,' said Durand.
'If there is to be an assassination attempt, we must be ready to
resist it. You must comply with all the precautions I suggest.'

'Must I?' said the other wearily. 'I have been threatened with
assassination for as long as I can remember. Most of those threats
have been hollow. Those that had substance were soon snuffed
out. A lot of men have gone to their deaths because they dared to
imagine they might be able to kill me.' He ran a finger around the
rim of his wine cup. 'Who could possibly have hatched this plot?
So few people know that I am even in this part of the country. No,'
he decided, on the move again, 'I will treat it with contempt.'

'But it comes from such a reliable source, my liege.'

'That is true. Ralph Delchard would not invent such a warning.
But how did he get wind of it? That's what I wish to know.'

'So do I,' said Durand. 'I mean to press him hard on the
subject.'

'As you wish. But all that I will agree to is an extra guard
posted outside my room at night. Who could penetrate a fortress
like this? You have worked hard to strengthen it. We could repel a
thousand assassins from inside these walls, yet Ralph was talking

of a lone killer. One man is up against hopeless odds, Durand,' he said, putting his cup down on the table. 'I refuse to lose a wink sleep over this supposed threat.'

'You will not need to, my liege. I will protect you.'

William gave him a pat of thanks on the arm and they move slowly towards the door. The heavy tread of the King's feet gav ample warning. Several seconds before they left the hall, th person who had been listening outside the door was able to fl away to a hiding place.

Chapter Twelve

After leaving some of his men at the quayside to search all boats coming downriver, Ralph Delchard led the way back to the abbey at a steady trot. He and Gervase Bret believed that, in their eagerness to follow the trail of the kidnapper, they had overlooked some vital clues there.

'I'd like to speak to those novices again,' said Ralph as they rode through the crowded streets. 'Kenelm and Elaf. I'm not sure that they told us everything they knew.'

'No,' agreed Gervase. 'Kenelm in particular. I sensed that he might be holding something back. We need to get him on his own. When we questioned him before, we had Bishop Wulfstan and Brother Frewine there as well. It must have been very intimidating for him, facing the four of us like that. It drove him back into his shell.'

'I'll pull him out of it!'

'He won't be pulled, Ralph. He needs to be coaxed.'

'Coaxing takes too much time.'

They arrived at the abbey, dismounted and tethered their horses. When they went through the gate, the first people they met were Bishop Wulfstan and Hamelin of Lisieux, talking seriously together. Seeing the newcomers, they broke off their conversation.

'What news?' asked Wulfstan, shuffling across to them.

'We are making progress,' said Ralph, 'but it is slow, I fear.'

'Canon Hubert told me you had found the locksmith who made the duplicate key. A clever deduction on your part but a devastating one for Abbot Serlo to accept.'

'Yes,' said Hamelin solemnly. 'Bishop Wulfstan was just

243

relating the sad story to me. A key to the abbey. They are luc
they have only lost a few novices. If someone was able to come
and out of here at will, they could have borne off the gold a
silver plate, the holy vessels for the altar and the precious relic

Wulfstan was assertive. 'I would trade them all for the sa
return of those boys,' he said, plucking at his lambskin cloak a
dislodging some of its remaining fur. 'You cannot put a price
human life. Other items can be replaced. The abduction of thr
young boys is a far more heinous crime. That is why the kidnapp
must be run to ground.'

'He will be, Bishop Wulfstan,' said Ralph.

'In time,' added Gervase. 'But we are glad to find you her
Bishop Wulfstan. Our fear is that Owen was taken by someo
engaged in the slave trade. You have preached against that,
understand, and taken several measures to stamp it out.'

'I have, Master Bret.'

'It would help us to know what they are and to have some id
of how widespread the trade has been in this county.'

'This is private talk,' said Hamelin tactfully. 'I wish you luck
your pursuit of this villain but will not intrude. You obvious.
have much to discuss with Bishop Wulfstan.'

Hamelin of Lisieux took his leave and slipped out through th
front gate. Ralph and Gervase were surprised to find him at th
abbey. When they met him at the shire hall, he did not strike the
as a man of pious inclination. Wulfstan answered the questio
before they asked it.

'The lord Hamelin is a devout man,' he said gratefully, 'albe
somewhat late in the day. He was waiting for me when I returne
from the castle. He wishes to endow a new church in the Westbur
Hundred and wanted to discuss the procedure with me.'

'It sounds like a worthy enterprise,' said Ralph huffily, 'but
do think the lord Hamelin is being unduly hasty.'

'Hasty, my lord?'

'He is talking about building a church on land which has yet to be confirmed as his. The holdings in the Westbury Hundred are the subject of bitter dispute. Will his piety hold up if he is deprived of them?'

'He assured me that there was no question of that because his claim will certainly be upheld by you.'

'It remains to be seen,' said Gervase. 'At all events, it is heartening news for you, Bishop Wulfstan. The founding of a new church must always be an occasion of joy and it is to the lord Hamelin's credit that he is donating some of his wealth in this way.'

'Yes, Master Bret. He has acquired an unfortunate reputation in the past and is viewed by some as nothing short of a tyrant. I take him as I find him. A man with spiritual needs and philanthropic leanings.'

'That was not my estimate of him,' said Ralph.

'Oh?'

'When someone marries a woman like the lady Emma, spiritual needs obviously come second to more physical ones. But that is his business,' he said dismissively. 'Let us forget the lord Hamelin. Tell us about this trade in young boys, Bishop Wulfstan. How long has it been going on and where is it seated?'

'It has been going on far too long, my lord.'

'Years?'

'Several.'

'I understand that Archbishop Lanfranc is fighting against it.'

'He and I have exchanged many letters on the subject.'

'Have there been many victims in your diocese?'

'Alas, yes.'

'Which part?' asked Gervase.

'All over.'

'Mainly in Worcester?'

'No, Master Bret. This county has suffered far more. Abbot Serlo and I have been gravely concerned. There seems to be no way of eradicating the evil completely.' He sucked in air through

his teeth. 'We are convinced that the two boys who disappeare
from the abbey in the past were abducted by someone involved i
this abominable trade. And this latest victim, Owen, is no
following them into a life of misery.'

When he first heard the sound he thought it must have been mad
by an animal. It began as a light tapping then faded away. Owen'
mind turned back to his plight. He was defenceless. When Brothe
Nicholas was alive, he had someone to protect and care for him. I
was ironic that he had been seized when trying to pay his respect
once more to his friend. The grave which had become a shrine to
him had lured him to disaster. It was heart-rending. Owen sobbe
quietly to himself until the noise stopped him.

It was much clearer this time, more insistent and rhythmical.
Fear clutched at him. Only an animal of some size could make a
noise as loud as that. What if the creature made its way into his
part of the mill? Owen would stand no chance against it. He
would be a sacrificial victim. But the regularity of the sound
argued against a wild animal. Time and again, something was
banging hard against wood. When Owen realised what it must be,
he had his first moment of relief since being taken from the
abbey. He was not a lone victim. Somebody else was being held
at the mill, aware of his presence and trying to attract his attention.
Owen rolled on to the floor so that his back was to the wall. He
jabbed his feet back hard by way of reply. There was a pause,
followed by even more frenetic banging. Owen answered it with a
series of grateful kicks.

A flicker of hope came. He had a friend.

Bishop Wulfstan's account was a revelation. When he left them to
call on the abbot, Ralph and Gervase were very glad that they had
returned to the abbey. They now had a much clearer idea of what
they were up against and how much money was involved in the
trade. Gervase had listened to the bishop's impassioned speech

with special interest. He took out the list which had been compiled for him earlier by Abbot Serlo. Running his eye down it, he came to an immediate conclusion.

'That's how it was done, Ralph!' he declared.

'What do you mean?'

'That's how the victims were selected. I thought that the names were familiar when Bishop Wulfstan first mentioned them. You see?' he said, thrusting the scroll at Ralph. 'This is the list of the abbey holdings which Brother Nicholas used to visit. Over the last couple of years, most of those who were abducted came from one of these places. Brother Nicholas was the scout for the slave traders. He not only provided them with an occasional novice from the abbey. In the course of his travels, he would be able to spot other likely targets.'

'But some of the victims didn't come from abbey properties at all.'

'Maybe not,' said Gervase, 'but I'll wager they lived on land that the rent collector passed through while discharging his duties. He was in the perfect position, Ralph.'

'Alone and unsupervised.'

'Completely trusted because he was a monk.'

'Though not always liked.'

'He could be affable when he wanted to be,' recalled Gervase. 'Think of Caradoc whom we met in one of the abbey's outliers. He and his wife thought Nicholas a jolly fellow. So did his four sons.'

'Yet that other sub-tenant, Osgot, had nothing but scorn for the rent collector. And we know why. Osgot feared for his son.'

'He didn't fear that the boy would be abducted, Ralph, because he could not have suspected for a moment that a monk would be involved in the slave trade. What he feared was that Brother Nicholas would befriend the lad and lead him astray in other ways.'

'Who can blame him?'

'As for Caradoc, I think we can guess why his sons were not a
risk. If they were built like their father, they would be strong and
lusty, too likely to resist an attempt to snatch them. Bishop
Wulfstan pointed out how young the victims always were,' said
Gervase, taking the list back from him. 'Young and unable to
defend themselves. Like Owen.'

'Quite so, Gervase. And their youth would increase their value.'

'Value?'

'When they were sold,' explained Ralph. 'The younger the victim
the longer the service a new master would get out of him. I think
you have hit the mark, Gervase. The rent collector was the hub of
the wheel. He told his accomplice when and where to strike.'

'Carefully choosing his victims from a widespread area so that
no link would be made between them.'

'Exactly.'

'And making sure that not all came from abbey lands for fear
that a pattern would be detected.' He held up the list. 'But there is
pattern enough here. Or, indeed, in this abbey itself. Note how he
spaced his victims out over a period of time, Ralph.'

'Yes. First, it was Siward. Then almost a year elapsed before
the second boy was taken.'

'And a further year before Owen.'

'Brother Nicholas was as cautious as he was cunning.'

'So why was he murdered?'

'He must have fallen out with his accomplice.'

'Yet he was the provider, Ralph. Why kill a man who is such a
vital part of your trade? The next rent collector will not be as
corrupt and unscrupulous. The accomplice will have to look
elsewhere for help.'

'Perhaps he did not need Brother Nicholas any more,' said
Ralph thoughtfully. 'Perhaps it was time to look further afield for
victims, on land that had no connection with the abbey and which
Nicholas had no cause to visit. In short, he'd outlived his
usefulness.'

'I wonder.'

'The rent collector was murdered and some of the money he'd arned was stolen from the hiding place in the bell tower. Jnknown to the killer, Nicholas had a second horde in his cell.'

They speculated for some time before coming to agreement. Jervase was just putting the list away again when an animated figure came bursting through the abbey gate. Abraham the Priest was in a hurry. He gave a sigh of relief when he saw them.

'Thank heaven I found you!'

'What is the trouble?' asked Gervase.

'They have gone.'

'Who have?'

'I took your advice, Master Bret, and sought to prevent the attempt on the King's life. But the person I needed to see is no longer in the place where he was hiding.'

'What's this?' said Ralph, angering. 'Have you been riding off to see your confederates?'

'Friends, my lord. Not confederates.'

'They are one and the same.'

'It was at my suggestion,' explained Gervase. 'But the archdeacon was too late. We cannot blame him for that.'

'I rode back as fast as I could to warn you,' said Abraham. 'It means that the attempt will go ahead. Have you warned the King?'

'Yes,' said Ralph sharply, 'and if he knew where the information came from, he'd have you hanging from the nearest tree. You gave enough information for a warning but none whatsoever for an arrest.'

'I hoped to avert this crime by myself.'

'And failed.'

'Yes, my lord. I own it willingly.'

Abraham was contrite but Ralph continued to abuse him until Gervase came to the man's rescue, pointing out that security at the castle was now so tight that fears of a successful assassination attempt could be discounted. Owen's real predicament, he argued,

was far more important than the rumoured danger to the Kin
The others quickly came to the same view. Gervase explained
the archdeacon what they had learned from Bishop Wulfsta
When he heard about Brother Nicholas's role as the supplier
victims, the Welshman searched avidly through his own memo
of abductions.

At long last, the name of a possible suspect emerged.

'Strang the Dane!' he murmured.

Ralph was taken aback. 'Strang?'

'I have had my suspicions for some time, my lord, but lacke
the proof I needed. He is the man we want, I am certain of it.'

'But he is wealthy enough without getting involved in this vil
business. What could be the attraction to someone in his position'

'Rich men always want more and this trade is very lucrative
Look at his circumstances,' reasoned Abraham. 'He has holding
scattered all over the county and in the Welsh commotes so he ha
a legitimate excuse to travel around. The iron mines in the Fores
of Dean provide him with ore which he ships downriver so he ha
regular sailings to Bristol. But I believe he carries an additiona
cargo.'

'I am not persuaded,' said Ralph.

'One moment,' recalled Gervase. 'Think back to their appear
ance in the shire hall, Ralph. When they first heard that the
archdeacon was to challenge their claim to land in the Westbury
Hundred, both of them were discomfited. Strang was irate and
Balki was plainly worried.' He turned to Abraham. 'Were they
aware of your suspicions?'

'They were certainly aware of my campaign against the slave
trade. I spoke freely and openly on the subject. Strang would have
known that I was on the alert.'

'Another factor comes in here. Strang is desperate to regain
land which would give him direct access to the river. I thought he
wanted to defray the cost of transporting his ore overland but his
eagerness may be the result of a secondary motive. The river is his

best way of moving any kidnap victims. Who can stop a boat when it is surging along in the middle of the Severn?' Gervase pieced it together in his mind. 'The most obvious clue passed us by. Strang the *Dane*. Who else would trade with the Irish Vikings but one who spoke their language? You have given us the name we needed, Archdeacon. Strang must be apprehended.'

'But he has already sailed from Gloucester,' said Ralph.

Abraham started. 'Sailed? Today?'

'Yes, we saw him off from the quayside ourselves.'

'But he may have had the boy aboard his boat, my lord.'

'No, he didn't. Gervase searched it thoroughly.'

'Balki helped me,' confirmed Gervase. 'Before they set sail.'

'Balki?' The archdeacon was puzzled. 'He is the estate reeve, is he not? Why should Balki be sailing a boat when he should be looking after his master's holdings? Strang surely employs sailors to take his vessel up and down the river.'

Ralph was impressed. 'That is sound reasoning, Archdeacon. We were blind not to see what was in front of our eyes. Not only was Balki hoisting the sail, Strang himself was at the tiller.'

'A man in his position doing such a menial task?'

'Ordinarily, he would not,' decided Gervase, 'but this time he will be carrying more than iron ore so he cannot entrust the cargo to anyone else. He has to supervise the transaction in Bristol himself. That is why he was so furious at the delay in our proceedings, Ralph. He was anxious to get Owen aboard a ship to Ireland and on his way to slavery.'

'But you searched his boat,' said Ralph. 'Owen was not there.'

'Not when it left Gloucester.'

'They mean to pick him up on the way,' said Abraham.

'Where?'

'There is only one way to find out, my lord.'

It was a strange way to make conversation but it brought Owen a mild sense of pleasure. When he kicked the wall, he heard a response from the other side of the mill. If someone was thumping the wall, it was likely that they, too, were bound and gagged and unable to communicate in any other way. Both were imprisoned in the abandoned mill but a shared fate was somehow easier to bear. Although his legs were aching, Owen kept up steady contact with his unseen friend. It stopped him from dwelling too much on what horrors might lie ahead.

Another sound intruded and it caused him to break off at once. Owen tried to sit up so that he could listen more carefully. His fellow prisoner had also heard the noise because he, too, had stopped banging the wall. Too weak and tired to be able to get himself upright again, Owen abandoned the attempt and lay there on the rotting floor. The sounds grew louder until he was able to identify them. Someone was coming. A boat thudded into the bank outside. Voices could be heard. Owen's hopes rose. His ordeal was over. Rescue was at hand.

Then the two men came into the mill. The older of the two, a thickset individual with a grey beard, ordered his companion to carry the boy aboard then went swiftly out. Owen squirmed and kicked as much as he could but his resistance was futile. The spare man with the straggly red beard cuffed him into obedience, lifted him bodily and flung him over his shoulder. Owen was taken out to the waiting boat and carried aboard before being lowered roughly to the deck. A second boy emerged from another part of the mill, trussed up like Owen and slung over the shoulder of the other man. He, too, was dumped aboard. The two victims lay side by side, unable to move. The man with the straggly red beard pulled a tarpaulin over them so that they could no longer see.

Fresh sounds penetrated the sudden darkness. They were muffled by the tarpaulin but were soon easy to identify. Horses were coming at a gallop. The thickset man was yelling and his companion was making frantic efforts to cast off and set sail. The two boys were bewildered.

* * *

Ralph Delchard's horse was galloping hell-for-leather along the bank with Gervase Bret and Abraham the Priest close behind. Four of Ralph's men formed an escort, their swords already out, their blood up at the promise of action. They had spotted the boat from two miles away. When its sail was seen turning into the tributary where the mill was located, they knew that they had their only chance to catch it. Once in midstream, it would be beyond their reach.

Strang the Dane was bellowing orders, but they only helped to confuse Balki, who was still struggling with the mooring rope when the horses thundered up. For once Ralph overcame his fear of water. As the boat pulled away from the bank, he leaped down from his horse and flung himself headfirst after the vessel, catching the bulwark and hauling himself aboard. Balki grabbed an oar to try to push him away but he was no match for Ralph. Tearing the oar from the man's hands, Ralph flung it overboard then hurled Balki after it into the water. Gervase did not hesitate. Ralph's men would fight shy of the river in their heavy hauberks, but he was not handicapped by armour. Diving into the water, he swam towards the steward and grappled with him.

Ralph, meanwhile, confronted a more formidable opponent. Strang the Dane had a dagger in his hand and was circling him menacingly.

'The game is up,' said Ralph, one eye on the blade. 'I'm arresting you for the murder of Brother Nicholas and the abduction of several boys. Put up your weapon. You have no chance.'

'Nor do you, my lord,' said Strang, advancing slowly.

Ralph backed away. The advantage lay with Strang. In the seconds it would take Ralph to pull his sword from its scabbard, his adversary's dagger would be thrust into him. The boat was now drifting helplessly towards the other bank, too far away for his men to reach it without risking the deep water. Ralph decided that his wisest response was to keep both hands free in the hope of catching Strang's wrist when the weapon flashed. Even then he knew that his chances were slim.

Two things came to his aid. Hearing the sounds of the rescue attempt, Owen began to buck and twitch violently under the tarpaulin in order to attract attention. Strang was momentarily diverted. At exactly the same time, the prow of the boat thudded into the bank and caused both men to stumble forward. Ralph was the first to recover, throwing himself at Strang and seizing the hand which held the dagger. There was a violent struggle and both fell to the deck, rolling over, kicking and punching, using all their strength to subdue the other. Strang was a powerful man but Ralph was fired with anger and revulsion. It put extra strength into his arms and enabled him to twist the dagger free.

Pummelling his face, he beat Strang into submission then rose to his feet. Ralph drew his sword and held it at the Dane's throat but there was no further resistance. The man was exhausted. His face was covered in blood and his hand had been gashed when Ralph snatched away his weapon. Ralph looked across at the tarpaulin, still moving as if by its own volition. He used the point of his sword to flip it back from its cargo. Owen and the other boy blinked as they saw daylight again.

Ralph grinned warmly. 'You're safe now, lads.'

Threshing sounds took his attention back to the river. Gervase had overpowered Balki but was having difficulty dragging him ashore. Help was at hand. Divesting himself of his Benedictine habit, Abraham the Priest jumped naked into the water and swam strongly across to lend his help. Gervase was grateful and Ralph hugely amused.

'Delivering babies,' he called, 'and saving two drowning men. Is there anything you can't do, Archdeacon?'

Suddenly Ralph became aware that he was aboard a boat which was starting to drift into midstream again. His fear of the water returned at once. 'What do I do *now*?' he roared. 'Help!'

* * *

Hamelin of Lisieux was talking to his wife when the visitor arrived. They were staying not far from Gloucester in the manor house of a friend. Nigel the Reeve knew exactly where to find them. After a token exchange of civilities, he broke the news about the arrest and imprisonment of Strang the Dane. The lady Emma was horrified to learn that the man had been involved in the slave trade, but her husband immediately saw how it advantaged him.

'This will speed things up at the shire hall,' he said cheerily. 'To be honest, Strang was the only person who might have ousted me from those holdings. I did, after all, take them from him in the first place.'

Nigel curled a lip. 'He will have no need of land now.'

'I will spare him enough for a burial plot.'

'Does this mean that the commissioners will resume their work?' asked the lady Emma. 'Has any time been set?'

'Yes, my lady,' said Nigel. 'Tomorrow morning. Soon after Prime.'

'We will be there.'

'Both of us,' added Hamelin. 'Unless there is a further delay. No chance, I suppose, of Ralph Delchard being invited to the castle to take part in the King's council?'

'None, my lord.'

'Good.'

'From what I hear, their business is all but complete.'

'That was the impression I got from Bishop Wulfstan when I spoke to him at the abbey. They are to confer again this evening then the King will away at dawn. A pity. I would have valued time with him myself. Well, thank you, Nigel,' he said, indicating that the conversation was over. 'It was good of you to bring the tidings, especially as they make my claim to that land irresistible now. Be off about your business. I am sure that you have to inform Querengar and Abraham the Priest of the new developments.'

'Only the Breton, my lord.'

'Oh?'

'The archdeacon was involved in the rescue of the boys.'

'Something good has come out of Wales at last!' sneered Hamelin. 'That leaves Querengar. Is it really worth his while to turn up at the shire hall tomorrow? Advise him to ride home, Nigel. He will be spared a deal of humiliation that way.'

After bidding them farewell, the reeve withdrew. Hamelin looked across at his wife. 'If he were not so useful to me, I could enjoy hating that man. He is an objectionable fellow.'

'That's too kind a judgement.'

'Yet he brought excellent news, I'll grant him that. It seems that our visit to Gloucester has been very worthwhile.'

She smiled gently. 'So far.'

Abbot Serlo was glowing with pleasure and throbbing with gratitude. He looked around the assembled faces and spoke with deep feeling.

'This is one of the most satisfying days of my life,' he said. 'A murder has been solved, a novice has been rescued from slavery and a second kidnap victim has been restored to his parents.' He beamed at Ralph Delchard. 'It is all thanks to you and Master Bret.'

'And the Archdeacon of Gwent,' noted Gervase. 'He not only dived into the river to help me, he swam after the boat and clambered abroad to steer it back to the shore. Abraham the Priest is a born sailor.'

Canon Hubert snorted. 'And all this when he was stark naked? Hardly fit behaviour for a monk. I suppose that we may be glad that he did not feel obliged to deliver another baby at the same time.'

'A baby, Canon Hubert?' queried the abbot.

'A private jest, Abbot Serlo.'

'We are sorry that you were not there with us, Hubert,' teased Ralph. 'Our efforts really needed the controlling hand of the leader of the murder investigation.'

There were five visitors in the abbot's lodging. Ralph, Gervase and Hubert had been joined by Bishop Wulfstan and Brother Frewine. The two older men heaped their own congratulations on the commissioners.

'No mercy will be shown to them,' promised Wulfstan. 'Strang the Dane and his henchman will be tried, convicted and hanged. A lot of parents will sleep more soundly after this day's work.'

'So will the monks of this abbey,' said Frewine softly. 'With your permission, Father Abbot, I would like to put a question of my own to these three heroes.' Hubert basked in his inclusion. 'We now know that it was Strang who was seen arguing with Brother Nicholas and that he killed our holy brother. But why? The motive is unclear.'

'It was to us,' admitted Gervase. 'At first.'

'But I got the truth out of him,' boasted Ralph. 'It is amazing how willing some people are to talk when they have a swordpoint at their throat. Strang was furious with Brother Nicholas. He had waited patiently until it was safe to abduct another novice from the abbey, knowing that your rent collector would have won the confidence of his next victim. But Nicholas betrayed him. Having befriended Owen for the purpose of selling him to Strang, he grew to like the boy too much and Owen, in turn, became fond of him. They were like father and son, meeting in secret at night in the bell tower just to be together. When Strang tried to force Nicholas to hand the boy over, he refused. He could not bear to part with a child he had come to love.'

'He had some glimmer of humanity, then,' observed Wulfstan.

'Yes,' said Gervase. 'Owen adored him. He would not hear a word against his friend. Brother Nicholas, apparently, gave him a coin as a memento. It was the most precious thing Owen possessed. He told us that he buried it in the grave.'

Abbot Serlo was troubled. 'That is a commendable gesture but it concerns me that a novice should believe that money is more

precious than serving God in all humility. Owen has much t
learn.'

'Adversity has already been a strict teacher,' said Frewine. 'Bu
do continue, my lord,' he invited, turning to Ralph again. 'I do no
believe that you finished what you were saying.'

'Gervase has told you the bulk of it, Brother Frewine,' said
Ralph. 'And let me confess to you all that I misjudged your ren
collector. When I heard the rumours about him, I thought his
interest in young boys had an unnatural side to it. Which it did, in
a sense, because what is more unnatural than selling them into
slavery? But he had no designs on their innocence, Owen assured
us of that. They just sat together and talked. Nothing more
occurred. The closeness of their friendship may have annoyed
Strang but it also gave him his opportunity.'

'In what way?' said Hubert.

'He knew that Owen would want to mourn Brother Nicholas.
The only way that he could do that alone was to visit the grave or
the church at night. Strang rightly guessed that the boy might be
on the loose and he lay in ambush.' He touched the bruise on his
chin. 'Strang is a powerful man, I can vouch for that. Owen had
no chance against him.'

'This has all ended most satisfactorily,' said Abbot Serlo. 'I am
so grateful that Canon Hubert took an interest in this whole
business.'

'My colleagues are the real heroes,' said Hubert with false
modesty. 'But I like to feel that I set everything in train. What
pleases me is that my earlier judgement was proved sound.'

'What earlier judgement?'

'The same one you made yourself, Abbot Serlo. That the killer
could not possibly have been a Benedictine monk?'

'Yet he was,' said Ralph. 'When he committed murder and
abducted a novice, Strang the Dane was wearing a cowl. To all
intents and purposes, he was one of you.'

A loud chorus of protest came from Serlo, Wulfstan, Hubert

and Frewine. It was left to Gervase to provide the balm to their injured pride.

'*Cuchullus non facit monachum*,' he said.

The quartet smiled instantly and clapped in approval.

'What does it mean, Gervase?' asked Ralph.

'The hood does not make a monk.'

When he was summoned that evening by the Master of the Novices, Kenelm walked towards Brother Paul's lodging on unsteady feet. He was certain that a long overdue punishment would now be administered. It was not only because he had twice ventured out of the dormitory at night that he feared reprisal. What terrified him most was the thought that the strong-armed Brother Paul had caught wind of his earlier vow to flee from the abbey. Kenelm had changed his mind about that but he doubted if the master would give him time to explain. The mere suggestion of him absconding would be enough to stir his ire. As he knocked on Brother Paul's door, Kenelm could almost hear the swish of the birch rod. Sweat ran freely down his back like so much blood.

The door opened and the bushy eyebrows lifted with pleasure.

'Kenelm!' greeted Brother Paul. 'Come on in!'

He stood back to reveal another visitor. Seated in a corner was the waif-like figure of Owen, released from his torment and restored once more to the abbey. Kenelm was so pleased to see him again that he burst into tears. Brother Paul eased him forward.

'Why not give him a proper welcome?' he suggested.

Kenelm darted forward as Owen rose to his feet. They embraced warmly and held each other for a long time. Kenelm was thrilled to see him back in the safety of the cloister but it was Owen who had the greater delight. In that involuntary hug, a whole list of past slights was forgotten and forgiven. Kenelm liked him now. Owen had a new friend.

It was a splendid feast with an appropriate air of celebration this time. His business in Gloucester concluded, King William was able to relax, and he presided happily over the banquet in the hall at the castle. They were all there: Durand the Sheriff, the nominal host, sat beside the King, with his wife on the other side of their guest. The other three members of the council were in attendance, Bishop Wulfstan among them, at last persuaded, to the advantage of all within reach of him, to remove his malodorous cloak while he was at table. Ralph, Gervase and Golde sat together. Canon Hubert had accepted the invitation to join them, as had Abbot Serlo, but Brother Simon had not dared to quit the abbey. Hubert felt his decision wise. Among the other guests were Hamelin of Lisieux and his wife. Unable to take his own eyes from the lady Emma, Hubert kept telling himself how much the scribe would be suffering if he were there.

Though the King was the guest of honour, he graciously directed attention to the commissioners, praising them for their good offices in solving two crimes and liberating the abbey from the grip of fear. Serlo was pleased with all he heard, but Hubert was peeved that his name was not mentioned and Durand was positively writhing with suppressed fury at the way Ralph and Gervase were garlanded for succeeding in duties that rightly fell to him. The sheriff's fury was increased when he saw that Nigel the Reeve was enjoying his discomfiture so openly.

When the festivities finally ended, the guests slowly began to depart. King William came across to put a congratulatory arm around Ralph's shoulders. He gave a chuckle.

'I should take some credit myself,' he observed.

'Credit, my liege?'

'Yes,' said William. 'Who was it who sent you to Gloucester in its hour of need? You came at exactly the right time, Ralph.'

'But not to get embroiled in murder and abduction. We came here as commissioners, my liege. As it happens,' he said, seizing a unique opportunity, 'your own arrival here could not have been more timely. Tomorrow morning we sit in judgement on two men who have royal charters to what appears to be the same holdings.'

'That will test your mettle.'

'I was hoping you could save us an immense amount of trouble, my liege. All that you need do is glance at the two charters and tell us which one takes precedence.'

'And rob you of the pleasure of working it out for yourselves?' William's chuckle was even riper this time. 'I am sorry, Ralph. By the time you sit in the shire hall, I will be riding back to Winchester. A momentous decision was made in this hall earlier on. It needs to be implemented with all celerity.' He walked away. 'Farewell, my friend. Sleep well, for tomorrow you'll be put through your paces.'

Before Ralph could detain him, the King was gone to speak to Bishop Wulfstan, before quitting the room with the sheriff, who escorted him to his apartment. As he watched them leave, Ralph remembered the warning from Abraham the Priest. There was no reason to doubt its sincerity. In view of the immense help given to them by the archdeacon, he no longer suspected him of complicity in the plot, and Ralph knew that he would be lurking outside the castle that night in the hope of intercepting the impetuous Welshman he feared might be trying to get in. Ideally, the assassin would be turned away.

Ralph's attention shifted to the lady Emma. She was looking more beautiful than ever and he was pleased to see that she and her husband were spending the night at the castle, raising the possibility that they might meet again over breakfast. He was still drooling over the prospect when Golde came up to nudge him out of his reverie. Smiling at his sudden display of interest in her, she linked arms with him and led him out. In the privacy of their bed, he would forget all about the lady Emma. Golde was content. On their way up the stairs, they met Durand. The sheriff was dark-eyed and tight-lipped. Ralph could not resist enraging him even further.

'All your assumptions about the murder were wrong, my lord

sheriff,' he said cheerily. 'If you had not misled us so at the start, we'd have solved the crime for you in half the time.'

'It is solved, my lord. That is the main thing.'

'By two commissioners and a naked archdeacon.'

'I would have effected the same arrests in due course.'

'But you were preoccupied here with affairs of state.'

'Good night, my lord.' A cold smile for Golde. 'My lady.'

'Good night,' she replied. 'Thank you for your hospitality.'

'You are most welcome.'

'And the King?' asked Ralph. 'Is he well guarded?'

'Of course,' said Durand testily. 'I have seen to that. Go back to your own work, my lord. This is my castle and I am responsible for everything which happens under its roof. You will not take my office on again. I resent it. I deplore it. I forbid it!'

Abraham the Priest kept up his lonely vigil well into the night. Even when those leaving the castle had finally departed, he remained at his post, close enough to keep the castle under surveillance while keeping out of sight of the sentries who patrolled the ramparts with flaming torches. It was a warm night but low cloud was blocking out the moon. That fact alone, he feared, might tempt Madog to fulfil his threat. The archdeacon strained his eyes to penetrate the gloom but it was his ears which alerted him. There was a padding sound far off to the right, as if someone were keeping to the shadows and heading towards the castle walls. He moved stealthily forward until he caught sight of the man.

A hunched figure was conjured out of the darkness. Abraham did not hesitate. Scurrying up behind him, he threw a restraining arm around his neck and clapped his other hand over his mouth to prevent a yelp which would have alerted the guards. He dragged the assassin away.

The hoot of an owl brought him awake. Ralph was suddenly

alarmed. He got out of bed at once and reached for his dagger, sensing that something was amiss without quite knowing why. Golde was fast asleep. He unbolted the door and let himself out. The steps felt cold beneath his bare feet but he did not dare to make a sound. It was dark at the top of the staircase but candles burned close to the apartment at the bottom where King William slept. Outside the room, he knew, would be an armed guard who was relieved at regular intervals by a deputy. Ralph crept on until he saw the first flickers of light reflected on the walls. He relaxed. All was well. The candles burned, the guard was in place, the King was in no danger. His alarm was groundless.

Then the fingers of flame disappeared from the wall with dramatic suddenness. Someone had extinguished the candles. Gripping his dagger more tightly, he went on down the stairs with a mixture of urgency and apprehension. When he reached the bottom, he almost tripped over something and realised that it was the guard. More than the candle had been snuffed out. As he knelt beside the man, he could feel the blood gushing from the slit throat. Ralph needed no more prompting. The assassination attempt *was* taking place after all. He flung open the door and charged into the room.

A single candle burned beside the bed but it contained no King of England. A sack of something had been placed beneath the blanket to give the impression that the bed was occupied. The man who had stabbed so viciously at the sleeping King now stood back in amazement and stared down at the empty bed. Ralph was on him in an instant, knocking him flat with the impetus of his attack, then trying to disarm him. But the assassin was a more wily opponent than Strang the Dane. He recovered at once to jab at his adversary and inflicted a flesh wound in Ralph's arm. Dropping his dagger, Ralph jumped up and used his foot to deliver a kick to the other's face. A loud grunt showed that his aim was accurate. Ignoring the trickle of blood from his arm, Ralph leaned over to blow out the candle and plunge the room into darkness.

They were on more even terms now. The assassin was armed
but Ralph was elusive, darting around him as he rose from the
floor and waiting for the moment to attack. It soon arrived. Alerted
by the sounds of the struggle, guards came running. A blaze of
light appeared in the doorway. It illumined a tall figure in a black
cowl. Caught between the desire to kill Ralph and the need to
escape, the man hesitated for a fatal second. Ralph was on him,
seizing his wrist and bowling him to the ground before punching
him with his other hand. Bright light bathed them and a dozen
swords brought their struggle to an end.

'Stop!' yelled a peremptory voice. 'Stand back, Ralph!'

Reluctant to get up, Ralph obeyed the King, wondering how he
had just come through the door of the apartment in which he was
supposed to be sleeping. But his main interest was in the identity
of the man he had fought. Seeing the hopelessness of his position,
the latter had dropped his dagger and was cowering on the floor.
Ralph reached down to throw back his hood, expecting to see the
face of a Welsh assassin.

But it was Hamelin of Lisieux who glowered up at him.

'I am glad that I decided to quit this chamber,' said the King.
'He would have been a murderous bedfellow. Take him away!'

Hamelin was dragged out quickly by the guards, Ralph still
trying to overcome his amazement. King William gave a weary
smile.

'Once again, I am in your debt, Ralph. You warned us that there
would be an attempt on my life. I took the best precaution I could
and moved from the bed he would expect me to be in.'

'I never suspected Hamelin of Lisieux,' admitted Ralph.

'That is because you do not know his wife as well as I do.'

'The lady Emma?'

'A beautiful but ambitious lady.'

'Is she involved in this plot?'

'My guess is that she probably instigated it,' said William.
'That is why I did not allow her husband at the council table. Do

you know what we discussed here in Gloucester?'

'No, my liege.'

'The invasion of the Vexin.'

'I begin to see the connection.'

'Guess from which part of France the lady Emma hails?'

'The Vexin.'

'Correct.' He saw the blood on Ralph's arm. 'But you are injured. The wound must be bathed and dressed.'

'It is nothing, my liege,' he said, stemming the flow with the palm of his other hand. 'Tell me more about the lord Hamelin.'

'There is little more to tell beyond the fact that I have doubted his loyalty for some time. It was given out that he spent much time in Normandy but my intelligencers say that he crossed into the Vexin with his wife.' He glanced at the bed. 'Now we know why. And to come in the guise of a monk shows his cunning. The guard outside the door would not have had suspicion of him until it was too late. Hamelin of Lisieux was a treacherous monk.'

'*Cuchullus non facit monachum*.' said Ralph with a smile.

'I did not take you for a Latin scholar.'

'I have many talents. But what will happen to his wife?'

'She will be executed alongside him. Would you like to have the pleasure of seeing the lady arrested in her chamber?'

'It is a temptation I will resist,' said Ralph. 'A more beautiful woman awaits me in my own apartment. More beautiful and more loyal to her King. Besides,' he added, holding up his arm, 'with a wound like this to display, I can be assured of unlimited sympathy.'

Other guards now waited for orders at the door. Before Ralph could ease past them, the King stopped him with a final question.

'Who did you think the assassin *would* be?' he asked.

'Someone else.'

Canon Hubert and Brother Simon were the first to arrive at the shire hall the following morning. Unaware of nocturnal events at the castle, Hubert had reached the conclusion that Hamelin of Lisieux had a legal right to the holdings which he had seized from Strang the Dane. He was aghast, therefore, when Ralph Delchard walked in with his arm in a sling and told him of the bungled assassination. Simon was almost as horrified at the injuries to his colleague as he was at the notion of an attempt on the King's life. Ralph was touched by his concern.

'It does simplify matters,' Gervase pointed out.

'Does it?' said Hubert.

'Yes. Strang the Dane has been removed from the race and the lord Hamelin has also fallen. The choice now rests between a Breton and a Welshman. Which would you choose?'

'Neither, if I am honest.'

'No decision is required of you, Hubert,' said Ralph. 'It has already been made by a higher authority.'

'God?'

'Not that high.'

'King William,' explained Gervase. 'He was so grateful to Ralph for his brave intervention that he deigned to settle this dispute for us. He confirmed the charter to Querengar. The holdings go to the Breton.'

'Summary justice,' observed Hubert. 'Will the King resolve all our disputes like that? He will save us a great deal of time if he does.'

'He rode out of Gloucester at dawn,' said Ralph. 'Let us put the two surviving claimants out of their misery, shall we? Then we may move swiftly on to the other disputes before shaking the dust of this fair city from our shoes. When I looked into the jaundiced eye of the sheriff this morning, I had a feeling that we'd already outstayed our welcome.'

Querengar the Breton and Abraham the Priest were brought in to hear the verdict. Both sat in dignified silence, showing no emotion when Ralph awarded the holdings to Querengar. The Welshman congratulated him without rancour. When the two men

ft, Ralph followed them out so that he could have a parting word
ith Abraham.

'I am sorry to disappoint you, Archdeacon,' he began.

'It was a fair judgement.'

'You will not revile us because of it?'

'I have too much respect for you and Master Bret to do that.
ou helped to capture men who have been terrorising the Welsh
ommotes with their abductions. That reward alone was well worth
he ride from Gwent. The news will be received joyfully when I
nnounce it.'

'Good. But what happened to your assassin?'

'Ah,' said the other. 'You may well ask.'

'Did he not even make it over the castle wall?'

'He did not even arrive, my lord,' confided Abraham. 'I mounted
uard myself until I saw someone sneak up in the dark. Thinking
t might be the man I feared, I jumped on him.'

'You are an aggressive man when you are roused, Archdeacon.'

'Too aggressive for Tomos.'

'Tomos?'

'My companion. He fainted with fright. Since I had been out
f Gloucester for most of the day, he had come in search of me. I
nly wish I had spoken to him before because he could have saved
ne from my sentry duty.'

'How?'

'While I was away, he received word from our friends that the
lot had been abandoned. Wiser counsels had prevailed.'

'Your disapproval forced them to reconsider.'

'Partly that, my lord, but the consequences weighed most
eavily with them, I suspect. In the excitement of the moment,
hey felt that they would be striking a blow for Wales by assassina-
ing King William. They would be national heroes, lifting the
oreign yoke from their native land.'

'A complete illusion.'

'I think they came to realise that. Had the plan been successful, it would not have liberated Wales at all, only subjected it to wor barbarities. One king would be dead but a more vengeful o would take his place.' He heaved a sigh. 'I am glad that my frien recognised that.'

'So am I, Archdeacon.'

'It means that they went of their own volition and not becau I betrayed them to you. I can ride home with a clear conscienc He looked deep into Ralph's eye. 'Thank you for all you ha done, my lord.'

'My thanks are due to you,' said Ralph earnestly. 'And not on because you rescued me from that boat. You acquitted yourse nobly in the shire hall.' His face split into a broad grin. 'This is wondrous event. I am, for once, actually sorry to see a Welshm going home.'

'I will give your regards to Archdeacon Idwal!' teased the oth Ralph's grin vanished. His anger flared.

'Goodbye!' he yelled. 'Ride hard!'

Epilogue

'Tomorrow, Golde!' There was deep disappointment in her sister's voice. 'You are leaving tomorrow?'

'At first light, Aelgar.'

'But why?'

'The commissioners will have concluded their deliberations.'

'They have been in Gloucester barely a week.'

'Nine days in all,' said Golde. 'Don't forget that we arrived here well before you and Forne. Time has certainly not dragged. Those nine days have flown past.'

'I wish that you could stay another nine,' said Forne with clear affection. 'Just when I am getting to know you properly, you leave us.'

'It is not my decision. I must go where they go. I am simply part of the baggage.' Golde gave a smile. 'It always surprises me that Ralph does not strap me across one of the sumpter horses.'

Aelgar was shocked. 'He would never do that to his wife. Baggage, indeed! You set too low a value on yourself. Ralph would be lost without you. He more or less admitted that when he was here.'

'I am sorry we did not see more of him,' said Forne. 'I fear that I was a little rude to him when we met.'

'Extremely rude,' scolded Aelgar.

'With some cause.'

'There is never any cause for abusing our guests, Forne.'

'I did not abuse the lord Ralph.'

'You are doing it now when you call him that,' said Golde amiably. 'I have told you before. If we are to be tied by family, no

269

formalities will exist. I am plain Golde and he is plain Ralph.'

'He's too handsome to be plain,' said her sister.

'I would agree with that.'

'What about me?' asked Forne, angling for a compliment.

'You are almost perfect.'

'Why only almost?'

'Because I have not trained you fully yet.'

'Oh, I am to be trained, am I?' he said coltishly. 'I did not realise that I was to be your pet animal when we married. I expected that it was I who had to do the training.'

'You will each school the other,' observed Golde fondly. 'It is called being in love and there is no better education.'

She had called at the house where they were staying to break the news of their departure and to apologise that Ralph could not make the visit with her. It was not simply a case of wanting to avoid any further friction with Forne. A final verdict needed to be given at the shire hall and he would be involved there until evening. Besides, since his arm was still heavily bandaged, Ralph did not wish to be put to the trouble of lying about the way he had received the wound. Forne and Aelgar could be told about the crimes at the abbey but word of the assassination attempt was being kept strictly within the walls of the castle. It was too sensitive a subject to be delivered to the local gossips. It upset Golde that she was not able to talk about her husband's courage in tackling the would-be assassin, but she appreciated the need for secrecy.

Aelgar came to a decision. She looked directly at Forne.

'We will see them off tomorrow.'

'That early?'

'At midnight,' she insisted, 'if that is when they choose to leave.'

'Dawn is challenge enough for me,' said Golde, 'but there is no need to haul you two out of your beds. That is why I came to take my leave of you now. Enjoy your sleep while you can.'

'How can I when my only sister is riding away from me?' said Aelgar with unusual vehemence. 'I will be there to wave you all off and Forne will be with me.'

He grinned. 'It is all part of my training.'

'It would be lovely to see you,' admitted Golde.

'Then you shall,' promised her sister. 'It will give Forne a chance to make a better impression on Ralph. He has much ground to make up.'

'Who does?' asked her betrothed. 'Ralph or me?'

'Both,' said Golde.

'How long will this go on?' wondered Aelgar.

'What?'

'This endless travelling you seem to do.'

'I have no idea. If it were left to Ralph, it would end tomorrow and we would enjoy the simple pleasure of staying in our own home. But the King's word must be obeyed.'

'We know that!' muttered Forne rebelliously.

'We go where Ralph and Gervase are sent.'

'Well, I hope you are sent in our direction again, Golde,' said her sister, reaching out to squeeze her hands. 'Short as it has been, this visit has brought us much joy. I am so glad that we made the effort to get to Gloucester while you were here.'

'So am I, Aelgar.'

The two sisters embraced then looked expectantly towards Forne.

'And so am I,' he said willingly. He gave a vacuous grin. 'You see, Aelgar? You have me trained already. I indulge your every whim.'

'Good,' she said sweetly. 'For I have a lot of them.'

The final day at the shire hall was punctuated by the small irritations they had learned to take in their stride. One witness lied, another tried to pretend he had forgotten a vital document, and a third changed his evidence so many times that they had no idea which claimant he was really supporting. Under Ralph's firm leadership, the last case was resolved and dispatched into history. After thanking his colleagues, he gathered up his papers to put into his satchel.

'A shorter visit than I anticipated,' said Hubert airily. 'Given the fact that we were distracted by other matters, I think that we showed exemplary efficiency.'

'You always do that, Canon Hubert,' said Brother Simon.

'Thank you.'

'Especially when leading a murder investigation,' noted Ralph.

'Do not mock,' said Gervase. 'Canon Hubert's presence at the abbey was critical. We were the outsiders, Ralph. But for the fact that he and Brother Simon stayed there, we might never have been drawn into this whole business at all.'

'I thank God that you were,' said Simon. 'The abbey was poisoned by those dreadful crimes. You and the lord Ralph helped to cleanse it.' He saw Hubert's grimace. 'With the assistance of Canon Hubert, that is.'

'Not to mention a little help from the Archdeacon of Gwent.'

'True, Gervase,' said Ralph, who had now come to appreciate to the full the Welshman's contribution. 'An extraordinary man. Whether acting as a midwife or swimming to my rescue.'

'He should restrict his activities to the pulpit,' said Hubert sniffily.

'You mean that all future babies should be delivered there?'

'No, my lord!'

'Can we leave this distressing subject?' begged Simon.

'Of course,' said Gervase. 'Ignore Ralph. He is being skittish now that our work is done here. But tell us this. How has the atmosphere been at the abbey since Strang and his accomplice were arrested?'

Simon smiled. 'It is a different place altogether.'

'It is as if a huge black cloud has been dispersed,' said Hubert.

'They know that you are leaving,' said Ralph.

'Abbot Serlo paid me the compliment of inviting me back at any time and Bishop Wulfstan was equally hospitable. Worcester Abbey is open to me whenever I happen to be in the county.'

'They recognised your true worth,' said Gervase without sarcasm. 'It is a pity that they were not able to evaluate Brother Nicholas's character more accurately. Had they done so, much pain and bloodshed would have been prevented.'

'Abbot Serlo appreciates that, Gervase. He will scrutinise his monks with far more care from now on. He and Brother Frewine both.'

'Yes,' said Ralph. 'The Precentor is worth his weight in gold. I liked him more than any of them. Kind, honest, decent, humble, but with a mind as sharp as the edge of my sword. No wonder the novices turn to him. He understands them.'

Hubert gave a flabby grin, forewarning them of a rare flight into humour. In a confidential whisper, he passed on information that caused none of them the slightest surprise.

'They have a nickname for Brother Frewine,' he said.

'Do they?' asked Simon obediently.

'Brother Owl.'

Gervase gave a dutiful laugh. 'Very appropriate.'

'Wise, old and feathered.'

'But not the only owl in Gloucester,' observed Ralph. 'Bishop Wulfstan could certainly lay claim to that nickname. So could Abbot Serlo. And there were moments when even Abraham the Priest showed the requisite wisdom. But there is only one owl of Gloucester for me.'

'Which one is that?' asked Gervase.

'The one whose hoot woke me in time to save the King. At least, that is what I believed I was doing. Accident or design? I'll never know. But that hoot outside my window helped me to catch Hamelin of Lisieux.'

'And his wife,' said Hubert grimly.

'Both of them. What a fall from grace for the lord Hamelin!

And for the lady Emma. Who would have believed that someo
so beautiful on the outside could be so ugly on the inside?
were all at fault there.'

'All of us, Ralph?' said Gervase.

'Yes,' he explained. 'We were vain enough to think that the l
Hamelin brought her here simply to dazzle us. Whereas she ca
on a much more pressing errand. The assassination of the Ki
The fact that she turned up at all should have alerted us to
darker purpose than tantalising three commissioners.'

'I was never tantalised, my lord!' howled Hubert.

'What we lacked was a woman's intuition.'

'Intuition?' repeated Simon.

'Golde had it. When she met the lady Emma, she knew at or
that there was something false about her, even though she co
not discern exactly what it was. Golde felt that she was in
castle for other reasons than simply calling on the sheriff's wi
So it proved,' he said. 'The lady Emma was there to spy out
land for her husband.'

'She will pay the ultimate penalty for it,' said Hube
'And rightly so. Well, I think we can make one proud boas
he continued airily. 'Thanks to our enterprise, we will lea
Gloucester in a far better condition than we found it.'

They all agreed. Chatting easily, they headed for the door.
was early evening and bright sun still gilded the shire hall wh
they stepped outside it. Ralph was sorry that Nigel the Reeve w
not at hand for a final curt reprimand. The latter's friendship w
Hamelin of Lisieux was now a cause of deep embarrassment
the reeve, and Ralph had intended to compound that feeling. Th
treat eluded him.

Canon Hubert blossomed in the sunshine and grew lyrical.

'Brother Owl was a bird of peace in a war-torn world,' he sa
'He sat, watched and waited with the wisdom of ages shini
from his eyes.' He turned to Simon. 'I fancy that *I* have somethi
of the owl about me.'

'Oh, yes, Canon Hubert,' endorsed the other.

Ralph was less obsequious. 'Does that mean you hunt at night and feed off vermin? Or that your feathers moult in summer? I know one thing, Hubert, if you are an owl, there is no bough you could perch on for there is not a tree which grows one big enough.'

Hubert was hurt. 'I was speaking in metaphors, my lord.'

'Oh, that is different.'

'Long experience *has* given me a degree of wisdom.'

'I could not agree more,' said Gervase. 'Our time in Gloucester has imparted a little wisdom to all of us. Even you, Ralph.'

'Me?' protested the other. 'What wisdom did I gain?'

'You learned the value of forethought.'

'Forethought?'

'When a man hates water as much as you do, he should take care never to go into it or even upon it. Be grateful to Abraham the Priest,' he said. 'The Owl of Gwent. If he had not rescued you from that boat, you would have sailed all the way to Normandy by now. What would your dear wife have said to that?'

Ralph needed only a second to find his answer. His eyes widened, his mouth narrowed to a circle and his arms went out like small wings.

'Too-wit, too-woo!'

The Wildcats of Exeter

Edward Marston

His business completed, Nicholas Picard rides home
in the gathering dusk of the Devonshire countryside.
Lost in his thoughts, he does not see the danger
ahead. And by the time he is aware of the snarling
wildcat it is too late. They find his body in the woods
– the claw marks on his face a hideous indication of
his attacker. But the laceration to his throat is the
work of a human hand.

The discovery of Picard's death complicates an
already difficult task for Ralph Delchard and Gervase
Bret. The murdered man was involved in one of the
land disputes they are in Exeter to adjudicate and
new claims are now made on the property in
question. Picard's wife, Catherine, views herself as
the obvious benefactor, but his mistress and the
mother of a previous owner have other ideas. So
determined is each woman to prove her claim that the
commissioners soon begin to wonder if this piece of
land could have driven one of them to murder. But
the root of the mystery lies far deeper than avarice . . .

'Delchard and Bret make an enterprising pair of
sleuths' *Sunday Telegraph*

0 7472 6055 9

HEADLINE

The Mask of Ra

Paul Doherty

His great battles against the sea raiders in the Nile Delta have left Pharaoh Tuthmosis II weak and frail, but he finds solace in victory and in the welcome he is sure to receive on his return to Thebes. Across the river from Thebes, however, there are those who do not relish his home-coming, and a group of assassins has taken a witch to pollute the Pharaoh's unfinished tomb.

Reunited with his wife, Hatusu, and his people, Tuthmosis stands before the statue of Amun-Ra, the roar of the crowd and the fanfare of trumpets ringing in his ears. But within an hour he is dead and the people of Thebes cannot forget the omen of the wounded doves flying overhead.

Rumour runs rife, speculation sweeps the royal city and Hatusu vows to uncover the truth. With the aid of Amerotke, a respected judge of Thebes, she embarks on a path destined to reveal the great secrets of Egypt.

'The best of its kind since the death of Ellis Peters' *Time Out*

'A lively sense of history' *New Statesman*

0 7472 5972 0

HEADLINE

If you enjoyed this book here is a selection of other bestselling titles from Headline